THE MURDER BALLAD

JANE HILL

WILLIAM HEINEMANN: LONDON

First published in the United Kingdom in 2006 by William Heinemann

1 3 5 7 9 10 8 6 4 2

Copyright © Jane Hill 2006

The right of Jane Hill to be identified as the author of this work has been asserted by her
in accordance with the Copyright, Designs and Patents Act, 1988

William Heinemann
The Random House Group Limited
20 Vauxhall Bridge Road, London, SW1V 2SA

Random House Australia (Pty) Limited
20 Alfred Street, Milsons Point, Sydney,
New South Wales 2061, Australia

Random House New Zealand Limited
18 Poland Road, Glenfield
Auckland 10, New Zealand

Random House (Pty) Limited
Isle of Houghton, Corner of Boundary Road & Carse O'Gowrie
Houghton 2198, South Africa

Random House Publishers India Private Limited
301 World Trade Tower, Hotel Intercontinental Grand Complex
Barakhamba Lane, New Delhi 110 001, India

The Random House Group Limited Reg. No. 954009
www.randomhouse.co.uk

A CIP catalogue record for this book is available from the British Library

Papers used by Random House are natural, recyclable products
made from wood grown in sustainable forests. The manufacturing processes
conform to the environmental regulations of the country of origin

Typeset in Monotype Fournier by SX Composing DTP, Rayleigh, Essex
Printed and bound in the United Kingdom by
Clays Ltd, St Ives plc

ISBN 9780434013227 (from Jan 2007)
ISBN 0 434 01322 6

THE MURDER BALLAD

Jane Hill was born and brought up in Portsmouth. She has worked in radio for twenty years, first as a journalist and then as head of programming for an award-winning group of commercial radio stations. She is now a freelance writer and broadcaster and is also pursuing a career as a stand-up comedian. She has a passion for live music and also for travelling, particularly in the USA.

Praise for *Grievous Angel*

'By turns playful and poignant, sexy and sinister, Hill's darkly comedic portrait of a woman scorned packs a captivating surprise' *Booklist*

'A new voice in psychological suspense fiction' *Daily Mail*

'A sensational new addition to the psychological thriller shelves' *Daily Record*

Also by Jane Hill

Grievous Angel

For my dad, who was proud of me.

Acknowledgements

Thank you to my agent Luigi Bonomi, for helping to make this happen, and to the supportive team at Random House, especially Nikola Scott and Cassie Chadderton. Thank you to my family and friends for their love and support, particularly my sister Jo who is a pillar of strength and a perceptive first reader.

Thanks to my friends Jan and Mark Keable for letting me curl up in the corner of the settee feeling musically inadequate at all those late night jam sessions in Barton-upon-Humber, particularly the one involving the brilliant Chris Smither and Jeffrey Foucault; also to John Lee, Steve 'the Sound' Ellis and to Keith Miller for the paper percussion.

My gratitude to the musicians I met in Asheville, North Carolina. Thanks to Bill Malone for his book *Country Music USA*; to John Alexander Williams for *Appalachia: a History* and to Wayne Erbsen for his books on old mountain music, particularly *Rural Roots of Bluegrass*. Thank you to Jean Ritchie for her version of 'Pretty Polly' on the album *Jean Ritchie and Doc Watson Live at Folk City*, and to Paul Burch, Lambchop, Kate Campbell and AKUS for bringing their own particular brands of country music to the UK.

Prologue

The first time I saw the river it didn't look like a killer. Soon after I arrived in my husband's home town I'd gone down there to sit on a flat rock in the middle of a clear shallow blue stream. I dangled my bare feet in the cool water, enjoying the sunshine of an idyllic summer afternoon. After the greyness of my London life – my cramped flat; the dull, damp weather; the loneliness and nagging, underlying grief that threatened never to go away – that moment felt like Paradise.

But now I know the true character of the river. After days of heavy rain, when the river is in full flood, the rock that I sat on that day disappears under a fierce torrent of rust-brown water, water that's decorated with creamy foam like the traceries of fat on streaky bacon. The river rushes headlong and deadly through the narrow channel in the rocks, filling every inch of the available space. Then it broadens and flattens out, skimming over the rocky bed, its surface deceptively smooth. It's as if it takes a breath – a pause – before hurling itself over the next ridge with exhilarating speed and strength. You can hear the *whoosh* from almost a mile away. Each wave that falls over the ridge sends up droplets as it hits its target at the bottom of the waterfall. The droplets reach ever higher into the sky, with what seems like uninhibited joy, like schoolkids doing star jumps from a vaulting horse, trying to outdo each other: 'Look, miss, how high I can jump!'

On the day I learned first-hand the damage that the river could do, patches of gaudy autumn colour were showing amongst the green curtain of the trees on either bank. But beyond the leaves I could see nothing. The mountains on either side of the narrow valley were completely obscured by fog. When my husband lured me to his home town high in the Appalachian Mountains he promised me crisp air, bright, clear days, and stunning views across the peaks of North Carolina and Tennessee. But he didn't tell me the whole story. The early settlers called the place Foggy Hollow. Older people living in the town still call it by that name, and it must have stuck for a reason. On days like those it's easy to believe that there is no wider world out there. The whole world shrinks to a small town in a narrow fold in the mountains, a kind of Appalachian Brigadoon.

I'm thinking about the river and what it can do. I know of two people who were killed in that river. I watched one of them die. I know what it's like to be caught up in its angry brown cascades, to feel its water slapping against your legs and lifting your feet off its bed. I know what it's like to feel the force of the river beating against the rocks, hurtling with all its strength towards the waterfall. For just a second you feel exhilarated, as if you're flying, and then terror takes over. Terror, and a fierce determination to survive, to hold on at all costs. I still have scars on my fingertips as a reminder.

B odie's Hollow. That's the town's proper name, although the designation Foggy Hollow lives on in the name of the ramshackle little-patronised motel a couple of miles out of town. Bodie's Hollow is a small, straggling cul-de-sac of a place, population 279: a crooked little finger pointing nowhere, lying in a forgotten corner of beautiful, mountainous but insignificant Campbell County. The maps tell you that it's an easy drive from Bodie's Hollow across to Asheville or Knoxville or even down to Nashville, but I've discovered that's a lie. Once you're off the interstate the roads cling to the crumpled contours of the land and you have to double or treble the time you expect every journey to take. It's as if God took the land, screwed it into a little ball, and then couldn't be bothered to flatten it out properly. Bodie's Hollow lurks in one of the creases. On those days when the fog stubbornly refused to lift; when wisps hung in the street like a giant's cigar smoke and you could almost reach out and touch them; when the fog hung over the narrow valley, obscuring the neighbouring mountain tops, cutting the town off from its surroundings like a roof or a lid or a wall: on those days it seemed that there was no way out of Bodie's Hollow.

When I first arrived, the town appeared more than half-dead to me. The signs of life my husband had excitedly told me about – the espresso-bar-cum-internet-café, the store selling scented candles and greetings cards, even the studio he had built – seemed fragile, like blooms that had shot up too early. It felt as if they could easily be snuffed out by the heavy sense of past that hovers over this town like the fog.

The town is overlooked by its graveyard, cut into the side of the steep hill that climbs out of the valley behind the Presbyterian church. The names on the mossy stones are prosaic ones: Henderson, Johnson, McDonald, Ferguson – my husband's family name – and many of the dates speak of short, hard lives. The name Ferguson appears most prominently on a tall, straight, plain memorial stone that stands near the centre of the graveyard. My husband's grandparents: Margaret Jean Yancey Ferguson; Clyde James Ferguson. A few yards away, tucked into a corner by the graveyard wall, there's another, much smaller stone: a young woman, who died aged just nineteen. Both these graves looked as though they were regularly and lovingly tended.

When I moved to the North Carolina mountains after my sudden marriage I had to learn quickly how to talk the Bodie's Hollow way. It's always 'holler', never 'hollow'. The mountains are usually just 'the mountains'. There are the Blue Ridge Mountains and the Black Mountains and the Great Smoky Mountains, and they're all part of a much bigger range; and if you must give that range its name, call it the Appalatch-uns, not the Appalay-shuns. 'Appalay-shun' is what the Northern folk say. I never dared mention the Civil War: it was the War Between the States or even, amongst the older, euphemistically minded townsfolk, those who seemed as if they could almost reach back and touch those times, the Late Unpleasantness. As for the music that the town was built on – that harsh uncompromising music, the music that was played on the porch of my husband's house, the music that led to so much of what was to happen – I'm still not sure what I should call it. It's not exactly bluegrass. It's not country, certainly not country and western. Mountain music maybe, or – and it's okay to use this word, they've reclaimed it – hillbilly music. Or maybe I should stick to the most descriptive term of all: old-time.

Because that's what it's all about, really: the old time. My husband, like many Americans, could trace his family history back further than any British person would want to. He could talk about the fierce, warlike Fergusons scratching a living on the Scottish borders in the late 1500s. They emigrated in about 1600 to what he would call Ulster and I would call Ireland, and then, a hundred or so years later, across to Pennsylvania with its promises of a better life and the freedom to practise their strict Presbyterianism. Then, like many of the so-called Scotch-Irish, they found their way south to the folds and peaks of the Appalachian Mountains, taking with them their folk songs about love and death, particularly violent death, particularly murder.

And I guess when you have that kind of history hanging over you, a death that happened less than twenty years ago seems like a recent event, a scar too freshly healed to be picked at.

There were, as I have said, days when Bodie's Hollow seemed liked Paradise after everything I'd lived through in London. But there were also many days when I felt hemmed in: by fog, by history, by the situation I'd stumbled into. Days when my husband was busy and preoccupied; silent, almost. Days when his workload, his emotionally needy ex-wife, the burden of his heritage, the weight of unspoken secrets came between us and threatened to split us apart. I told myself that it was only natural: I didn't know him very well, after all. I was bound to feel lonely and homesick, a stranger in a strange town. But the sliver of doubt that crept into my mind in the days before my wedding soon turned into a thicker wedge: what on earth had possessed me to leave my home, my friends and everything that was familiar to marry a man I barely knew?

1

I married a man I barely knew, within two months of meeting him. I should have been wiser about it, of course: more sensible, more cautious. I should have thought it through. Marry in haste, repent at leisure, the old saying goes. But I married him quickly because I was afraid that the moment might pass, and because I was at a stage in my life when acting on a whim seemed better than almost any other option. I'd wasted enough time already. I wanted to change my life. I wanted to take a chance. I wanted to trust in fate, and when fate presents you with a beautiful, brilliant, vulnerable man with a charming smile and pale blue eyes who says that he loves you, you grab that chance with both hands. He swept me off my feet. It was what's generally known as a whirlwind romance.

I did take advice before I married him. I asked my friends what they thought. Should I marry him? Was it too soon? Was it a rebound thing? Was I being stupid to think I could just up and leave the country and settle into a new life abroad? Go for it, they said. Of course it's not too soon. You deserve some love in your life. He's lovely, he's gorgeous; you'll kick yourself if you let this one go. And it's only America; it's not as if you're moving to somewhere really foreign.

So I married my beautiful pale-eyed suitor and he whisked me off to his home town high in the heart of the Appalachian Mountains; which was where I realised I hadn't married just one man but a whole town full of ghosts and memories.

I met Trey Ferguson less than a year after my fiancé Martin died, so you could say that I was still emotionally fragile. I was working as a freelance journalist at the time. When Martin first became ill, I'd left my staff job as a magazine sub-editor so that I could spend as much time as possible looking after him. Eleven months after his death I was getting myself back on track. Friends and colleagues told me I was looking good and coping well; they seemed relieved that they didn't have to worry about me any more. I was thinking a lot about my future. I was getting fed up with the life of a freelance, writing women's-magazine articles on spec, and I was wondering if I should return to something a bit more secure, job-wise, so that I could upgrade my tiny flat and maybe even buy a house. I was looking for security and some direction in my life. I don't think I was looking for love.

Nick and Fiona invited me to go to a gig with them. That was how it all started. Big, blond, kind-hearted Nick had been Martin's best mate at the music magazine where they both worked: Nick as the features editor, Martin as the hotshot writer. Petite, lively, slightly annoying Fiona was Nick's wife, and we were, I suppose, good friends. We often used to go out as a foursome. Nick and Fiona had done their best to look out for me since Martin died, inviting me to go out with them whenever they thought I might be down. So when Nick was due to review an alternative country band at the Borderline that he thought would be right up my street, Fiona rang me and asked me to come with them.

One of the many misunderstandings in this story stems from the fact that I don't actually like country music, but Nick had long believed that I shared his passion for it and it seemed churlish to correct him. I grew up being forced to listen to my Irish father's collection of old-fashioned country and western records. The first time I met Nick he was impressed that I knew names like Ray Price and George Jones, and the misapprehension that I liked country music stuck in his head. Without it, I would never have met Trey Ferguson.

He was the supporting act, and Nick was more excited about seeing him than the main band. 'He's the grandson of CJ Ferguson,' he said urgently in the pub beforehand. Fiona raised her eyebrows at me, as if to say, 'Please humour him.' So I said, 'Really?' I had no idea who CJ Ferguson was.

'Apparently he's been making a living as a session musician in Nashville but recently he's decided to go back to his roots. He's just recorded a solo album. Very traditional bluegrass style. A mix of his own songs and some old stuff that his grandfather did. He's a brilliant musician, so tonight should be good.'

'Is he related to Missy Ferguson?' asked Fiona, bringing up a name that I knew would be anathema to

Nick. Missy Ferguson, the latest country-crossover sensation, was last seen on *Top of the Pops* wearing a pair of
leather chaps and belting out a Diane Warren power
ballad. Nick hated her with a passion, seeing her as
emblematic of everything that was slick and crass and
overtly commercial about the modern-day country-music
industry. He shuddered and shook his head. 'God, no,' he
said, in a horrified voice. 'Jesus, I hope not.'

He looked like he was about to launch into his usual
tirade so I quickly said, 'So, tell us about this CJ
Ferguson, then.'

Nick's eyes lit up. There was nothing he liked more
than sharing his musical passions with people. He cleared
his throat and began. 'CJ Ferguson was the Preacherman.
That's what everyone called him. Kind of a man in black
before Johnny Cash ever got the idea. He was an early
country superstar, sort of a dark flip side to the Carter
Family.'

I nodded. I'd heard of the Carter Family. The name
conjured up Sunday-best suits and faded floral dresses,
guitars strummed on a front porch somewhere in a poor
mountain community in the American South.

Nick continued. 'CJ Ferguson appeared on radio
shows throughout the late twenties and thirties, all
through the Depression era. He recorded thousands of
songs, a lot of religious stuff but also a lot of traditional
folk songs. He specialised in murder ballads, those grim
songs from Scotland and Ireland about people killing their
loved ones, usually down by the river. You know the kind
of thing I mean.'

'Like "Banks of the Ohio"?' I asked, thinking of the 1970s Olivia Newton-John hit that my dad had had on an eight-track cartridge.

'Exactly,' said Nick. 'Loads of the early bluegrass musicians recorded versions of that song. That and "Knoxville Girl" are probably the best-known murder ballads.'

'Oooh,' said Fiona, excitedly. 'That Richard Marx song – "Hazard". That's got a murder in it. I love that one.'

Nick threw her a look of complete bafflement. He cleared his throat again. 'Anyway, back to CJ Ferguson. He's not that well known these days, but he was hugely influential in his own way. Very dark and Gothic. Quite haunting, actually.'

'So there you have it, Maeve,' said Fiona. 'I bet you're really glad you came.'

Trey Ferguson emerged on stage with very little fanfare. In fact, he sauntered out from the wings while the lights were still up, just him and a Gibson guitar, and until he spoke I think most of us in the audience assumed that he was one of the stage crew. Nick, Fiona and I were standing near the front, which was significant as I discovered later that Trey was so short-sighted he probably wouldn't have noticed me if I'd been further back. He seemed to wink at me as he introduced himself. 'My name is both a burden and a heritage,' he said in a courtly Southern accent, his sweet, honeyed vowel sounds tempered by a slight rasp. 'I hope to share something of that heritage tonight, while also giving you a taste of my own songs.'

Trey was very tall and he seemed ungainly, with slightly hunched shoulders as if he were embarrassed by his height. He was wearing a crumpled dark suit that seemed almost Victorian, with a high-buttoning jacket over a white shirt worn without a tie. I looked at his feet, expecting to see cowboy boots, but instead he had on a pair of filthy scuffed red Converse baseball boots. He had dark hair, untidy and long, down almost to his shoulders, and thick, stylishly heavy-framed glasses. His face was pale, with sharp cheekbones and a surprisingly full Cupid's bow of a mouth.

It was just him, on his own, with his guitar and a mandolin that a gofer brought out for him. Later the same guy fetched a weird primitive-looking wooden instrument that I now know to be an Appalachian dulcimer, which Trey played sitting down, his long hair tucked behind his ears. He sang some songs that I thought I knew, songs about God and fair maidens and cabins in the hills, and others that I guess he wrote himself, about roads and motels and being lonesome.

It must be tough being a supporting artist. Most people were there to see the Moonshine Boys, the main act, so to start with there was a lot of foot-shuffling and whispering, and people were still drinking at the bar. But once Trey started to sing most of the fidgeting stopped. His voice was not a conventionally good one: it was slightly gravelly and ragged around the edges, and when he stretched towards the high notes it turned into a kind of nasal yodel. But it had a harsh kind of purity and was strangely moving. He hit notes as if he was slicing into them from an acute angle. Once he hit the note, he held it – no curlicues or fancy bits in his singing. In between the songs he told funny stories about them. 'My ex-wife's a singer,' he said, introducing one of his own songs. 'Her name's Missy. Maybe you've heard of her?' There was a ripple of laughter, some catcalls and a couple of isolated jeers.

Fiona dug her elbow into Nick's ribs and said, 'See?' I tried to work out how this diffident guy could possibly ever have been married to the big-haired country diva. 'I wrote this song for her,' he said. 'She never recorded it.' He smiled in an aw-shucks kind of way as he launched into the song. Looking back, I think that was the moment when I slowly, almost imperceptibly, began to fall under his spell; although I didn't notice it until much later.

On stage, Trey had begun singing a different song, a song he introduced as 'Pretty Polly'. Nick tapped me on the shoulder. 'It's a murder ballad,' he whispered. 'One of the oldest there is.'

Trey leaned over his dulcimer and began to strum a strange, frantic, relentless, almost discordant tune. The song, which he sang near the top of his register, was very simple in contrast, and seemed almost unconnected to the music. 'Oh Polly, pretty Polly, come along with me,' it began, innocuously enough, but the instrumental accompaniment gave it an underlying sense of threat. About halfway through there was a line that Trey sang so plainly and simply that it sent a chill down my spine: 'I dug on your grave the biggest part of last night.'

I shivered, enjoying the menacing sensation. He continued with a bit about plunging a 'fatal knife' deep into Polly's bosom, and all of a sudden a faint memory stirred: of an old folk song we used to sing in music lessons at junior school, with all the boys sniggering at the word 'bosom'. I'd gone along with the sniggers and the class's snide remarks but secretly I'd loved it, that beautiful, mournful tune: something about a lily-white maiden killed by her one true love. For years afterwards I'd remember snatches of its haunting melody.

I'd closed my eyes, focusing on the memory, and now I looked up at the stage again. The technician must have done something to the lights. There was just one spotlight shining on Trey, a cold, hard beam like moonlight. His glasses cast a heavy shadow on his sharp cheekbones. He sang the final lines of the song: 'Now to the devil a debt I must pay, for killing sweet Polly and running away,' and there was something haunted and desolate about his eyes, his face: as if he knew exactly what he was singing about.

And that's when it happened. Somehow, the combination of Trey Ferguson's pure sad voice and that look on his face reached right inside me and did something to me. I'd learned to keep my grief about Martin in a box, the lid firmly bolted down: it was something I occasionally allowed out when I was by myself and wanted to be a little self-indulgent. But that night it managed to escape without warning. I found my eyes filling with tears. I tried to use my hands to wipe them away. Fiona noticed, and passed me a tissue. But it wasn't enough. Embarrassingly, before I could stop it, a sob – an audible sob – emerged, and at that point Trey looked up, saw me crying, actually stopped playing the dulcimer and mouthed, 'Are you all right?'

His eyes looked so concerned that I felt myself blush to the roots of my hair and I had to swallow hard to dislodge the lump that had somehow found its way into the base of my throat.

I was at the bar during the interval with Nick and Fiona, drinking a pint of bitter and feeling embarrassed about the fuss that I'd caused, when I felt someone grip my elbow from behind. I looked up and saw Nick's face, his eyes wide with astonishment. I turned around and realised that it was Trey Ferguson who'd touched me. 'I'm sorry I made you cry,' he said.

Although I'm quite tall I had to crick my neck to look up at him. He was well over six feet. 'It's okay,' I said. 'It wasn't your fault. Don't worry about it.'

'Can I buy you dinner to say sorry?' He had a cute, eager look on his face.

'I can't. I'm with my friends. Nick's here to review the Moonshine Boys.'

'Hey, don't worry about us,' said Nick. 'You should go.' He had a dazed look on his face, as if amazed that the grandson of the Preacherman would ask me for dinner.

'Come on,' said Trey to me. 'You don't want to see the Moonshine Boys. They suck. Big time.'

'Do they?'

'Well, no, not really. But I'm trying to make dinner with me seem more of an attractive proposition. Please come?'

'Why?'

'Because I made a beautiful woman cry and I want to say sorry.'

And with that incredibly corny chat-up line my fate was sealed.

2

Trey Ferguson could be a real silver-tongued charmer, you know. The truth is, I'm not, nor ever have been, beautiful. I'm in my mid-thirties with reddish brown hair that falls into untidy corkscrew curls unless I use industrial-strength straightening products. I'm on the heavy side of average, but as I'm fairly tall – five-eight – I like to think I can carry it. I wear dramatic clothes well. I look good wearing velvet in rich colours, with shawls and throws and deep V-necks, but I really wish I could wear jeans and skimpy T-shirts without feeling fat. That fateful night I was wearing wide-legged black linen trousers with a drawstring waist and a loose lime-green linen shirt: a good look for me, but not in any way glamorous.

I have what's known as a high colour. I blush easily, and the blush runs quickly down my neck and across my chest like the map of an undiscovered country. I have greenish-brown eyes, round cheeks and a mouth that's the saviour of my face, big and curvy with large, even, white teeth. I get by. I don't scare the horses. But I don't usually get called beautiful. At least, not by strangely attractive men who used to be married to gorgeous singing superstars. Trey called me beautiful, so of course I agreed to have dinner with him.

The Borderline is on the edge of Soho, so we ducked through an alleyway and straight out onto a busy street full of restaurants. Trey was still holding my elbow, but gently. He had a strange uncoordinated walk, as if he'd only just grown to his full height and hadn't got used to it yet. Somehow we ended up in a booth at the back of a dark cave of an Italian trattoria, with red-checked tablecloths and Chianti bottles on the wall. He took off his jacket and rolled up his shirtsleeves, revealing long, sinewy fore-arms, whose dark hair curled over smooth, shockingly white skin that looked as if it had never seen daylight. Over indifferent Italian food we talked about a lot of stuff, hesitantly at first, taking ages to meet each other's eyes. I asked him about his ex-wife. 'She e-mailed me last year to tell me she was marrying her bass player,' he told me.

'I'm sorry,' I said as sympathetically as I could. 'Was it a shock?'

'The bass player? Yeah. I thought it was the drummer she was after. Oh well, she's always had a thing for rhythm sections.'

I laughed. Trey laughed too. 'I'm sorry,' I said. 'It must have been tough.'

'It's okay. It was always a matter of time with Missy. We managed to stick together for – what – seventeen years? That's more than I ever expected.'

I was shocked. 'Seventeen years?' Missy had always looked so young whenever I'd seen her on TV.

'We married straight out of high school. We were both sixteen.'

'Wow,' was all I could think to say to that. I did a quick calculation. That made Trey a year or so younger than me.

'What about you?' he asked, just as I stuffed my mouth with a forkful of pasta. 'Are you married? With someone?'

I shook my head, and when I'd finished the mouthful I said, 'I was going to get married, but he got ill and then he died, so I didn't. Obviously.'

It was his turn to say, 'I'm sorry.' He took a deep breath and seemed about to say something else but didn't. He played with his wineglass, running his finger around the rim. Then finally he said, 'Is that what made you cry?'

I still had my fork in my hand so I studied it very carefully, scratching a bit of pasta sauce from one of the tines with a fingernail. I shrugged my shoulders. 'Maybe. I don't know. It was nearly a year ago so I should be okay.'

I put my fork down, took a deep breath and pressed the tips of my fingers over my eyes, trying hard not to start crying again. I sat like that for a while, and then Trey touched my hand very gently. Leaning across the table, he used his thumb to wipe away the tears that had appeared at the corners of my eyes.

I took him back to my cramped ground-floor flat in south London, hacked out of the front room of a big

Victorian terraced house. Trey looked around, and I saw it with his eyes. The divan bed with its desperately cheery ethnic throw, the old settee and the dining table that doubled as my desk, piled high with newspapers and books, all fighting for space in the high-ceilinged, bay-windowed room. 'This is homey,' he said, but I think he was just being kind. I went into my tiny cupboard of a kitchen to make coffee as he stumbled around the flat, looking at things. I heard the sound of the stereo being switched on, and then the distinctive opening chords of Joni Mitchell's album *Blue* filled the room. As I poured water onto the coffee I was surprised to find that my hands were shaking: it'd been a long time since I'd invited a strange man back to my flat, and I wasn't totally sure how the script was supposed to go.

Trey appeared in the doorway of the kitchen. He stood there, slightly stooped, one hand on the lintel above the doorway, just looking at me. I put the kettle down and looked back at him: at his dishevelled hair, so dark against his skin; at his blue eyes, sparkling behind his glasses; at that choirboy's mouth. I felt my blush return, warm and almost liquid, pouring itself across my face and chest. Trey's mouth twitched and turned into a smile. And then suddenly the moment came: the moment I guess I had been waiting for since he'd first touched my hand in the restaurant. He had my face in his hands and he was kissing me, his lips gentle yet insistent on my forehead, my nose, my eyes, my mouth.

I forgot about the coffee and responded. Trey's glasses clanked against my nose so I took them off and put them on the kitchen worktop. Jokingly I said, 'Why, Miss Jones, you're . . .'

'Blind as a bat,' he responded, and as if to prove it he hit his head on one of the overhead cupboards as he stepped forwards, pinning me against the worktop. He barely winced. 'But to compensate,' he said, 'I have been granted an amazing sense of touch.'

Trey was right. His long-fingered hands quickly found their way inside my shirt. The tips of his fingers were rough and callused, particularly on his left hand, and felt harshly erotic against my skin. I ran my hand through his hair and brought his face even closer to mine, exploring his mouth with my tongue. Then his mouth was on my neck and he was fumbling with my bra strap, those callused fingertips on my spine. I felt the warm liquid feeling spread through my entire body but I felt something else as well: fear? Apprehension? Guilt? I put my hand flat on his chest as if to say, 'Stop.' He pulled away from me, his mouth still slightly open. We looked at each other for a few seconds, as if we were trying to read each other's minds. Then I decided. I took hold of his wrist and led him to my bed.

We took each other's clothes off. To his credit, Trey gasped when he saw my breasts, my only truly impressive feature. Under his shabby suit he turned out to have a beautiful body, long and lean and pale, with narrow hips and a line of dark hair from his navel to his dick. He kissed me virtually all over my body, saying my name 'Maeve, Maeve,' as he did so, the M and the V sounds making his lips vibrate on my body. He burrowed down under the duvet and tenderly, insistently licked me, bringing me almost but not quite to orgasm. Then he kissed me full on my mouth so I could taste myself on him. He straddled me, and I could see his erection. 'Do you have something?' he whispered, and I fumbled in the drawer of the bedside cabinet and pulled out a condom.

When I woke, Trey's arms were wrapped around me, his face buried in the back of my neck. I'm not usually the kind of woman who likes to be held all night, but as I ran my fingers gently through the hair on Trey's forearms and he snuggled closer to me, I realised that it felt right, comfortable, familiar; as if we'd known each other for years.

As I got breakfast in the kitchen I heard a sound that I hadn't heard in more than a year: the discordant twang of a guitar being tuned, a sound that reminded me so strongly of Martin that I felt the hairs on the back of my neck stand on end. I looked across and saw Trey sitting on the edge of the bed, leaning over a guitar. Martin's guitar: the guitar that he used to play almost every evening; the guitar that had been sitting in the corner of the room gathering dust since he'd gone. I felt my throat constrict and for a second I was angry. I wanted to tell Trey to put it down. But then I saw how tender his fingers were as they plucked the strings, how closely he was listening to the notes that he played. He smiled: not at me but to himself; his whole face radiant and absorbed. He began to play. It was a song I knew, from the Joni Mitchell album we'd played the night before. And so, instead of telling him to stop, I joined in, singing in my passably tuneful, acceptable school-choir-standard voice. Trey looked up at me as if he'd forgotten I was there, smiled again and added a harmony. It sounded surprisingly good: he actually managed to make my voice sound okay. And from that moment sprang one of those niggling mis-understandings at the heart of our marriage: Trey thought I was musical.

He'd rummaged through the huge CD collection the night before and assumed it was mine, but it wasn't. The Delta-blues compilations; the classic rock – the Stones, Led Zep, Jimi Hendrix, Nirvana; the cool stuff from the 1960s and 1970s – the Band, the Byrds, Buffalo Springfield: anything in the collection that was remotely credible had belonged to Martin. My CDs were a paltry collection of female singer-songwriters – chick music, Martin used to call it. Kate Bush, Sheryl Crow, Dido. The only artist we'd both loved was Joni Mitchell. And then the guitar: Trey had immediately thought that it was mine. He should have realised it wasn't – it was dusty and out of tune. But he'd looked at me, smiling, as I'd started to sing. Music was obviously such an important part of his life, and so when we sang together on that first morning Trey must have assumed that I shared his passion. At the time I really didn't think anything of it. But maybe – I'm not sure, but maybe – that was one of the reasons he wanted to see me again.

3

As far as I was concerned it was a one-night stand. That's what I kept telling myself that morning: a one-night stand. It was something I'd needed to do: a rite of passage; another step forward in my recovery after Martin's death. It was fun, and I felt adored and appreciated for a while. Trey Ferguson was a safe choice, because he was someone I was never likely to see again. Yes, he was lovely, and in the pre-Martin days I might have wanted to see more of him, maybe pursue a relationship, because he was charming and funny and quirkily good-looking. But at that point I didn't think I was in the market for a relationship. It'd been a good night. Maybe even a great night. The sex had been good and he'd used a condom. He seemed like a nice guy. We'd both enjoyed ourselves. All in all, a thoroughly satis-factory night's work.

That wasn't how Trey saw it. He asked me if he could have my e-mail address.

'Why?' I could feel my defences rising. I'm sure a blush was sweeping across my neck and chest. I was trying to keep a close watch on my heart.

'Duh,' he said, hitting his forehead with the heel of his hand. 'So I can e-mail you. You know, send you one of those new-fangled electronic message thingamajigs?' His expression was deadpan; his eyes were sparkling.

'Oh.' I could feel the blush rising to my face. We were standing in the open doorway of my flat saying goodbye, and one of my upstairs neighbours, a good-looking young guy I often exchanged a few words with, came bouncing down the stairs at that point. He winked at me on his way out of the front door.

Trey took hold of my left hand. 'I'm flying home tomorrow, but I want to get to know you better. Is that okay?'

I was so surprised that I didn't know what to say.

Trey laughed. 'Hey, I know it was only supposed to be a one-nighter, but I really like you. I think we have a connection. I think we should take this further.'

He squeezed my hand and leaned into me, and we kissed for a long time. I could feel his erection and I felt a definite tingle, but I put the palm of my hand flat on his chest, said, 'Hold on a moment,' and went and rummaged through the papers on my desk until I found a copy of my business card.

He held it as if it was something precious. He pushed his glasses up onto his forehead, brought the card close to his face and read it out loud. 'Maeve O'Mara.'

Then he pushed his glasses back down, put the card in his jacket pocket and took my face in his hands. He kissed me again and then said, 'Maeve O'Mara. What a wonder-ful name. I'll be in touch.'

He touched his right index finger to his forehead in a kind of salute, and he walked away, whistling.

A couple of hours later Fiona rang, wanting details.
'So?' she asked, breathlessly.

'So what?' I said, deliberately obtuse.

'What happened? You know, with Trey Ferguson?'

'What do you think happened?'

'Oh Maeve, I'm so pleased for you.' As if I'd just passed
my driving test or something similar. 'Do you want to
have lunch today? I'm meeting some of the girls at that
place by the river in Richmond.'

I hate girlie lunches. I hate girlie chat. Call it the legacy
of being brought up with two brothers by my widowed
Irish father. The thought of sitting around a table with
Fiona and her friends, analysing my night with Trey
Ferguson, made me shudder. 'I can't, Fiona, I've got that
piece to finish. Loads to do . . .' I trailed off vaguely.

'OK, no probs,' she said, brightly. 'I'll let you get on.'
She paused. Then, 'Are you going to see him again?'

I laughed at the predictability of the question. She
asked it as if it had been an afterthought, but I knew that it
was all she wanted to know. 'Fiona, he lives in America.
He's flying home tomorrow.'

'Oh well, never mind,' she said, in a comforting voice.
'I'm so pleased you had a good time last night.'

After I put the phone down I thought: did I actually tell
her I had a good time last night? Then I realised I must be
getting better, getting back to normal, because Fiona was
beginning to piss me off. Straight after Martin's death I'd
been glad of her solicitousness and friendship; now it felt
patronising. I smiled to myself. Two big achievements
within twenty-four hours: good sex with a nice guy, and

turning down one of Fiona's lunch invitations. Perhaps I was finally recovered. Feeling better than I'd done all year, I went out into the early summer sunshine, bought the Sunday paper and walked to the friendly organic café two streets away where I ate a mound of amorphous cheesy lentil stuff while reading the *Observer* magazine.

Trey's first e-mail came that evening. I was on-line, digging up pseudo-scientific research I could use for a magazine piece I was writing about women who drink alone. Ironically I had a large glass of wine within reach of my right hand. Not really expecting anything, I clicked on the mailbox icon and got the familiar 'ping' of incoming mail. The sender, Trey Ferguson. Time received, just a few hours after he'd left. He was keen.

Hey, Maeve . . .
Thanks for a wonderful night. I thought it was great – hope you did too.
Here I am in my lonely hotel room, getting ready to go back home after five weeks on the road, and all I can think about is whether I'll see you again some time. I may be back in Britain later this summer and I'm really hoping we can hook up again. Anyway, e me and let me know how you're getting on. I'd love to hear from you . . .
Take care, Trey x

I read the message several times. It seemed – nice. Not

obsessive or anything. Okay, the 'all I can think about . . .' gave me pause for thought, but generally I got a good feeling about it. He liked me. He liked me a lot, but I wasn't picking up any kind of weird vibe.

I decided to reply. 'Hey yourself,' I began. Not a phrase I'd use in normal speech, but it seemed the right way to begin an e-mail to an American who used phrases like 'e me'.

Hey yourself . . .
Nice to hear from you. I had a great time too. I'm quite busy this summer but if you're over here it'd be really nice to meet up again. Let me know when.
Have a good flight home, and thanks again for last night.
Maeve x

Carefully non-committal, building in an excuse not to see him should I change my mind. I read it over a few times until I was happy with it, then I filed it in 'drafts' and resolved not to send it until a full twenty-four hours had passed since he'd sent his e-mail. A woman's instinct: even in this age of electronic communication, always play hard to get.

4

And so it began. Our e-mail romance, if that's what you want to call it. I'd send Trey an e-mail, then he'd reply the next day. The following day I'd e-mail back, and so it went on. Regular as clockwork. His messages made me smile and gave me a warm feeling inside. He told me how he'd recently moved back to his home town in North Carolina. Bodie's Hollow, it was called. 'Really,' he wrote. 'I know that sounds like a made-up name but it's a real place.'

I bought an American road atlas and found Bodie's Hollow, eventually: a tiny speck on a back road deep in the Appalachians. Trey told me that he'd moved back to what he called the 'old Ferguson homestead,' and how all the townspeople treated him like a kid, because they remembered him simply as CJ Ferguson's little grandson. 'The lack of respect is good for me,' he wrote. 'I tell myself it's character-forming to go into the café and have the waitress pinch my cheek and ask me if I still like chocolate ice cream.'

He told me that he'd built a recording studio in the old family home. He said he was doing his best to breathe some new life into the town. He told me how beautiful it was, how clear the air, how much I'd love it there. I read that as an invitation to visit, to which I didn't respond. I kept my e-mails light. I told him what I was up to at work, what articles I was planning to write. I described a couple of gigs that Nick and Fiona had taken me to. I told him about an interesting documentary on BBC4 about Joni Mitchell, about a French film I'd seen at the cinema, about a really bad new restaurant I'd been to. Nothing personal, nothing emotional: just keeping the channels open, keeping in touch.

I found myself buying Trey Ferguson's album and listening to it quite a bit. He had one of those voices that get inside your head: husky and intimate, recorded – I imagined – very close to the microphone; naked, almost. I Googled his name, and voraciously read all I could find about him. I was surprised by his long list of recording credits. He'd played acoustic guitar and mandolin on all sorts of people's records. Mainstream country mostly, but also a surprising smattering of other stuff: cool indie groups, hip singer-songwriters and even a few famous rock stars. He'd produced quite a few records too, including four albums for – surprise, surprise – Missy Ferguson. He'd even won a handful of Grammies, both as a musician and a producer. Trey Ferguson was more successful than I'd imagined.

I checked out CJ Ferguson too. Nick had been right when he'd called him 'very dark'. He even looked scary: tall and thin with a cadaverous face and a black suit, steadfastly refusing to smile for the camera. I ordered a CD of his songs from Amazon, and found it haunting and unsettling. A deep voice, half-singer, half-hellfire preacher. A harshly strummed guitar offered sparse accompaniment. He sang funereally slow songs about death, particularly violent death, particularly murder. I recognised 'Pretty Polly'. Scarier and perhaps less sorrowful than Trey's version, nonetheless it still moved me to tears.

And yes, of course, I did what any woman would do. I Googled Trey's ex-wife and found her homepage. There she was, all poised and perfect, her hair with its marmalade-coloured streaks hanging sleekly around her heart-shaped face, her chin balanced pertly on the back of one hand. 'Missy Ferguson was born and raised in the tiny mountain community of Bodie's Hollow, NC,' said her biography. 'She was greatly privileged to have learned to sing under the tutelage of the legendary CJ Ferguson,' it continued clumsily. 'At just sixteen, Missy married CJ Ferguson's grandson Trey Ferguson, himself one of the foremost living exponents of traditional mountain music. The young couple soon took Nashville by storm.'

It didn't mention their divorce, but why should it have? That would have ruined the fairy tale. I looked at the photos of Missy, compared her manicured hands to my chunky nail-bitten ones, and wondered why Trey was the slightest bit interested in me.

My relationship with Trey, if you can call it that, came to a head after about three weeks of regular e-mails. I got a call from an editor friend of mine asking me if I wanted to interview Carly Rose, the sixteen-year-old

American actress who was in London promoting her new film. Of course I didn't want to, but — as any freelance would — I jumped at the offer of work. The interview was set for four o'clock at a new boutique hotel not far from Covent Garden. At five o'clock I was still waiting on a trendy but uncomfortable purple sofa in the hotel lobby. It was a horrible day, unseasonably wet, and I was cold and bored. Eventually, ninety minutes late, the little madam deigned to see me. Her nose was red and runny, which she blamed on hay fever, and she snuffled her way through the interview. I asked her the usual questions but I was distracted by her breasts, which were twice the size they'd been in the film, and had a tell-tale inch of shiny stretched skin between them. After an indifferent ten-minute interview, the PR woman wound things up and I was back out on the rainy streets before I'd plucked up the courage to ask Carly Rose about her boob job.

I remembered that I had no food in the flat, so I ran through the rain to the branch of Marks and Spencer opposite Covent Garden Tube station, where I loaded a basket with ready meals and pre-prepared vegetables and joined the long, long queue at the checkouts. The line snaked all the way back through the yogurt and dairy-produce aisle. The shelves bore the marks of people who'd given up waiting: packs of chicken breasts dumped in the middle of the cheese section, frozen peas gently thawing next to the fancy French butter. As my basket became ever heavier, I whiled away the time working the interview up into an anecdote about Carly Rose's boob job and coke habit, smiling to myself like a mad person.

And then it suddenly hit me what I was doing: I was planning what I'd tell Martin when I got home, planning how I'd make him laugh with stories about my day. And what struck me particularly was this: he wouldn't even know who Carly Rose was. That was how long he'd been dead. People had had whole careers since Martin had died. There were teenage superstars on the covers of magazines who'd been anonymous schoolkids when Martin had been alive. Groups he'd never heard of were playing at Glastonbury this summer. The whole world was moving on and he wasn't here to see it.

I nearly lost it, there in the dairy aisle of the Covent Garden Marks and Sparks. I nearly dropped my basket, nearly slumped to the floor and started crying out loud. Instead, I pressed my hand to my mouth, pushed my shoulders back and took a deep breath. I thought about Trey Ferguson. There'd be an e-mail waiting for me when I got back to the flat. That was a good thing, something to look forward to. I started to think about what I'd write about in my next e-mail to him. I'd tell him about Carly Rose. I could make it really funny. He'd enjoy reading about it. Thinking about Trey made me feel a little happier inside, and that kept me going as the queue inched its way forward, and then as my carrier bags of shopping cut into my hands on the way home on the packed Tube.

Bedraggled by the rain, I let myself into the flat. I dumped my shopping in the kitchen and turned on my computer. As I waited for it to boot up, I took off my soaking-wet jacket, filled the kettle and threw a tea bag in a mug. I went back to the screen, dialled up my internet connection and clicked on my mailbox.

Nothing. No new mail. Nothing from Trey Ferguson.

I checked back through the inbox and noted the regularity of his previous correspondence. Every two days, no mistake. I checked the 'sent' file. Again, every two days. Yes, I'd sent him an e-mail the day before. He should have replied by now. I read through my last e-mail to him again. Was there something in it that had caused him not to reply? I couldn't see anything. Just a nice, normal, chatty message. Signed off with a 'Write soon! Maeve x', just as usual.

I'm ashamed to say that was when I really did lose it. I sat down heavily on the floor, my back against the end of my bed, and I sobbed my heart out. I was crying about Martin, of course, and about the rain and being lonely. I was crying about the ugliness of London and the length of the queues in the shops, and about a sad, arrogant little teenage girl called Carly Rose who was already ruining her life. But mostly I was crying because I'd accidentally let someone into my heart, accidentally started caring about someone again, and that could only lead to heartbreak.

5

Trey rang me. That night. He didn't e-mail me; he rang me. All that fuss about nothing, as if I were a teenage girl in love for the first time. I'd sobbed for about half an hour, until I'd run out of tears and self-pity, and then I'd looked at my watch and remembered I hadn't put the food away in the fridge. I was standing in front of the microwave working out how long a radiation blast my moussaka would need when the phone rang and I nearly dropped the plastic container of food on to the floor. I was still too emotional to answer the phone in a normal manner so I let the machine pick up, and then I heard a gravelly American voice, with a distinctive Southern accent, say, 'Hey, Maeve O'Mara . . .'

I ran to the phone, tears forgotten. 'Hi! How are you?'

'I'm good, very good. You?'

'I'm . . . fine.' An awkward pause. Then we both spoke at once. 'So . . .'

Trey laughed. 'Go on, you first,' he said.

'I was just going to ask what you're up to, I mean, what time is it there? Where are you?' Stop gabbling, Maeve.

'Well, I'm at home in Bodie's Holler. It's about three o'clock, and I was just sitting here at my computer writing you an e-mail. And then I figured that maybe you'd be at home, and I thought it would be cool to talk to you, so I found your number on your business card and rang you instead. Is that okay?'

He sounded nervous.

'Yeah,' I said, as reassuringly as I could. 'It's great.' I pulled the phone towards me and curled up in a corner of the settee.

'So, like I said, I'm coming to Britain soon. Probably for a couple of weeks or so. I've got some people I need to see in London, and I was thinking that maybe if I was over there I could come and see you and we could, you know, hang out? You could show me round London, maybe? You know, only if you want to. If you're not too busy.'

Trey's hesitancy was endearing. Perhaps if he'd been surer of himself I would have said no. But he sounded so sweet, so nervous, as if he'd had to pluck up his courage to make the call, that I found myself agreeing to meet him at Gatwick in a week's time and even invited him to stay in my flat.

I drove myself mad with anxiety that week. What had I done by inviting Trey to stay? Was this suddenly a relationship? If so, was I ready? How had I got myself into this? I'd been so guarded since Martin had died. I'd been so protective of my heart, of myself, of my hard-won recovery that I'd barely let anyone get close to me. A thousand times I wanted to phone Trey and cancel the invitation. I wanted to retreat, to lock my door, to tell him that I just wasn't ready for whatever it was he wanted from me. But I didn't. Instead I dithered. I distracted myself from the big questions and got wound up about trivial things. The hot water wasn't working properly: would there be enough for two people to have showers? What kind of food did he eat? Would I need to make proper coffee for him, or could he cope with instant?

I cleaned the bathroom and the kitchen, and hoovered the floors several times. I tried to tidy up, but found that there wasn't enough room to put everything. I opened the wardrobe doors and stared for a long time at Martin's clothes in there. Finally, I decided it was time. I bundled his shirts and jeans into dustbin liners and dropped them in the charity clothes-recycling bin at my nearest super-market. I was trembling as I did it. I wanted someone to hug me or congratulate me. I guess it was the modern-day equivalent of coming out of mourning. It was only when I got back home that I realised the anniversary of Martin's death had been and gone a couple of days before, and I hadn't actually noticed it.

On the day of Trey's arrival I dressed carefully. The same black linen trousers that I'd been wearing the night we'd first met, topped with a fuchsia-pink wrap-around cardigan over a deep orange vest. Clashing colours, sure, and if I blushed the clash would be even worse, but they made me feel vibrant and happy. I put on lipstick and mascara and pulled my hair back in a ponytail, allowing a few carefully chosen corkscrew curls free to dangle around my face. I looked as good as I possibly could without it seeming as if I'd made a special effort.

I stood in the Gatwick arrivals area carrying a cardboard sign I'd made: 'Trey Ferguson' in thick black marker pen. It made me smile and I hoped it would make him smile, too. At the very least it would be an ice-breaker. I thought we needed one. I was so nervous I'd thrown up my breakfast.

He came bounding – lolloping, almost – through the gate, like a marionette being operated by a trainee puppeteer. He was even taller than I remembered. He was carrying a huge backpack – the sort that students take to Australia in their gap years. He had a big black guitar case slung from one shoulder and what I guessed was a mandolin case from the other. He was wearing baggy jeans. Not stylish-baggy, just baggy-baggy. A faded orange T-shirt with a tourist message on it: 'I've been to Grandfather Mountain'. An old corduroy jacket, beige, with leather elbow patches, too short in the sleeves. On his feet, those same Converse sneakers. His long hair was caught up in some kind of ponytail, loose strands flying around his face or tucked untidily under the arms of his glasses: a kind of accidental twin of my own hairstyle. It took him a few moments to see me, then – squinting – he did. He grinned hugely, stopped in his tracks and turned towards me, nearly decapitating an elderly Chinese woman with his guitar case as he did so.

Trey kissed me across the barrier. We kissed each other. He pushed his glasses to his forehead and surrendered to the kiss, eyes closed, hands on my face like a blind man. I was on tiptoe, straining into him, wondering why I'd ever been nervous. Then we pulled away for breath. He pushed his glasses back on his nose and, attempting to keep hold of my hand over the heads of everyone, he walked round the barrier and came to where I was standing. 'I love the sign,' he said. 'Were you afraid I wouldn't recognise you?'

'Of course not. I'm very memorable. I was just afraid that I wouldn't recognise *you*.'

He threw his head back and laughed, I guess at the absurdity of the notion.

'Have you?' I said.

'Have I what?'

'Been to Grandfather Mountain.'

He looked puzzled. I pointed at his T-shirt. He laughed again, loudly: an unembarrassed laugh that got people staring at him.

'Oh yeah. I mean, this is a thrift-store shirt, but yeah. When I was a kid. My aunts took me. Big treat.' Trey's eyes lit up with the memory, and it struck me that he was still pretty much a kid. Hard to believe that he'd been married for seventeen years.

As we walked across the airport concourse pushing the trolley piled with Trey's luggage, he threw his arm around me. His hip rubbed against my waist, my hip against his thigh: it felt familiar and comfortable, and reminded me of walking home from the pictures with my first boyfriend. Trey took one look at my sturdy, unfashionable Volvo estate, smiled, said, 'Hey, it's roomy,' and hurled his guitar and backpack into the back. He curled himself into the passenger seat, pushing it as far back as it would go, and promptly fell asleep.

6

And then we fell in love.

That sounds absurdly romantic, I know, but I think it's true. Put it another way: over the next week Trey and I moved from feeling warm about each other to talking seriously about spending the rest of our lives together. Is that a description of falling in love? From my admittedly limited experience, I think it might be.

The first thing I noticed was how quickly we felt at ease together. The first couple of days we did tourist things – the London Eye, a double-decker-bus tour (Trey's idea, and he loved it) – but mostly we just hung out together. We went to the supermarket and the pub together. We sat on a bench in the local park and people-watched. We talked and talked, mostly about nothing. We touched each other a lot: holding hands, brushing each other's hair from our faces, even that good old teenage standby: the hand in the back pocket of the other person's jeans. When I needed to get some work done, Trey sprawled on the settee with a book or a newspaper or his guitar. In the evenings we watched trash TV together, and I discovered Trey's flip, deadpan humour. We'd be watching some American cop series and he'd gesture at the characters and say something like, 'I could be wrong, but I'm sensing some unresolved sexual tension here,' and he'd say it so straight-faced that it would take me a beat or two (and a glance at his eyes, always a give-away) to see that he was being funny. He had a droll, understated sense of humour, of the sort that we Brits tend to assume Americans don't have.

We discovered that we had things in common. For one thing, we were both orphans. I told Trey about my Irish father, who'd come to London to work on the roads but had done well for himself, setting up his own building business and becoming virtually middle-class in the process. I told him about my mother, how she'd died when I was five. 'I've always assumed it was cancer. Dad never told us when we were growing up, and since he died four years ago there's no one left to ask.'

In fact, I had tried asking him once, when I was a teenager. 'How did Mum die?' was the way I'd put it, and my father had deliberately misunderstood me and said, 'Peacefully.' I never asked again.

Trey told me about his parents. 'Have you ever heard of Junior Ferguson?' he asked. I shook my head. 'My father,' he said, with what seemed like a heavy dose of bitterness. 'A very fine musician, apparently, but he squandered his talent, so the family story goes, on drink and drugs and fast cars. Apparently he arrived back in Bodie's Holler from LA with a pregnant flower child in tow. My aunts tell me she was dark-haired and beautiful, with hair hanging down below her waist, and went by the name of Liberty. She gave birth to me, they hung around for a few months, and then they drifted away back to California, leaving me behind. A year or so later they were both killed in a car crash somewhere on the coastal highway between LA and San Francisco. My grandfather and my aunts brought me up.'

'So your parents just abandoned you?'

Trey looked at me with narrowed eyes, then down at the floor and then back at me. He shrugged and then shook his head. 'No, not really. They left me with people they knew would look after me. I had a good childhood with people who loved me. I was lucky.'

Something about his manner suggested he'd said that before. 'I was lucky.' It sounded like something he had trained himself to say.

'Do you know anything more about your mother?' I asked. 'What about her family? Have you ever met them?'

He shook his head. 'I thought about tracing them once. I asked my aunts to tell me all about my mother. But they didn't know anything so I figured: she walked out on me when I was just a baby, so why should I care?' It was the first time I'd heard hardness in his voice. It didn't suit him.

'Christ,' I said. Trey winced. I'd noticed he did that whenever I said it. I found it almost sweet.

I wanted a second opinion on Trey. Was he as wonderful as he seemed? I took him to the Irish pub where my cute but feckless kid brother Mickey, who affects an Irish accent and likes to think that he's in touch with his heritage, was playing bodhrán in a ceilidh band. They bonded on sight. Trey took a turn on the fiddle. 'It's not really my instrument,' he said modestly, before his fingers flew up and down the neck producing amazing shimmering strings of notes.

Mickey extended an open invitation to 'jam any time you like, mate,' and they exchanged a macho brotherly hug.

Nick and Fiona loved Trey too. They invited us for dinner, and once Nick had got over being star-struck we had a great night. Nick plays guitar, so there was more jamming. I noticed that Trey watched Nick closely, letting him lead, making Nick's guitar-playing seem better than it was. Fiona, pink-faced from too much wine, said to me in a stage whisper, 'Maeve, he's gorgeous. Hold on to this one,' and I wondered what she meant by that: as if I had deliberately let Martin go?

The real clincher was my old school friend Helen, a tough person to please. She'd never liked Martin, for example, but had done her best to understand why we were together and how he meant so much to me.

Helen and I had met on the first day at secondary school, at the posh, fee-paying girls' school my newly middle-class father thought I ought to attend. Helen Oliver, Maeve O'Mara: we were next to each other in the alphabet so the teacher made us sit together. I wasn't happy about it; I wanted to be friends with the cool, pretty popular girls, and Helen had a narrow stern face, pale ginger hair in tight plaits, and sensible lace-up brown shoes. I soon discovered that she was funny, clever and secretly subversive, and the most dedicated friend anyone could hope to have. Helen's a Methodist minister now, a sharp, waspish minister who leads a quietly good life and doesn't suffer fools gladly. She's single through choice – happily so: she doesn't see why she should make compromises in order to have a husband. I was desperate to know what she thought of Trey so I invited her round for dinner.

She quizzed him on lots of things. She asked him about his ex-wife ('She wanted to be free to wear leather pants on MTV' was his explanation of the divorce), his upbringing ('Just like *The Waltons*, if John-Boy Walton had been an orphaned only child,' he said) and how old he was. Helen noticed things. 'You don't like it when Maeve says "Oh God" or "Jesus", do you?'

Trey looked embarrassed. 'Not really, no.'

'Why not?'

'It's how I was brought up. My grand-daddy was what you'd call a God-fearing man. He would hot-sauce me if he heard me take the Lord's name in vain. So I learned not to.'

'Hot-sauce?' I heard it as 'hot source', and thought it sounded like something to do with the internet.

'Hot-sauce, yeah.' Trey grinned. 'Hot-saucing. Tongue-slapping. Maybe it's an American thing? I mean, if he heard me take the Lord's name in vain he'd put Tabasco sauce on my tongue and make me close my mouth. It soon beat the habit out of me. And now it's so engrained it actually sounds wrong when someone close to me does it.'

Helen stared at him with wide eyes. I did, too. I looked hard at him. He wasn't joking this time, I could tell. 'You mean, your grandfather actually put Tabasco sauce on your tongue when you were just a little kid? That's weird. God. I mean, Jesus. Christ. Shit,' I said, covered in confusion. 'I'm going to have to teach myself some new swear words.' I looked at Trey and smiled. I pressed my knee against his under the table. Someone close to me, he'd called me.

Later, as Helen helped me with the washing-up, I whispered, 'What do you think?'

She went bright red, right to the tips of her ears. 'Oh Maeve, he's lovely. Seriously lovely. He's funny and he's cute and he's – okay, this is going to sound old-fashioned, but it's true – he's a gentleman. A gentle man. A properly good, decent man. I love that he still cares about his ex-wife – you can tell that, even though he jokes about it. But let me tell you this. He loves you. Like crazy. He adores you. You should see the way he looks at you. You should marry this man. And if you don't, I will.'

The next morning I was in the kitchen waiting for the kettle to boil when Trey walked in, wearing boxers and another of his thrift-store T-shirts, a purple one endorsing the joys of Spring Break '95 at Lake Havasu. He was rubbing the sleep out of his eyes and his hair was dishevelled. Actually, 'dishevelled' is too mild a word. His hair was a complete mess, sticking up in wild angles all over his head. We'd had very energetic sex the night before. He looked so cute that I felt my heart leap. He pulled himself up to sit on the work surface, leaning forward at an uncomfortable angle to avoid hitting his head on the wall-mounted cabinets. He watched me for a while, and then said, 'Maeve, would you be seriously freaked out if I asked you to marry me?'

I stood still for a while, balancing a spoonful of instant coffee. I felt my hand start to shake so I quickly dumped the coffee into a mug and put the spoon down. I took a deep breath, and then turned towards Trey. I could feel my entire face and neck engulfed in a deep red flush. He was watching me carefully. 'Have I spoken too soon?'

I nodded. Then I shook my head, and then I burst into tears.

7

'When?' I said.

'When what?'

'When did you decide you wanted to marry me?'

We were sitting at opposite ends of the settee, looking at each other. I had a box of tissues on my lap and was working my way through them, tearing them into little pieces. Trey said: 'I think it was the first time I saw you. I think it was love at first sight.'

I shivered. 'Why?'

'What do you mean, "why"?'

'Why love at first sight? Why did you fall in love with me?'

'Why not?' He laughed uneasily.

'No, I'm serious, Trey. I really need to know. Why did you fall in love with me the first time you saw me?' I pulled my knees up to my chest. I knew my body language was defensive, but I couldn't help it.

'It was your shirt I noticed first, that bright yellow one . . .'

'Green.'

My voice must have sounded harsher than I intended, because he blinked and looked startled for a moment.

'Sorry, green. Anyway, you were standing right at the front and you had your arms wrapped around yourself and I looked up at your face and you didn't want to be there. It was so clear in your eyes. I thought maybe you were a big fan of the Moonshine Boys and hadn't expected there to be an opening act, something like that. And then something happened to your face. You responded to my music. So many amazing expressions flooded over your face. You couldn't hide them. You didn't try to hide them. I felt we'd really connected. When you're a musician that's what you live for, that kind of response. And I thought, I love this woman. I have to meet her. We're meant for each other. That's what I mean. Love at first sight.'

'I don't believe in love at first sight.'

'Don't you?' Trey's voice was gentle and concerned. I shook my head vigorously. 'Why not?'

I tore up another tissue and bit my bottom lip. 'I think I need to tell you more about Martin.'

If love at first sight really happens, then why didn't it happen with Martin? It took me six years to fall in love with Martin. Six wasted years. I think it was the waste of time that was the biggest tragedy of our life together. We could have got married; we could have had children. Yes, he'd still be dead now. But we would have had time to create a life together, not just this cheap shoddy flat and a run-down Volvo, a dusty guitar and a couple of years' worth of memories.

Martin and I hated each other at first sight, and kept hating each other for years. We worked together at the same magazine. He was the whizz-kid new writer and I was the sub-editor who had to rip his prose to shreds. Not a relationship made in heaven. I thought he was over-rated, and that his writing was shallow and meretricious. In person, I thought he was even worse. Shorter than me, skinny but pugnacious: small-man syndrome, I told friends. Badly cut mid-brown hair. Bad skin, still prone to outbreaks of acne. Shiny suits that he appeared to get from Mr Byrite. He had what I assumed was an exaggerated cockney accent, and an infuriating way of adopting unpopular viewpoints just to get a rise out of people. Chips on both shoulders, and anywhere else it was possible to have a chip. I figured that he'd been a clever kid at school and hadn't worked out how to translate his skills into adult life.

He thought I was a snooty cow. Years later, he told me that he enjoyed getting me angry so he could listen out for the precise moment at which my posh accent started to crack. Even after we stopped working together, we still moved in the same circles. We often found ourselves in the same pub, having interminable arguments about music or films or politics, or anything. We argued so much that friends used to tell me that I was obviously in love with him and just didn't want to admit it to myself. I told them that was nonsense.

One day I bumped into Martin in the street near the offices of his magazine. He was standing in a doorway smoking, looking very pissed off. He raised his hand in curt greeting. I was in no hurry so I stopped and said, 'What's up?'

'Jesus, Maevo. What the fuck am I doing with my life?' He dropped his cigarette on the ground and angrily stamped it out.

'What do you mean?'

'I mean, what the fuck am I doing with my life? Did you know I'm thirty-three tomorrow?'

He said that as if it was supposed to mean something.

'Martin, that's ancient. Thirty-three and what have you achieved? Absolutely nothing. You might as well kill yourself right now.'

He was rummaging in his pocket for his pack of cigarettes as I said this. He looked up suddenly and saw that my eyes were laughing. And then, for the first time since I met him, he laughed too: a huge, unexpected belly laugh. 'Christ, Maevo, I'm so glad there's you. What the fuck would I do without you?'

Martin stared at me. I stared back. Something was happening. I wasn't sure what. Then he kissed me. I flinched slightly, at the taste of cigarettes, and then kissed him back. A week later he moved into my flat, and we seemed to be the only ones who were surprised.

Given his thirty-a-day smoking habit, it should have been lung cancer that got him, but in fact it was a brain tumour that went undetected for months. By the time Martin finally admitted to me that yes, yes, something was wrong, he was more bad-tempered than usual because he kept getting headaches, maybe he should get his eyes tested or something, it was too late.

'The thing about me and Martin,' I told Trey after giving him the condensed version of the story, 'was that we were so alike. We were two bright, scared kids who'd had tough childhoods and it seemed like everyone else around us had been given the script but we just had to make things up as we went along. I know I'm not explaining it very well but . . .'

I had to stop there because a huge ball of grief was trying to explode out of my chest and I could hardly breathe. 'Oh Jesus, Trey, I'm sorry,' I said as I broke down in sobs. 'I didn't mean to do this. It's not fair on you. But I miss him so much and it's so fucking unfair that he had to die, and if anyone had to fall in love with me at first sight then I wish it had been him. I'm sorry.'

Trey held me as I sobbed on his shoulder, which I guess wasn't what he'd imagined happening when he came into the kitchen that morning to ask me to marry him. 'Shhh,' he whispered, and 'It's okay, it's okay,' and other generically comforting phrases like that. Then he put his cheek against mine, ran his hand through my hair and spoke gently into my ear. 'Maeve,' he said, 'I know what it's like. Trust me. I know what it's like to lose someone you love.'

That made me angry. How dare he assume that he knew how I felt? Getting divorced from your childhood sweetheart, while no doubt traumatic, is scarcely equivalent to watching the man you love slowly losing his battle to keep living. Death trumps divorce every time. I pushed him away. 'Yeah, but you got divorced. That's not really the same, is it?'

Trey opened his mouth as if to say something, then seemed to think better of it. If only he had said something then. If only he'd told me the full story then, when he first thought about sharing it with me, so many things would have been different. But instead he said, 'I know that my marriage ended after seventeen years but I'm not afraid to try it again.'

'Christ, Trey, for a musician you've got lousy timing.'

He sat back and smiled at me. 'You're not ready, are you?'

I blew my nose and wiped my eyes again. 'Of course I'm not ready. Look at me. I'm an emotional wreck.'

Trey frowned; a frown like a small child would do after being told off, with a sulky stuck-out bottom lip and a vertical line between his eyebrows. He sat like that for a while, then stood up, took a pile of clothes into the bathroom and shut the door. He was dressed when he came out. 'I'm going out for a while,' he said. 'I think you need to be on your own.'

8

I thought I'd lost him. He went out and I didn't know where he'd gone. I sat on the settee, curled in a ball, and wondered if he was coming back. Maybe that was what he intended: to make me see what I'd lose if I let him go. I looked around at the flat, at the paper peeling from the walls, at the bed and settee that had seen better days, at Martin's CD collection gathering dust. Nearly half my life gone, and what had I got to show for it?

I had a shower, gathered my wet hair back into a ponytail and pulled on jeans and a T-shirt. I finished making the cup of coffee I'd been planning when Trey had interrupted me with his bombshell. I sat down on the settee again and thought about things. What I thought about mostly was this: why on earth can't blokes propose properly? Aren't they supposed to take you out to posh restaurants and kneel at your feet, or maybe drop the engagement ring into a glass of champagne for you to find? I was trying to decide if Trey's proposal was better or worse than Martin's had been.

To be honest, Martin didn't propose, exactly. He came in from the office one day, saw me at the computer and said, 'I've been thinking. We get on really well together, don't we?'

'Yeah.'

'I thought it might be nice to have kids or something.'

Or something? Like what? A dog? A potted plant? I nodded, wondering what was coming next.

He said, 'If we wanted to have kids, then maybe we should make it official, you know, like get married.'

I raised my eyebrows and said, 'Okay.'

A couple of days later he sheepishly handed me something small, wrapped up in a bit of cotton wool. I opened it, puzzled. It wasn't like Martin to give me gifts. Nestled in the cotton wool was an old, slightly tarnished engagement ring. 'It was my grandmother's,' he said.

'It's lovely,' I said, lying, and tried to fit it onto the ring finger of my left hand. It didn't fit, of course it didn't. Since then I'd worn the ring on a chain around my neck.

I loved Martin so much. It was a weird kind of love, like a harsh metallic thing. We clanked and sparked against each other, never gave an inch. Even when he was ill. 'Jesus, Maevo, your hair looks like shit,' he'd say.

'Well, at least I've got some. You still puking your guts out?'

Even those closest to us didn't really understand how much we loved each other. The last time I saw Martin was in his hospital room with his no-nonsense mother and his sister Karen. We all knew this was the last time, and Martin's mum and Karen were in floods of tears, inconsolable. I stood and looked at Martin, trying to memorise his face. I think I saw his eyes flicker. I thought he might have been looking at me. His right hand was lying on the bed in front of him, with wires and tubes coming out of it. I remember reaching out my left hand and touching the top of his hand with my ring finger, the finger that should have been wearing the engagement ring but wasn't. As I did this, I looked at him again and realised that of course he couldn't see me; he had no idea I was there. I was seized by a sudden sense of pointlessness. I wanted to swear and shout and scream, but instead I just walked out of the door and kept walking down the corridor and out to my car. All the while I kept my arms wrapped tightly around me, because I felt that if I didn't, all my internal organs would fall out, just slither onto the floor to form a bloody pile.

I'd always got on well with Martin's family, but after that, and at the funeral, they seemed to shun me; as if, because I didn't cry as much as them, I couldn't have loved him as much.

I stretched out on the settee and felt for the ring, still on its chain around my neck. I always knew where I was with Martin. I was myself, hard-edged and clearly defined. I thought about how Trey made me feel. Adored. That was the first word that came into my mind, and it made me shiver. That was the word Helen used. Adored. What's so wrong with that? Why should that scare me? Trey made me feel soft and squishy; I felt like a different person with him. I smiled more, twirled my fingers in my hair, and acted like a love-struck girl. With him my emotions – my joy, my grief – seemed closer to the surface. We couldn't keep our hands off each other. Everyone said it; everyone could tell we loved each other. Is that what I was afraid of? Going soft? Dissolving? Succumbing?

Trey's rucksack was propped up against the end of the bed, and from one of the outside pockets I could see a wallet of photographs poking out. I pulled out the wallet and looked through the pictures. A white wooden house with a front porch, complete with a swing: just as he'd said, like something out of *The Waltons*. The back of the house: another porch, gingham curtains at the windows. A view of a small town nestled in a valley, surrounded by tree-covered mountains receding into the distance. I looked around at my flat again, and then back at the photos. All of a sudden I wanted to live there. I thought to myself: what's so bad about succumbing?

I picked up the phone and rang Helen. 'Hi,' I said. 'Trey's just asked me to marry him.'

I had to hold the phone away from my ear because Helen's scream was so loud and piercing.

'I don't know what to say. I think I might say yes, but I'm worried that's just because he's got a lovely home.'

'Oh Maeve, what can I say? You know that I think you should marry him. He's wonderful. But, of course, it's up to you.'

'I think he wants me to go to America with him.'

'How exciting,' said Helen. 'It would be a wonderful new start for you. You deserve it, you really do.'

And I thought, how strange. My best friend thinks that I should leave the country. But I could see what she meant. London – and particularly this flat – would always mean Martin to me. Here was a chance to change my life and marry a lovely, sensitive, talented man. Of course I should say yes. What on earth was I scared of?

Trey came back an hour or so later, by which point I had made up my mind and was desperate to tell him what I'd decided, before I had time for second thoughts. The instant he walked through the door I said, 'Okay then.'

'Okay what?' He looked nervous.

'Okay, I'll marry you.'

His face went through three distinct emotions, as clear as if a caricaturist had drawn them. Confusion – a wrinkled brow. Disbelief – a wrinkled brow with raised eyebrows. And then, happiness – a huge, huge smile. He grabbed me in a hug and started to lift me off the floor. I remembered suddenly how heavy I was and how thin he was, and jumped down from his arms somewhat sheepishly. Then Trey looked at me again, with a question on his face. 'Yes,' I said. Then I flung my arms around him, jumped up and down and said it again. 'Yes, yes, yes.'

He held me at arm's length. 'Whoa,' he said. 'I didn't expect that. I mean, technically I haven't even asked you yet. All I've done is ask you if you'd mind if I asked you.'

He looked at me, I think expecting a smile, but instead I frowned at him. 'Sorry, sorry,' he said. 'I'm nervous, is all. Just babbling. Sorry.'

'Go on, then. Propose to me.'

So he grinned, got down on one knee, took my hand in

his and said, 'Maeve O'Mara, will you do me the great
honour of becoming my wife?'

As Trey knelt at my feet I found myself fumbling for
Martin's ring, then tucking it under the neckline of my T-
shirt. 'Please don't let him have his grandmother's ring to
give me,' I said to myself. I have fingers like sausages, and
there's no way an antique ring will ever fit me. But he said
nothing about a ring, just stood up and stretched. Then,
'Hey, you found the photos. What do you think of the old
Ferguson homestead?'

'It's beautiful. I can't wait to go there.'

So we celebrated our engagement by sitting at my
dining table looking at photos of Trey's house and his
home town. He pushed his glasses up onto his forehead
and his eyes took on a dreamy romantic faraway look. I
thought then that he was imagining our life together, but
I know now it was just the look that extremely short-
sighted men get when they haven't got their glasses on.
But then, as I've already said, this is a story full of
misunderstandings.

9

They make you wait at least fifteen days before you can get married. I suppose we could have flown to Vegas or Reno or somewhere, and done it straight away. But we'd decided that it would be nice for me to get married in London, at my local register office, with friends and family around me, so we just had to wait for the next available appointment. We were, apparently, lucky. Because it wasn't one of those architecturally charming register offices in a fashionable part of London, and because we didn't mind getting married on a Monday morning, we fixed the date for a little over three weeks ahead. And I guess waiting for a little over three weeks is probably a good idea when it turns out that you don't even know your future husband's real name.

It was only when we met with the registrar to organise the wedding that I realised. Trey. I suppose I had half-wondered if it was short for something. Terence perhaps. Maybe Travis. Or, God forbid, Tracey, which I knew was a man's name in the American South. I just hadn't got around to asking him. The registrar, a brisk woman with heavily freckled arms, said, 'Full name, please,' and Trey said, 'Clyde James Ferguson. Clyde James Ferguson the third.'

I felt my mouth open with surprise and then I closed it again quickly. I thought the registrar might notice my surprise and then assume it was some kind of hastily organised marriage of convenience to allow Trey to stay in the country or something. I mean, what kind of woman marries a man whose name she doesn't know?

Afterwards I asked him how the hell Trey could be short for Clyde James. He looked at me, puzzled. 'It isn't.'

'So how come you're called Trey?'

'Because I'm the third Clyde James. Third. Hence, Trey.'

'Oh.' I tried to think of any other Treys I'd heard of. The only one I could think of was Charlotte's impotent husband in *Sex and the City*. 'Is that what Trey always means?'

'Pretty much,' he said. He looked at me with great surprise. 'It's funny you didn't know that.'

'So, let me get this straight. Americans called Trey are always Something Something the third?'

'Yeah, pretty much. Sometimes they're called Trip, but in my case – Trey. Simple as that.'

We walked along for a moment, hand in hand, as I digested this information. Trey looked at me. 'Hey, is it a problem?'

'No,' I said, kissing his hand. 'I'm just trying to come to terms with the fact I'm about to marry a man called Clyde, that's all.'

Three weeks. It was enough time for me to buy a dress I didn't much like, and to summon my older brother Sean from his home in Italy to give me away. Enough time to arrange for an agent to look at my flat with a view to renting it out. (Not putting it on the market – was this a sign that I wasn't sure about what I was about to do?) Enough time to talk to a few editors I knew about the possibility of a monthly column about life in a small American town in the Appalachian Mountains. (They looked at me as if I'd gone mad. One of them said, 'Maeve – one word. *Deliverance*. Are you sure you know what you're doing?') Enough time to persuade my local pub, which has delusions of gastro status, to host the wedding reception, at which Mickey's ceilidh band, of course, would play.

It was also enough time for Trey to fly home to 'tie up some loose ends'.

'Like what?' I said, perhaps more sharply than I'd intended.

He stared at me, as if momentarily nonplussed. 'Well, you know, it'd be kinda nice to let my friends and neighbours know I'm getting married before I return home with a strange woman in tow. Also, now I come to think of it, I'm not at all sure I washed the dishes before I left in such a hurry to see you. I'd hate to carry you over the threshold only for you to find out what a slob I am.'

In fact, I was glad he went home. Absence makes the heart grow fonder, they say. Although I don't think I could have been any fonder of Trey and we were very much in love, I did have a sort of strange, irrational underlying fear: that I might somehow run out of love for him before we actually got married. With him away, my stock of love would be preserved and maybe even increased.

Okay, yes, I admit it. I still had my doubts. Was I doing the right thing? I asked everyone who knew me well and no one – not one single person – thought that I was making a mistake. Even Sean, the person I most love and respect, the nearest thing I have to a parent; even Sean, when I spoke to him on the phone, was thrilled. But then, what else should I expect from a guy who flew to Italy for a two-week language course, fell in love with his teacher and never came home? In fact, when I came to think about it, perhaps this whole whirlwind-romance-with-a-gorgeous-foreigner thing ran in the family?

Things weren't made any easier for me by the fact that Missy Ferguson's face suddenly seemed to be staring at me everywhere I looked. It is absolutely true what they say, about how once you start fixating on a name or a face you see it everywhere. I suppose it was just a weird coincidence that her record company had decided to push her album particularly hard at exactly the same moment I'd decided to marry her ex-husband. She'd been in London a couple of months previously doing interviews, and besides seeing her on *Top of the Pops* I'd barely noticed her. But now her face was all over the place: on the side of a bus that passed me as I tried to cross the road at Piccadilly Circus; blown up on posters liberally plastered in the corridors of every Tube station; newspapers, record stores, magazine covers – everywhere. She was even modelling jeans for Gap. I did a huge double-take when I saw that poster in the shop window. I was with Nick at the time. We'd just had lunch and he was on his way back to the office while I had an afternoon of form-filling at the US embassy to look forward to. We walked past the shop and then I realised what I'd seen. I stopped suddenly, turned and then stood and looked at the poster. 'See that?' I said to Nick.

He frowned. He didn't have a clue what I meant.

I gestured at the picture. Missy, her dark red hair piled haphazardly on top of her pert little head, looking coy, girlish and incredibly slim in a pair of cropped jeans and a bright pink sweater. In comparison, I was wearing one of those bias-cut skirts that are popularly supposed to flatter the larger-hipped woman and a sun-top stretched to full capacity. I stabbed at the poster with my finger: 'That woman,' I said. 'The man who used to be married to her is now going to marry me.'

A couple of streaky-haired teenage girls were passing and gave me a disbelieving look as I said that. Nick merely shrugged: 'And?'

'Well . . .' I said, and stood beside the poster so that he could do a comparison. A girlfriend would have said, 'The scrawny bitch. Obviously Trey wants a real woman,' or words to that effect.

Instead Nick said, 'Maeve, he loves you,' which was of strangely little comfort.

Trey and I had never really spoken about Missy. He'd made a few flip remarks about the divorce, that was all. But then, I'd never really asked him about her. The closest we came was when we had the conversation. You know the one, the conversation that couples – particularly couples in their mid-to-late thirties – are supposed to have before they even contemplate marriage. It occurred to me that we'd never talked about children. Trey seemed like the kind of guy who'd have children. He'd been married for seventeen years to a country singer. Don't country singers generally favour big families? He ought to have a whole string of little fair-haired kids (although why they'd be fair-haired when Trey was so dark and his ex-wife was a redhead I don't know) with cute, made-up names like Clancy and Casey and Tyler. And of course, Clyde James. What would the fourth get called? Quart?

Over dinner in a little Vietnamese restaurant near my flat, just before Trey flew back to the States, I broached the issue. 'Do you have kids? I mean, you and Missy?'

He looked down at the table, seeming uncomfortable with the question. 'No. No, we don't.' He shrugged. 'What can I say? We were never . . . blessed.'

The religious word took me by surprise. I found it quite touching. Trey was looking at the table, around the restaurant, anywhere but at me. Clearly I'd touched a nerve. There was a story here that I needed to know. I thought for a moment. Missy Ferguson. I'd seen her on television and she seemed like a very ambitious woman. Maybe it was her decision not to have children. Maybe that was really why they split up. I needed to tread carefully, but I also needed to know. 'Trey, would you like to have children?'

The corner of his mouth twitched, and I could see a smile spread across his face. 'Yeah. Yeah, I would.' And then he looked at me and quickly added, 'But, you know, only if you do too.'

I reached for his hand under the table and our fingers interlocked. Would I like to have children? This was a tough question for me. I have the reputation of not liking kids, mostly because I'm not the kind of person who coos and gurgles and gushes when colleagues on maternity leave bring their newborn babies into the office to show them off. But I do like children. In fact, I love them. Possibly too much. I'm scared of having children because they are such vulnerable little things and I wouldn't want to let any children of mine out of my sight. I'd smother them with love.

I know how vulnerable children are. I know how much pain children can feel. I was five when my mother died, but it's not my pain and vulnerability I remember. It's that of my brother Sean. I remember him at nine, ten, eleven: carefully pulling out the front-door key he wore on a cord around his neck, letting us in the house after school. I remember his concentration as he measured Nesquik into mugs and opened packets of biscuits, to keep us happy as we watched *Blue Peter* and waited for our father to come home from work. It wouldn't be allowed now, would it? Social services would have taken us into care. But there was Sean, with his tongue stuck out of the corner of his mouth, taking care of Mickey and me. All it takes is for me to catch sight of the back of a little boy's neck, a little boy who's had his hair cut too short, for me to think: no, I can't have kids, because suppose something awful happens?

But there was Trey, himself still half a kid: a little abandoned orphan boy who grew too tall too soon, a little boy whose grandfather punished him in weird, stern, Biblical ways. He wanted to have children. He believed it would be okay. I thought about the photographs of Trey's home town. I tried to imagine a bunch of little Treys running around in nappies in a meadow full of daisies: gurgling streams, friendly Southern folk, the safety of small-town America. Cute. Yeah, maybe I could do it. I told him: 'Maybe. Maybe. Yes, I think I would. Not absolutely desperately in a "my life would be over if I didn't" kind of a way. But I guess I always thought that if the circumstances were right, then it would be really nice to have a family.'

'And are the circumstances right?'

I looked across at Trey and studied his face. His eyes were wide, and alight with the childlike enthusiasm that I was beginning to know well. What an easy man to love. 'Yes,' I said, 'Yes, they are now.'

Trey squeezed my hand, and then leaned across the table and kissed me.

10

I suppose every woman sleeps badly the night before her wedding, but I think I probably slept worse than most. I was alone in my almost empty flat – in a last-ditch bid to respect at least one tradition, Trey had opted to spend the night in a hotel. The previous week I'd packed up my belongings – just a few boxes full – and sent them off to the States so that they'd be ready for me when Trey and I arrived. There was very little left in my flat. Nick had been in a couple of days before to pick up Martin's guitar and CD collection. He was going to look after them until I decided what to do with them. Pretty much the only things still in my flat were my suitcase and my overnight bag and – hanging ghostlike on a peg on the back of my door – my hastily-chosen wedding dress.

So of course I had bad dreams. Par for the course. My brain was working overtime. I was leaving the flat where Martin and I had spent our time together and heading for a place I'd never seen. I didn't dream about Martin, exactly. Instead, I dreamed about my dad, leading me by the arm down the aisle of a church that soon turned into the crematorium where Martin's funeral had taken. Trey was standing by the coffin waiting for me, his back towards me. In my dream he was about to turn around and look at me, but then I realised that I couldn't remember what his face looked like and I woke in a panic.

I must have gone back to sleep because in my next dream I was sitting at a big wooden kitchen table. There were a lot of people around the table: CJ Ferguson, who I recognised from the photo on the album sleeve, and two women in old-fashioned floral frocks, Trey's aunts, I guess. Trey was sitting next to me and we were all holding hands for grace, when suddenly Trey's grandfather pointed at me, looking a bit like that famous poster of Lord Kitchener, and boomed: 'Who is that woman?'

Everyone was staring at me, including Missy Ferguson who was suddenly also sitting at the table, immaculately coiffed and wearing the sort of glittery evening dress that cabaret singers wear. Trey turned to his grandfather and said, 'This is my sister.' Missy smiled, and a shiver went through me, until I noticed that the man sitting next to me wasn't Trey at all but my brother Sean.

I gave up trying to sleep after that. The clock next to my bed told me it was gone five in the morning, so I got up, made coffee, watched *News 24* for a bit and then started the long battle to make myself look beautiful.

The formal part of our wedding went according to plan. We smiled at each other and made our vows in clear voices in front of the same freckled-armed registrar who'd first asked us for Trey's full name. Ten minutes later we were standing hand in hand on the steps of the town hall as our friends threw confetti at us, and then we all walked round the corner to the pub. Trey and I barely found time to speak to each other. I was almost stunned into silence by the hugeness of what we'd just done.

Our wedding reception was a more raucous affair, involving copious pints of Guinness and lots of dancing to swirly Irish music. I felt ugly and uncomfortable in my dress, a heavy cream beaded thing from Monsoon that managed the impossible feat of turning this large-breasted big-hipped woman into a shapeless column, and dug into my shoulders and my armpits. It was a warm overcast day, and as the pub got hotter and the music got swirlier all I could think about was how shiny my forehead was and how much I was sweating.

Trey, in contrast, looked amazing. He'd found a cream linen suit in a vintage clothes shop in Camden that was only slightly too short in the legs and sleeves. He wore it over a flowery blue open-necked shirt that matched the colour of his eyes, and he'd abandoned his usual sneakers for an old pair of tan suede desert boots.

Some of Trey's friends had flown over for the wedding. There was Jerry, the best man, a stringy, fair-haired taciturn guy in his early thirties with a shy country-bumpkin smile. Trey introduced him to me as a luthier. I'd never heard the word before and thought I'd probably misheard. Lootier. 'I'm sorry?' I said, struggling to hear above the Irish music.

'I'm a luthier,' he said. 'I make some of Trey's instruments.'

'That must be interesting,' I ventured inanely.

'Yes,' he said, and fell silent after that. Then he cleared

his throat and said, 'You know, you're not at all like Missy.'

'Is that a good thing or a bad thing?' I asked, as lightly and as frivolously as I could.

Jerry blushed, and mumbled something into his beer. It felt too awkward to ask him to repeat himself and besides, I didn't really want to hear the answer. We looked at each other for a while, both embarrassed, and then I pretended to see someone I knew at the other side of the pub.

Then there was Kevin, who I sort of recognised as the lead singer of a weird American country-punk band that Martin had been a big fan of. In fact, he'd interviewed him a couple of years ago. Martin had always disliked interviewing people whose music he rated because they so often disappointed him. He would come in, throw down his tape recorder, say something like 'tosser' or 'wanker', and never listen to their music again. But when he interviewed this Kevin guy he came home glowing and said, 'Top bloke. Spot on,' which was praise indeed from Martin. I got a warm feeling standing at the bar next to him, and wanted him to remember Martin. I said, 'A friend of mine interviewed you a couple of years ago – Martin Davis?'

I mentioned the name of the magazine he'd worked for. Kevin thought for a while, and then his face cleared. 'Oh yeah, I remember. Jesus, how could I forget? Funny-looking guy. The Artful Dodger, we called him. Kinda strange. Smoked a lot. Is he here?'

And suddenly I didn't know why I'd even raised the issue.

Brides are supposed to be the centre of attention at weddings. They're supposed to glow – that's the word, isn't it? Everyone is supposed to say how beautiful she looks; every eye should be drawn to her. At my wedding, it was the groom who was glowing, while I just sweated and felt lumpy. Everywhere I looked, there was Trey. There he was hugging people, people who were my friends, who he'd only just met. Then I spotted him dancing with my beautiful twelve-year-old Italian niece, who'd arrived at my flat that morning with my brother Sean, clutching her first communion dress and offering her services as my bridesmaid. Giulia had obviously fallen in love with Trey at first sight. I noticed Trey's body language, the way he leaned into people, touched their arms as he spoke to them, the way he seemed to give them his full attention. He could charm the pants off anyone. There was Trey, deep in conversation with Fiona and Nick, and then Trey with Helen, and Helen's face going pink and girlie. Trey buying huge rounds of Guinness at the bar; gesticulating wildly while eating wedding cake; and most of all, standing on the makeshift stage with Mickey's band, playing an extraordinary array of different musical instruments.

I was happy just watching him, metaphorically pinching myself every once in a while and saying to myself: that's my husband. That really is my husband. At one point Sean sidled up to me and put his arm around my waist. I looked at him. For all his years in Italy he still looked like a red-faced red-haired London-Irish boy, only now he was a red-faced red-haired London-Irish boy in a sharp suit and good shoes. 'Have you had your "Oh my God" moment yet?' he asked.

'What do you mean?'

'The "Oh my God, what have I done?" moment.'

I laughed. 'Sean, the whole of the last two weeks has been an "Oh my God" moment.'

'But in a good way, yeah?'

I looked at Sean, and then looked across at Trey who was still standing on the makeshift stage playing with the band. I looked at Sean again. 'Oh yeah, definitely in a good way.'

Trey caught my eye and beckoned me over with a nod of his head. I thought he wanted to dance, so I walked across to the stage and expected him to step down and take me in his arms. Instead he helped me onto the stage and handed me a tambourine. That's how I spent the last hour or so of my wedding reception: playing in a weird, ad hoc band featuring a bunch of pseudo-Irish musicians, my brilliant bluegrass husband and the lead singer of my late fiancé's favourite country-punk combo, beating out the rhythm for Clash and Dylan cover versions so hard on the tambourine that I ended up with bruises on my thigh.

Blurrily in the crowd I could make out the familiar faces I was leaving: Nick, tall and fair; Sean, propped up at the bar with his pint of Guinness; the curly auburn head of Mickey, deep in conversation with my old school friend Helen. I sneaked sideways glances at Trey, pale and intense at the microphone beside me. My new husband. I bashed away on the tambourine, as if the harder I banged it, the less scared I'd be about the new life I was beginning.

11

Scared. Yeah, I know. I'm not the type to get scared. 'You're so brave.' That's what Fiona said to me at my wedding. Or rather, 'You're *sooo* brave,' in that gushy, confiding, insinuating manner of hers that really annoys me. She came up to me at one point during the afternoon as I was standing at the bar watching Trey. She put a hand on my shoulder and whispered in my ear. 'You know, we all really admire you for what you're doing. I can't think of anyone else who'd do it.'

Brave. That's me. Brave Maeve. I'm not afraid of anything. Or at least that's the part I've always played. I was the kid who'd climb the tree to get the ball back, who'd run straight into the icy-cold sea despite the huge waves, who'd pick up spiders with my bare hands. A motherless kid with two brothers, I was, if not quite a tomboy, distinctly tough and self-reliant. Every day of my childhood I wanted to prove that I was as brave as – braver than – Mickey and Sean.

The reputation has followed me into adulthood. I'm sure it's at least partly because of the way I look. I'm big, physically imposing. I'm popularly supposed to 'cut the crap', to 'take no prisoners', those phrases that are bandied about not entirely in admiration. I'm the woman who backpacked around India on my own when my lovesick, homesick friend flew home two weeks into the trip. I'm the woman who stayed calm, didn't cry and remembered all the right questions to ask the doctors when my fiancé was diagnosed with a brain tumour. I'm the woman who married a man she barely knew.

Of course I was scared. I was bloody scared. Who wouldn't be? The courage was just a front, of course. But I'd reasoned with myself. What was there to be scared of? What's the worst that could happen? That's what I asked myself. Yeah, maybe Trey could turn out to be a mad axe-murderer, but that didn't seem likely. And if he did reveal himself to be a complete and utter bastard, I told myself it would be no big deal. I could fly straight home and get a divorce. I'd coped with worse.

Or was I actually scared of small-town America? Particularly small-town America in the Appalachian Mountains? All those jokes my friends and colleagues made about *Deliverance* and 'Duelling Banjos' and toothless yokels in dungarees sitting on front porches spitting tobacco at me were bound to have had an impact. I'd never lived in a small town before. I'd never lived anywhere but London; and for all they say that London's really just a collection of villages, that's actually complete rubbish. I'd lived in my flat for four years and still the guy behind the counter at my local newsagent's didn't know my name.

The day after our wedding Trey and I woke under the thin duvet in my flat in South London to a brutally early alarm clock. I had to run to the bathroom to be sick, but I blamed that on the amount I'd drunk the day before: nothing to do with nerves. We'd decided against a honeymoon: Trey wanted to get back to work quickly, and I couldn't wait to see my new home. A taxi took us to Gatwick, still bleary-eyed and hung-over. Our mid-morning flight to Charlotte, North Carolina, landed in the sticky, syrupy heat of a Southern summer afternoon. I had a long queue at Immigration, herded by fat Customs officials with unflattering uniforms and no sense of humour. I began to realise what a giant step I'd taken. I was an immigrant. This was my Ellis Island, and I had to convince officials that I was genuine. I imagined it would be like the film *Green Card*, and they'd test me on trivia about Trey: the name of his childhood pet, his favourite colour, his date of birth. I would fail the test horribly. As I stood in line I thought to myself: my God, I'm not even sure when my husband's birthday is. I repeated his name under my breath: Clyde James Ferguson the third. Clyde James Ferguson the third. I was convinced that I'd forget it.

Eventually I was through, and it was on to another flight, this time on a small plane where the blonde honey-voiced stewardess greeted Trey like a long-lost friend. 'This is my beautiful new wife,' he said to introduce me, flinging his arm around me and clutching me to him. The stewardess threw me what looked like an incredulous glance, as if to say: 'You mean this fat, blotchy lump of a woman is the best you could get to replace the gorgeous Missy?' I never look my best on aeroplanes. My hair goes lank, my forehead goes shiny. And besides, I was tired and still very hung-over.

I sat outside Asheville Airport in the warmth of the evening, surrounded by suitcases, and waited for Trey to fetch the car. I stretched my legs out and took deep breaths of the mountain air. The sun was low in the sky, and in the time it took my new husband to remember where he'd parked a week ago it was beginning to slip down below the highest ridge of the mountains that edged the horizon, streaking the blue sky with delicate feathers of pink and orange. Eventually Trey pulled up in a dusty old red truck, leaped out and helped me hurl the suitcases into the back.

I don't know what it was – jet-lag, hangover, post-wedding jitters – but the longer the journey went on, the more I started to panic. Asheville – what I'd seen of it, anyway – had looked like a fairly big town, the kind of place that would have decent shops and restaurants and a cinema; maybe even a university, that guarantee of some kind of cultural life. Although I knew from the maps I'd studied that Trey's home was deep in the Appalachians, I'd still clung on to the hope that it would be an easy drive from civilisation, and for a while we followed a four-lane highway and I remained hopeful. But after nearly an hour of driving we took a small turning to the right some miles north of Asheville and followed a series of narrow roads that climbed slowly upwards, twisting and turning as they did so. Every so often there was a clearing: a valley dotted with houses and ugly mobile homes – trailers, I guess the American word is. The trailers had a look of permanence, as if they'd rooted themselves into the hillside, growing porches and fences and outbuildings in the process. Or there'd be a small strip mall with a gas station and a couple of shops. Then suddenly we'd be in the depths of the countryside again, the road lined on both sides by trees.

To begin with, the sky was still light enough for me to be able to admire the jagged range of mountains that surrounded us. But as the sun finally set and the night began, I started to lose my sense of direction. I felt as if I'd come adrift from my anchorage. I felt as if this journey had been going on for ever, and would never end. The mountains seemed to move closer as the sky got darker, and it felt as if the trees were encroaching on the road. I tried to remember the road journey so far, every kink of every little mountain road we'd taken; tried to retrace it in my head, as if that would give me an escape route should I need one. I looked across at Trey. He was leaning forward in the driver's seat, concentrating on the road, squinting in the dark. I wanted him to reach across and squeeze my hand, or rest his hand on my leg, some kind of reassurance that everything would be all right. But he was clutching the steering wheel so hard that it seemed it would be dangerous to disturb him. I felt my stomach lurch into my mouth. I wanted to throw up, or throw the door of the truck open and run away, back down the mountains to Asheville and then home. Who was this man sitting beside me, this man who was driving me away from everything I knew?

Y ou wouldn't know Bodie's Hollow was there unless
you were looking for it. The first hint was a small
country store, set back from the road, with two petrol
pumps, some old tyres and a sign on the forecourt
promising 'Cold beer, live bait.' Next to the store was the
Foggy Hollow Motel: two rows of wooden cabins, L-
shaped around a mossy parking lot. Paint was peeling
from the woodwork and although the two white plastic
chairs outside each cabin suggested that it was still in
business, it actually looked as if it hadn't seen a paying
guest in years. Trey took a sharp left turn at an unmarked
junction just beyond the motel, and then turned to me and
said proudly, 'Here we are: Bodie's Hollow.'

I looked out of the window and saw another strip mall,
this one smaller and shabbier than any I'd seen before,
with a supermarket, a post office and a pizza restaurant
ranged around the concrete parking lot, grass and weeds
growing from the cracks in the concrete. Then, big and
new and floodlit, a red-brick Baptist church with a low-
pitched white roof. Trey's truck crested a ridge, and then
we followed the road downwards and to the left, through
overhanging trees, before it straightened out to form an
old-fashioned main street. Through the darkness I could
make out shop windows on either side of the road, and
small streets of white wooden houses climbing the hill to
our right. Even in the dark I could tell that the town was
run-down. The road was full of potholes and half the
street lights weren't working. One large window to our
left was lit up: a café, with a handful of customers, caught
in a static moment, as if in an Edward Hopper painting.

Any moment now he'll pull over and we'll be home, I told myself, and everything will be all right.

But he didn't pull over. Instead we drove right through the town, past a much older church that stood sentry on a rise at the far end of the main street and past a small cemetery, the gravestones white in the pale moonlight. At the point where it seemed as if the road was about to run out Trey steered the truck onto a rutted dirt road that wound upwards behind the church, back into the wooded mountainside, back into the overhanging trees. The road – such as it was – twisted upwards for another half-mile or so before finally, finally, Trey brought the truck to a lurching stop.

He came round to my side, opened the door and helped me out. I felt the crunch of gravel under my feet and looked around me. It felt as if we were miles from anywhere. Below us I could just about make out the faint lights of Bodie's Hollow. There was almost total silence. I turned around and there, perched on a hill above us, stood a white building, looming ghostly in the darkness. It was squat and square, with a front door and four windows, like a child's drawing of a house. It was my new home.

12

Trey carried me over the threshold. I tried to stop him, worried about how he'd cope with the burden of my eleven stone plus. But although he bashed my head on the doorpost as he carried me in, his wiry arms proved surprisingly strong. As he dumped me with some relief inside the dark hallway I rubbed my head with my hand, and then quickly had to clamp my hand over my mouth instead. I gagged violently and nearly threw up. Trey noticed. 'Are you okay?'

I nodded, but I wasn't. There was a fusty smell in the house that had hit me with sudden force, and the nausea kept coming back to me in waves. The smell had the staleness of air that had been circulating in a dark closed house in hot weather. It smelled like an old person's house. But it was worse than that. There was an under-current to the smell that I couldn't put my finger on: stale cooking or food gone off or rancid milk, perhaps. I gagged again, and then I felt a shiver go down the back of my neck. I turned, and realised it was just a draught. Trey was in the hallway behind me, pulling the front door shut after bringing our luggage in. He seemed oblivious to the smell. He turned on the light and all I could do was stare at my new home.

You know those television property programmes, where someone buys an old house at auction without looking around it or even getting a survey done? And then they stand in shock, open-mouthed, looking around the wreck they've just bought while the presenter – almost gloatingly – tells them how much it's going to cost to put everything right? I suppose it was like that, only far, far worse. Because this wasn't just some development project: this was my new home, the home for which I had given up my life in London – such as it was.

The ceiling was claustrophobically low. It was painted a dull yellowy-cream colour, as were the walls. They felt damp and clammy to the touch. To my left was a closed door; to my right an open door led to an empty room – completely empty, nothing but bare floorboards and a boarded-up fireplace. Ahead and slightly to the left there was a staircase, its faded threadbare carpet coming dangerously loose from the runners in several places. Underfoot in the hallway was patterned yellow lino; in places it had worn through to the floorboards. But what drew my eye most of all was the right-hand wall. The whole upper half of the wall, between the ceiling and the dado rail, was covered with photographs, every single one of them of CJ Ferguson.

He glowered unsmiling in black and white from every frame, his eyes seeming to follow me as I walked slowly down the hallway. In some of the photos he was a young man, skinny and solemn with his guitar strung around his neck. In others he was older, his features more gaunt and haggard, but his gaze was as fierce as ever. There were full-length sepia photos of the young CJ Ferguson standing behind old-fashioned microphones. There were studio shots too, head-and-shoulders pictures of the Preacherman, his dark shirt buttoned to the neck. In one photograph he had his arm around a younger man, equally fierce, also dressed in black. I looked closer and recognised Johnny Cash. I looked from the pictures to where Trey stood, still hovering in the doorway, his stare fixed on me. I traced the resemblance between him and his grandfather: the pale skin, the sharply defined cheek-bones, the harshness made softer in my husband's face. Most of all, I noticed the eyes. CJ Ferguson's eyes were exceptionally pale, surprising under such heavy dark brows. Like Trey's eyes, I suppose, except altogether clearer and colder and harder.

One photo in particular drew my attention. Once again, the unmistakable figure of CJ Ferguson, older than in the other photos and now with snowy-white hair and ferocious eyebrows, but still tall and still impressive. He stood on stage, holding a guitar, behind a large micro-phone emblazoned with a radio station's call letters. He was wearing a dark high-buttoning formal suit. But what caught my eye was this: in the bottom right-hand corner of the photo was a skinny, scared-looking boy, no more than six or seven, with a pale face and his eyes screwed up, either closed tight or in deep concentration. He was wearing long shorts and a shirt buttoned to the neck and he had his arms wrapped around his grandfather's leg, as if clinging on for dear life. Trey saw me staring at the picture and he looked down at the ground, running his hand over his face as if embarrassed. 'Oh, babes,' I said. 'That's you.'

'Uh-huh.'

'That's so sweet.' I looked more closely at his grandfather in the picture. 'That suit he's wearing. Is that the same suit you were wearing when I saw you at the Borderline?'

Trey nodded. 'Yeah, it is.'

'So you wear your grandfather's suits on stage?'

'Sometimes, yeah.'

'Why?'

'It's a heritage thing, I guess. Tradition. It makes me feel he's watching over me, approving of what I'm doing.'

I looked closely at Trey, at his eyes in particular, looking for a glint, a sparkle, some sign that he wasn't being entirely serious; some sign that it would be okay for me to laugh. But there was nothing. I felt another shiver go down my spine – and this time it wasn't a draught.

13

Trey picked up the heavy suitcases and led me up the rickety stairs. Ahead of me I could see his shoulders hunching together as he ducked under the low ceiling. In fact the ceiling was so low that I felt myself ducking too. There were bare floorboards upstairs, and again those yellowy-cream distempered walls. I poked my nose into two tiny rooms, neither of them much bigger than a cupboard, both of them completely empty. In each room a bare light bulb hung in the centre of the ceiling and the fireplace was boarded up.

Trey showed me the bathroom. I walked in and closed the door behind me, glad of a moment alone. The suite was big and square, pale green porcelain, art deco-style. It looked like it might have been expensive originally. Big clunky chrome taps, tarnished and misshapen by lime scale. Black and white tiles, lined with mould. The bath, basin and toilet were dirty in a way that only a man's bathroom can ever be, a man who doesn't realise that a good scrub and a spot of bleach will remove almost any tidemark. On the windowsill stood a splayed-out toothbrush, a capless tube of toothpaste and a rusty can of antiperspirant, and the wooden window frame was black with mould. I rinsed my face and looked at it in the old spotty mirror above the basin, trying not to cry. Oh shit, I thought. This is my new home.

Trey was waiting for me in the main bedroom. It stood under the sloping roof at the front of the house, and a beam transected the ceiling above the big wooden bed. The floor was covered with a dark, heavily patterned carpet, threadbare in many places. The walls were dark, too, with small cream flowers on a green background, and the wallpaper was peeling in places, revealing strata of paper, paint and plaster underneath. A huge chest of drawers filled one wall, and Trey's clothes were spilling haphazardly out of the half-open drawers. The top of the chest was covered with a large white lace doily and some old china ornaments. There was a Toby jug that I picked up to have a closer look. 'George Washington,' said Trey. 'It's been in the family for generations.'

I put it straight down again, afraid I might break it. There were two china bulldogs, and a kitschy ornament of a little boy with a donkey. The donkey was pulling a cart, and in the cart there were some buttons, some keys and a rusty hairpin, all covered in decades of dust. It seemed that no one had touched the room in years. 'This was my grand-daddy's bedroom,' Trey announced as he walked backwards into the wooden beam that transected the low ceiling.

'And your grandmother's,' I said, as I fingered the hairpin in the donkey cart.

'Well, yes, but she died before I was born.'

I put down the hairpin, suddenly realising how old it was. I felt myself start to gag again. The room was hot and

stuffy and smelled as if the air hadn't moved in decades. I
went over to the small sash window and opened it to let in
the night air. I stuck my head out of the window and
breathed deeply. Outside, a slight breeze rustled the trees
and I could hear nothing else but the sound of unfamiliar
birds and insects. We could have been the only two people
left in the world. I took some more deep breaths. I had
broken one of the cardinal rules of relationships: never get
involved with a man until you've seen where – and how –
he lives. And here I was not just involved but actually
married to him.

Pull yourself together, I told myself. He only got
divorced last year. Why should I have expected something out of *Ideal Home* magazine? After all, Trey had
described my little flat as 'homey' so I should have
realised his comfort standards were low. 'When did you
move back here?' I asked Trey as casually as I could.

'At the start of the year. I guess eight or nine months
ago.'

'Really?' I was surprised. That seemed long enough to
have made the house more comfortable. A lick of paint, at
least.

Trey obviously heard the surprise in my voice because
he sounded defensive. 'It'd been empty for nearly twenty
years before then.'

'Why so long?'

'That's when my grand-daddy died.'

'So no one's lived here since?' That also surprised me.
'What about your aunts?'

'They moved away,' Trey said, with what sounded like

a chill in his voice. 'That's why so many of the rooms are
empty. They took what they wanted and moved away.'

'It's 1930s, isn't it?' I asked as we made our way down
the creaky wooden staircase. It came out louder than
I'd planned and more abrupt, sounding almost like an
accusation.

Trey stopped suddenly. 'How did you know?' His
voice sounded surprised.

'The style. The design. The woodwork – these
banisters, for example. This chunky, squared-off
design . . .' My voice drifted off, jet-lagged, too tired to
elaborate further. 'I was expecting it to be older.'

'Disappointed?'

'No.' Not by the age of the house, anyway. 'No, just
surprised. When you described it as the old Ferguson
homestead I was imagining it'd been here for centuries.'

'My grand-daddy built it. He knocked down the old
cabin that stood here and built this house when he first
became successful. He wanted to provide somewhere
solid and substantial for his family.'

'And nothing's been touched since then?'

'Hardly,' he said.

At the bottom of the stairs I gestured at the closed door.
'What's in there?'

'That? That's my grandparents' front parlour.' He
paused and hunched his shoulders, looking uncomfortable. 'I don't use it. I tend to spend most of my time
out back in the kitchen.'

I think it was the state of the kitchen that upset me the most. So the rest of the house was smelly, bare, dirty, uncared for. Well, okay. Trey was a recently divorced guy living in an old house that had been empty for twenty years. I guess I couldn't blame him for the state of it. But the kitchen: if he spent most of his time there, surely it would be light and warm and inviting? It wasn't.

It had potential, certainly. It was a big room, stretching the whole width of the house. There was a big old range, apparently unused in years, which badly needed to be cleaned and fired up. There was a huge butler sink and a long, scarred wooden table in the middle of the room. A range of decrepit cabinets and cupboards ran along the three walls to my left, some of them with what looked like real marble work surfaces. Straight ahead of me, French doors that I presumed led out onto some kind of back porch. To the right, a collection of items that made my heart sink: Trey's den.

A small fridge, a microwave, a coffee machine and some kind of electric grill thing, perched on a picnic table. A cheap pine-veneer chest of drawers, the sort you'd see in a bad bed-and-breakfast, with a television sitting on it. A bookcase with a few tatty paperbacks, piles of CDs and a stereo perched precariously on top. And along the right-hand wall, a truly horrible squishy orange 1970s couch.

I slumped heavily onto the couch and felt overwhelmed by something: tiredness, disappointment; disillusionment. Even close to despair. I tried hard not to cry. Trey could obviously read my body language, at least in part. 'I know,' he said. 'It's kind of old-fashioned, but – hey – it's just been me living here up till now, and it's cosy and comfortable so I've just ignored the rest of it.'

Cosy and comfortable. If this was Trey's idea of cosy and comfortable, then I'd made a big mistake in marrying him. I could feel the tears pricking the backs of my eyes. 'Loads of potential,' I said, feigning an enthusiasm I didn't feel.

Trey nodded, and then went across to the fridge. 'I asked my friend Brett and his wife to get us in some food for tonight.'

For a brief moment I let myself imagine some delicious home-cooked traditionally American food. Meat loaf, maybe. Chicken pot pie, whatever that was. I'd always wondered. Trey opened the fridge door and looked inside. He pulled two bottles of beer out and handed me one. Then, 'Uh-huh,' in a voice that nearly matched my own sense of disappointment. I turned and looked at him. He was standing there with two small boxes in his hands. Ready meals. 'Hey,' he said, with an ironic lift of his eyebrows. 'We have a real gourmet treat. I can offer you the choice of beef dinner or chicken dinner.'

And that was when I really did start crying. Trey put the food back in the fridge and rushed over to me. 'Hey,' he said, taking hold of my hand and interlocking our fingers. 'What's up?'

'I'm just tired,' I said. And, 'It's all been a bit too much excitement for one day.' And then I looked around a bit more and saw a huge bunch of lilies in a vase on the draining board by the kitchen sink. They seemed so out of place in that dark, ugly kitchen that I got up to have a closer look at them, despite my jet-lag and aching legs. And then I ended up doing what was probably the worst thing I could have done: I accidentally picked a fight about Trey's ex-wife.

14

She'd sent them, that huge, extravagant, flamboyant bouquet, far too big and showy for any room in the house. I suppose she couldn't possibly have known that I loathe lilies. It's the smell of them. It's more than a smell. It has a tangible quality: the perfume actually seems to absorb oxygen, so that you can't breathe. And there they were: these huge, smelly, overpowering flowers, and I wondered if they were kindly meant or not. There was a small card propped against the vase. I walked over to the sink and picked it up. My name – misspelled 'Mave' – was written on the front in loopy, schoolgirlish handwriting. I opened the envelope and pulled out a card. In the same handwriting it said, 'To dear Mave – good luck! Love, Missy' and then there was a long row of Xs and Os across the bottom of the card. Good luck, said Trey's ex-wife. Good luck. Was I being hypersensitive, or was that a strange message to send to your ex-husband's new wife? Was it some kind of sick joke about the state of the house? A comment on Trey's suitability or otherwise as a husband? I couldn't tell. I had no idea what she meant by it.

'Who are they from?' said Trey.

'Your ex-wife,' I said, wondering what reaction he'd have.

A huge smile was the answer. 'Hey, that's so thoughtful of her, isn't it?'

That wasn't the adjective that had sprung to *my* mind. Creepy, more like. I showed him the card. 'Is this her handwriting, or do you think it's the florist's?'

Trey squinted at it. 'Oh, that's Missy's writing,' he said, and sounded proud. Then he looked again. I hoped he'd comment on the message itself, but all he said was, 'Oh dear. I'll have to teach her how to spell your name.'

He reached out his arm and pulled me to him, nuzzling his cheek against mine. 'Trey, how did the flowers get here?'

'I guess they were delivered.'

'No, I mean, how did they get in the house while you were away?'

'Oh, I guess Brett and Linda Sue must have accepted the delivery when they came up here with the food.'

'And who are Brett and Linda Sue, exactly?'

'They're good friends of mine. They live just outside of town. They have a Christmas-tree plantation. Brett plays the banjo.' As if the fact that he played banjo explained everything.

'Oh.' Linda Sue? A Christmas tree plantation? What kind of place had I come to? But I suppose it made sense. Not much seemed to grow around here but trees. 'Oh,' I said again, unable to keep a note of relief out of my voice.

Trey must have heard it. 'Why? What were you worried about?'

'I was thinking you were about to tell me that Missy

had a key to the house or something,' and I laughed as I said it. But Trey wasn't laughing. His arm around my waist suddenly went rigid.

'Ah,' he said. 'She does. Is that a problem?'

'The thing you need to know about Missy is that she's part of my life. Always has been, always will be. She's one of my best friends. She's really important to me and you need to understand that.'

We were sitting at the kitchen table. Trey looked at me, across the table, as if to see how I was taking this. I was aware that I had my arms wrapped around me in my favourite defensive position, bracing myself for what was coming. This wasn't how I'd intended us to spend our first night together in the marital home. I don't suppose Trey was that happy about it either. I'd just shown him a side of me he hadn't seen before: I'd ranted and raved at him, jealous and shrewish and revealing what must have looked liked deep-seated insecurity.

Trey opened his mouth, seemed to think better of what he was about to say, and then closed it again. After a pause he said, 'Maybe Missy and I shouldn't have got married. Maybe we should have stayed as friends. It's difficult to explain, but it's as if we're kindred spirits. Perhaps we weren't supposed to be husband and wife, but I'm glad she's still in my life.'

'So why did you get married?' I still had my arms wrapped around me.

'We were kids. Sixteen years old. We both wanted

to leave home; we were very fond of each other. We got married. It seemed the right thing to do at the time.'

Trey told me that they'd been at school together, two little kids in a small town one-room schoolhouse. Church and Sunday school, too. They recognised something in each other. They both loved music, both dreamed of Nashville careers. He had music in his blood. She had one of the most beautiful voices he'd ever heard. He didn't regret a thing. He was still working with her, producing some tracks for her latest album. Even though she'd gone mainstream and he preferred traditional music, they were still very much on the same wavelength. He didn't want any of that to change just because they'd both gotten married to someone else.

'Look,' he said, reaching out and stroking my arm so that I finally started to relax. 'I've dated a couple of women since Missy and I split up, and they found it really difficult to cope. I just wanted you to know there's nothing to be jealous of. I love you, Maeve,' and he rubbed my hand with his thumb, 'and I think we have a very special future together, but Missy and I will always have something, I don't know what. Call it a connection. Anyway, that's what you need to know.'

I looked down at the kitchen table and traced the pattern of a knot in the wood with my finger. I wasn't entirely satisfied. 'I thought you'd only just moved back to this house, like, eight months ago.'

'I have.' Trey looked surprised at my sudden change of subject.

'Did you ever live in this house with Missy when you were married?'

'No. We lived just outside Nashville.'

'So why the hell has she got a door key?' I couldn't keep the sharpness out of my voice.

Trey took a deep breath, and then put his hands flat on the table in front of him and cleared his throat. 'Okay . . .' he said, as if he were about to explain something to an idiot or a small child. 'Like I said, Missy and I are working together on her new album.'

'Okay, I get that.'

'And we're doing some of the work here, in my studio up here.'

'Where is your studio?'

'In the basement. I'll show you tomorrow.'

I frowned at him, thinking about Trey and his ex-wife in the basement together.

He continued. 'It's a good place to write songs, record demos, that kind of thing. Missy likes to get away from Nashville sometimes and get back to her roots. Working here helps her. It inspires her, helps her reconnect with her heritage, I guess. That's all. It's no big deal. I promise you.'

Trey's left hand was flat on the table and he held his right hand in the air, as if he were taking the pledge in a courtroom. His face had taken on an almost comical look, like a child trying to avoid punishment. I was beginning to think that perhaps I'd been unreasonable. 'Thank you,' I said, 'I really appreciate your honesty, but . . .' and I could hear that my voice sounded constricted. I was jet-lagged and confused and still on the edge of tears. 'Why didn't you tell me this earlier?'

'I did, sort of. Remember how your friend Helen kept asking all those questions about Missy?'

Oh, okay, maybe I wasn't being unreasonable. I couldn't let him get away with that. 'You told Helen that you were still very protective of Missy, Trey. Those were your precise words. Very protective. Not 'Missy can come to my house any time she likes.' And besides . . .' I was on my high horse now. 'Besides, you told *Helen*. You didn't tell *me*. I told you all about Martin. It broke my heart, but I told you. Jesus, I virtually bared my soul to you. I can't believe you didn't find time, just one little moment before we got married, just to drop into the conversation, "Oh Maeve, by the way, my ex-wife has a key to my house and can let herself in any time she likes, I hope you don't mind." '

I took a deep breath, and Trey flinched slightly at this onslaught. 'What would you have said?'

'I'd have told you that I do mind, a lot.'

I think my voice must have sounded very English and squeakily indignant as I said that, because Trey suddenly laughed. 'Okay,' he said, 'I'll make her give the key back. I'm sure she'll understand.'

I looked across at him, this man I hardly knew, this man I'd married on a whim. His straight dark hair was plastered to his head from the long day of travelling. I noticed for the first time that his ears stuck out: the delicate white rims protruded slightly from his flattened hair. His shirt was crumpled, one sleeve rolled up further than the other. His eyes behind his glasses had a pleading look. He reached across and stroked my hand again with his thumb. 'Maeve, I am so sorry. I'm just really bad at understanding women. I love you so much. I know how lucky I am to have found you. Please forgive me.'

So I did. What else could I possibly do?

But when I woke with a start at four the next morning, as unfamiliar birds sang loudly in the trees outside our bedroom window and as fingers of sunlight made their way in through the gap in the curtains and across the carpet, I thought of something that Trey had said, something that rang a bell. 'Call it a connection.' That's how he'd described his relationship with Missy. And that's the word he'd used about me, the morning after our first night together. 'We have a connection,' he had said, as he kissed me goodbye and asked if we could see each other again.

Trey was lying behind me in his usual position, his chest against my back, his arms wrapped around my waist. I disentangled myself and quietly stepped out of bed and pulled on my dressing gown. I tiptoed down the creaky staircase, into the hallway and through to the kitchen. The scent of the lilies was so strong that I could almost taste it in the back of my throat, but at least it masked the fusty smell in the rest of the house. I wanted to take the flowers and throw them away, but I knew that would seem petulant and silly. Instead, I compromised. I picked up the card that was still propped up against the vase: 'To dear Mave – good luck! Love Missy XOXOXOXOX.'

Missy really did have childish handwriting. I tore the card into tiny pieces and rammed them down the plughole of the kitchen sink, one by one, until they were all gone. Then I wandered aimlessly back out into the dark hallway, glancing at the photos on the wall, peering into corners and cupboards. Back down the corridor there was the closed door that led to the front parlour. The doorknob was thick with dust. I pulled the sleeve of my dressing gown over my hand and turned the knob, pushing slightly as I did so. Nothing. Maybe it was just stuck. I jiggled the knob and tried again. Then I put my shoulder against the door and shoved. It didn't move. The door was locked tight.

I went back up to the bedroom, the stairs creaking under my weight. I'd ask Trey for the key. I'd open up the old room and we'd use it. Maybe it could be a study for me, or what they always call on property programmes a 'formal dining room'. The house was small enough already without blocking rooms off.

Trey stirred as I climbed back into bed. He half-opened his eyes and looked at me, a lazy smile on his lips. He reached out and touched my hair. He ran his right hand down the side of my face and on to my neck, and then he reached inside my dressing gown with his left hand. He ran his rough fingertips down the side of my right breast and found the nipple, tweaking it so hard that it hurt. I gasped as sexual desire flooded through me, my whole body feeling as if it had flushed bright red. I kissed him, tasting his morning mouth, feeling his unshaven cheeks rasp against mine. I reached my arms around his body, my fingers touching a small, ridged scar in the small of his back. I forgot Missy, forgot the locked room and surrendered to the moment.

Later, as we lay stretched out across the bed, Trey ran his fingers across my ample stomach and said, 'Mrs Ferguson, you're beautiful.'

'Um, Trey,' I began, unwilling to spoil the moment but needing to say something. 'I hadn't exactly planned on changing my last name.' Just another thing we hadn't discussed in our hurry to get married.

He looked at me, still with that lazy smile. He kissed my stomach and then kissed me on the lips. 'Maeve O'Mara,' he said. 'You are *so* modern.'

15

'I screwed up again, didn't I?'

'What do you mean?'

'Like when I asked you to marry me. You weren't ready for it. I keep doing stuff like this. I get carried away with an idea. I should have prepared you better. I should have warned you. We should have stayed the night in Asheville and driven up here in the daylight, because now it's all started off on the wrong foot.'

'Trey, what are you trying to say?' We were drinking coffee in the kitchen, and he was looking at me across the table, his most earnest look on his face.

'You don't like the house, do you?'

I wrapped my hands around my mug of coffee, stared at the surface of the kitchen table and tried to think how to answer the question. Some of my post-coital glow had worn off as I'd taken a fresh look around the untidy, unloved kitchen. I wondered what would happen if I said straight out that he was right, yes, I hated the house and wanted to leave. Would it be a deal-breaker? I fidgeted in my seat. 'It's . . . it's got potential,' I said, returning to my new favourite evasion.

That made him laugh with a sudden loud 'Ha!' 'Oh Maeve, that's so British of you. So stiff upper lip. Put a brave face on it. No, the truth is you hate this place. I can't say I blame you, either.' He looked around the room. 'It's not looking its best, is it?'

I needed to be honest with him. 'Trey, the problem is that it feels unloved. This is your childhood home. So I was expecting it to feel – well, you know – like a home. But it doesn't. It feels like an old empty house that's seen better days.'

His eyes lit up. 'Oh Maeve, you're so right. It's the atmosphere, isn't it? Of course, you're sensitive to atmosphere. I was forgetting about the Irish in you.'

I flinched at that. I hate it when people assign me supernatural abilities just because of my Irish name. Trey didn't seem to notice. He carried on: 'You felt it last night, didn't you? The way the house is dying? That's why you reacted like that.'

I did a kind of nod. He was sort of right, although I didn't want to admit to an over-sensitivity to atmosphere. I reacted like that mostly because of the pokiness of the house and that horrible fusty smell, and the fact that it obviously hadn't seen a duster or a vacuum cleaner in months. Years.

'Maeve, this house wasn't always a happy house. My childhood wasn't . . .' He scrunched up his eyes, looking for the right phrase to use. 'My childhood wasn't all that great, either. But my grand-daddy was a good man, and this was a good place. Good things happened in this house. Wonderful music was made here, in this house, in this place. And then it stopped. My grand-daddy died, my father – well, you know, he was long passed. I guess I was supposed to keep it going, keep the tradition going, but instead I left home and got married, and I can't help feeling that I abandoned this place and I shouldn't have done. Do you know what I mean?'

I nodded slowly, hesitantly. It seemed to be the correct response, as Trey smiled and continued. 'This house has nearly died, and it's our job, you and me together . . .' and he paused to lean over and kiss me once, twice on the lips. 'You and me, we're going to bring love and music back to this place, aren't we? We're going to make it a happy home.'

I stared at him, wide-eyed. So much passion about a house: an emotion I'd never felt. Maybe because the places I'd lived in had such sad associations: the house with its faint memories of my mother; the poky flat I'd shared with Martin. I'd never had such positive memories of a place. I wasn't sure what I felt. Was I scared? This seemed to be a different Trey from the one I'd known in London. Less of the light-hearted charmer. Darker, more passionate, more sincere. Maybe somewhat over-passionate? He smiled at me, that all-embracing smile, his stare anxiously searching my face, and I remembered all of a sudden that cold, wet day in London just a few weeks before, when I'd sat on the floor looking around at my flat, my shabby unloved flat – in truth, not much better than this house – and I'd wept from loneliness and frustration and because Trey hadn't sent me an e-mail. And then he'd phoned me and just hearing his voice had changed everything. He'd flown over to Britain to save me; and he'd swept me off my feet, and I'd let myself succumb.

And suddenly I could see what he meant. I could feel it, I really could. It was like a light going on. I wanted to share it with him, whatever 'it' was. I looked at him for a long time. I looked at the way his full rosebud lips fell slightly open, waiting eagerly for my response. I looked at the few fine dark hairs that had appeared on his unshaven chin, at the vulnerable white rims of his ears showing through his hair. I smiled at him, and his face broke into that huge smile of his.

'Wow.' It was a ridiculously inadequate word, but I couldn't think of anything else to say. I felt guilty and optimistic at the same time. I wanted to take back everything I'd thought about Trey and his house. No wonder he'd done nothing to redecorate. All his time, his effort, his energy – probably all his money – had gone into this: his studio, the studio he'd told me about, his dream studio here in the basement. And while I knew virtually nothing about recording studios, I could tell that it was a thing of beauty.

Running the full length and width of the house, the basement had been divided by a thick wall with a double-glazed window and a soundproof door. Inside the room created by the wall I could see an upright piano and some microphone stands. The main room was full of what I assumed must be the latest high-tech equipment: mixing desks with faders, computer monitors, more micro-phones. Hanging on pegs on the walls, guitars and mandolins added an endearingly old-fashioned note. The floor and walls were covered in a kind of pale green carpet, and from the ceiling recessed spotlights cast a bright glow on the shiny new equipment.

I perched on the edge of the mixing desk for a while and watched Trey as he walked around the studio, gesticulating with his awkward gangling grace. Yes, I know that sounds like an oxymoron, a contradiction in terms. I know 'grace' is a strange word to use about a clumsy, too-tall man-child who keeps walking into things, but that was the word that came to me that morning. Something about the way Trey moved in that space struck me as exactly right. There was a lightness, a floatiness, a freshness to his movements. His long-fingered hands tenderly stroked the faders and the knobs and the woodwork of the desk with the same grace that I'd seen him use to play the guitar. I thought of how those same hands had stroked my body just a couple of hours ago and I smiled to myself.

'So who uses the studio?'

'Well, I'm planning to make my next album here. Very much a one-man project. Although I'm still at the writing stage at the moment. And like I said, Missy's been doing some work here, but of course now I realise that would be very awkward for both of you, so, you know . . .'

I shrugged. 'Well, whatever . . .' I said, leaving it hanging, making it Trey's decision: not generous or foolish enough to say, 'Let her come'; not ungenerous or foolish enough to insist on banning her.

Trey gave me a sheepish smile. Then, 'Also, Kevin. You know, Kevin Strauss? He was at the wedding? He's planning a solo album and he wants to record some tracks up here. You'll like him. He's a great guy.'

Kevin Strauss. Of course. What was the name of his band? I thought for a moment. Goldbug, that was it. 'Martin was a big fan of Goldbug,' I managed to say.

'Was he? He had great taste.' Trey was looking at me with the kind of expression you'd use to encourage a child to give the answer to a difficult question.

I nodded and turned away, hiding the tears that were appearing at the corners of my eyes. Saying Martin's name out loud, just dropping it into the conversation, had been an experiment that still wasn't quite working for me. One day I'd like to be able to do it casually, as casually as Trey could mention Missy's name. To cover my embarrassment I ran my hand along the edge of the mixing desk. Some kind of pale wood frame kept all the components in place. Pale wood with beautifully finished details.

'This is a great bit of joinery,' I said in a completely different tone.

Trey laughed, looked at me, and laughed again.

'No, I'm being serious. This is a lovely bit of crafts-manship. Look at the detail of this dovetailing.'

Trey looked at me more closely. 'You *are* being serious, aren't you?'

'Of course I am.'

'You are so full of surprises, Maeve. Joinery. Dove-tailing. Those are very technical terms. And all that stuff last night about the house being 1930s. How come you know so much about this stuff?' He was smiling at me, his arms folded across his purple Lake Havasu T-shirt, his head on one side as if waiting for an explanation.

'My father was a builder,' I said, scanning the wall behind Trey critically. 'He started off working with his hands. It was his trade, what he did. I was the only one of his kids who actually took an interest in what he did. At one point when I was a teenager I even thought about going into the business with him, but then he sold up and retired and I went off to university instead. He went on to do some property development, just to keep his hand in. He'd buy old houses and bring them back to life. Restore their period details. I'd help him out sometimes and I got good at practical stuff like plastering, tiling, you know. We loved going around architectural salvage yards together, finding the right kind of fireplace or light fitting or door furniture. It's such a thrill, seeing old houses come back to life.'

I could feel my cheeks glowing bright red and I knew my eyes were shining. I realised I was now showing exactly the same kind of scary passion as Trey had done earlier. Trey's eyes were shining too. Something clicked in my head. I had never done much to the London flat. I'd always meant to redecorate, but then Martin had got ill, and after he'd died I had felt completely defeated by the place. But now a little flame started to flicker inside me. I was thinking about the beautiful geometric art deco detailing on the mantelpiece that I'd spotted in the front room. About stripping back the layers of thick paint, treating the woodwork and repainting it in glossy white. Unblocking the fireplaces and getting the chimneys swept. Then I thought about the butler sink and the marble worktops and the lovely old range in the kitchen, and that big room that could be so full of light. 'Trey, who did this joinery?'

'My good friend Brett and his son Lonnie.'

'Brett who runs the Christmas-tree plantation and plays the banjo?'

Trey laughed. 'That's the guy.'

'So does he do bespoke kitchen cabinets as well?'

'I guess,' he said. 'We'll ask him, shall we?'

'Trey, one more thing . . .' He was smiling at me still, nodding, full of excitement and encouragement. 'The old front parlour. I'd love to do something with that room, but it's locked. I tried the door earlier. Have you got the key somewhere?'

The smile dropped off his face. 'No,' he said in an expressionless voice. 'No key. Like I said, I don't use that room.'

'Well,' I began, about to say something like – no problem, I can just dismantle the old lock, it'll be easy – but then I looked hard at Trey. His shoulders were hunched and he had his arms wrapped around his chest. His face was as expressionless as his voice. No, not expressionless. Closed. Locked up. Forbidding. For a moment he looked just like the photographs of his grandfather.

16

My first sight of Bodie's Hollow in daylight was an almost physical shock, as if I'd been kicked in the stomach. I'd been so seduced by films and television. Small-town America. We all know what small-town America is like, don't we? Sure, yes, the people would be unfriendly to start with, despite Trey's repeated assurances. ('They'll love you.' 'Will they? Why?' 'Because I love you and I'm the town's favourite son.') But in my imagination the town would be neat and well-kept, with quaint shops and banks and cafés, and a white-painted church and a wooden schoolhouse. The reality? Bodie's Hollow was a dump, just one step up from a ghost town. There's no other way to describe it.

Main Street was cracked and rutted, but at least it was paved. The side streets were merely dirt and dust. The pavement – the sidewalk, as I guessed I'd have to get used to calling it – was uneven and also full of cracks and holes. It looked as though no money had been spent on it since it had been built. The old church at the top end of town was boarded up, and the overgrown churchyard had just a handful of neatly tended graves. The rows of shops that had looked promising as we'd driven through town the night before were a real let-down. They were built in

1950s concrete vernacular and, apart from the café, the only businesses were a hairdresser and beauty salon, with photos of ludicrously over-elaborate and outdated hairstyles in the window, and a drugstore with a display of incontinence pads and headache pills. To our left, the shops were older and faced onto a covered wooden boardwalk. They were quaint, I suppose, but only two shops in the row appeared to be in business: the internet café that Trey had told me about, and a brightly-painted gift shop. The others were in various states of disrepair – some with their windows still intact, others boarded up and almost falling down. Rising up the valley behind the shops, a few streets of wooden houses clung to the hill. Above them, trailers dotted the side of the valley. It was Wednesday lunchtime and the town seemed deserted. At the far end of town an old guy in a plaid shirt and a cap clambered into a truck and drove away. And that was it. It was almost as if we had wandered on to the set of a post-apocalyptic horror movie.

I clutched Trey's hand tightly. After the roller-coaster emotions of the last couple of days I didn't want to be forced into any further emotional pretence. I took a deep breath and said, 'Was it like this when you were growing up?'

'Like what?'

This deprived, was what I wanted to say. I searched my brain for another, less offensive word. I toyed with 'poor' but thought better of it. 'This quiet,' was what I came out with in the end.

'Well,' Trey said, drawing out the vowel sound to

Jimmy Stewart lengths. He rubbed his mouth and chin. He looked around him, as if he was seeing the town for the first time. 'I guess it's always been kinda quiet around here,' he said, and his eyes clued me in to the fact that I was supposed to smile. But I couldn't.

I know a lot about the history of Bodie's Hollow now. I spent a lot of time studying it while I was living there, looking for an angle, an idea for a feature that I could write; or simply for something to do. It's a good place for people with secrets, Bodie's Hollow. It lies in a narrow fold in the mountains with one road in and no roads out, as the local saying goes. Things kept passing it by, as though history itself didn't realise the town was there. Even the Blue Ridge Parkway, the scenic route that FDR decided to have cut through the mountains during the Great Depression, thus bringing tourist dollars to the area, bypassed Bodie's Hollow entirely, coming no closer than twenty miles away. Trey told me it was precisely that hiddenness, the secretiveness of the landscape, that drew the first settlers to Bodie's Hollow. I assumed he meant moonshiners, brewing their illegal hooch in makeshift stills before bootlegging it from county to county during the Prohibition era, but he quickly told me that that was an unhelpful Appalachian stereotype. What he meant was people like his ancestors: God-fearing, hardworking, self-reliant, mostly Presbyterian; the poor white working class, looking for somewhere to farm their own small plot of land, raise their families and practise their faith in private, without interference from the government. The hidden hollows and folds of the mountains meant they could do just that.

To begin with, Foggy Hollow was a collection of small cabins among the trees, each centred in a plot of land painstakingly cleared from the surrounding forest. Each family would grow a handful of crops: tobacco, corn, tomatoes, squash. There'd be a few chickens and turkeys, perhaps a couple of pigs and a milch cow, a phrase I had to look up in the dictionary when I first came across it during my research. The Fergusons, so Trey told me, had been one such family.

The Civil War tore families apart. Many of the poorer mountain folk sided with the North, distrusting the slave-owning rich folk who ran the tobacco plantations in the flat fertile land that made up most of North Carolina. The Appalachians became lawless, with groups of deserters hiding out in the caves and hollows. It was after the war that a carpet-bagger called Bodie gave the town his name. He was the man who started the first logging camp, taking advantage of the only true natural resources: trees and a river. Rowdy men, stripped to the waist, stripped the forest and sent the logs downstream. In the late nineteenth century the timber industry became more mechanised. Houses were built, quickly, for the influx of workers. A town grew up on the side of the river, with stores and bars and restaurants. But then the Depression hit and because the river that ran through Bodie's Hollow was too capricious (too shallow in the summer, too fierce in the winter) and because the railroad bypassed the town and the nearest railhead was too far away, the timber business slowly died, leaving a town that had very little reason to exist. In the 1960s and 1970s locals started moving out to the cities. Some stayed put but exchanged their old cabins for trailers, so much warmer and easier to look after. A handful of hippies and artists and musicians moved in, and many soon moved out again. As Trey said, the town had always been 'kinda quiet'.

It was characteristic of Bodie's Hollow that the river itself was now bypassed. The river, which gave the town its reason for being, had been relegated to an afterthought. The town had turned its back on the river and for most of the time you wouldn't even know that it was there. Maybe I should have read something into that. Maybe I should have realised it was significant that Trey himself never took me down to the river. But as far as I was concerned, it was just a river running peacefully through a small town in the Appalachian Mountains.

Such life as there is in Bodie's Hollow revolves around the brand-new Baptist Church and the local café. The Bodie's Hollow Café should not be confused with the new internet café-cum-coffee shop across the street, which has yet to convert the townsfolk to the joys of lattes, skinny frappachinos and easy access to the World Wide Web. If someone says they'll meet you at the café, they mean the one that's always been there, with its cracked red vinyl seats and peeling Formica-topped tables; with its row of stools lining the counter, and the day's specials ('meat loaf and two sides – $4.95') marked up on a whiteboard at one end of the counter; with its half-hearted souvenir stall in the corner, selling faded, curled postcards, Missy Ferguson CDs and gaudy wooden keyrings with names like Troy, Kurt and Tiffany engraved on them.

The smells that hit me as we entered the café that first time were of stewed coffee and lunchtime specials: cooked mince and boiled vegetables; and presumably at breakfast time the cooked-mince-and-boiled vegetable smell would be replaced by that of frying bacon. Trey held the door open for me, I walked in and I saw four pairs of eyes gazing at me with something that was closer to indifference than either hostility or interest. I was surprised. I suppose I'd been expecting some kind of welcome party. I'd imagined that the townspeople would be desperately interested to see Trey Ferguson's new wife, to see who he'd chosen to replace Missy, to bombard us with questions about how we had met. Instead, a few heads turned to look at me and then turned away.

An immensely fat woman with a pale doughy face was sitting at the booth nearest to the door together with a slender, hard-faced teenage girl who wore her hair scraped back from her face. 'Hey, Linda Sue,' said Trey, 'Hey, Kayla. This is my beautiful new wife Maeve.'

Mother and daughter looked at me judgementally for a moment, and then back to Trey. 'Was the food I got for you 'uns okay?' asked Linda Sue, her accent much harder and twangier than Trey's.

Trey made some polite non-committal remark and then asked, 'Hey, where's your boy Lonnie?'

'He's at Bible camp,' she said with some pride. 'Lonnie found the Lord.'

'Hallelujah,' added Kayla, dryly. I smirked, looked at her, caught her eye and we both smiled. Thank God, I thought, at least one person likes me, even if it's a teenage girl with too much eyeliner.

A comfortable-sized woman in late middle age stood behind the counter, dressed in a checked overall. Trey introduced her to me as Patsy. She looked at me with narrowed eyes, her head on one side. I held out my hand to her and, after a while, she tentatively shook it. Then, as if making an important decision, she stepped out from behind the counter, clasped my hands in hers, which were plump, white and freckled, looked me up and down and said, 'Oh yes.'

She looked across at Trey and nodded, and it seemed as if some secret communication had been passed between them. Then she gathered me to her in an enveloping hug. Her skin against my cheek was soft and powdery, and she smelled of pastry and lavender, which is what I imagine mothers must smell like. I swallowed hard. Maybe the townsfolk would take me to their hearts straight away.

Patsy poured me coffee and I sat at the counter to drink it. Trey was talking to Linda Sue again, and I found myself alone for a moment. An elderly man sat down on the stool next to mine. He had trousers hoisted up to his chest and an old suit jacket over a checked shirt. He had some kind of peaked cap perched on the top of his head: green, with mesh sides, with a yellow logo and the words 'John Deere' on the front. 'I've had half my lung removed,' he confided in me, as if it were a password in a spy movie. And then, 'That's Jerry's stool,' and I thought: so it begins. Now the townsfolk turn against me because I'm sitting in the wrong place. I made as if to move, but he put his hand on my arm to stop me. 'But Jerry's gone to Europe,' he said – pronouncing it 'Yurp' – 'so I reckon you can sit there.'

Patsy overheard, and called out to Trey, 'Did Jerry make it to the wedding?'

I noticed that everyone turned towards Trey to hear what he had to say, as if they were hanging on his every word. He laughed and said, 'Oh yeah, Jerry made it okay.' He looked across at me and explained, 'Jerry's never travelled before. He only got his passport a couple of days before our wedding. Anyway, he decided he'd stay over in Britain for a while. He's always wanted to see the Cotswolds.'

'The Cotswolds?' What on earth? 'Why the Cotswolds?'

'Jerry runs a little antiques business here as well as his guitar-making. Someone told him the Cotswolds were the antique capital of the world. So at this very moment he's probably sitting in a quaint ole teashop in a picturesque British village.'

I laughed, thinking about the shy little man who'd told me how different I was from Missy. 'Do you know, I've never been to the Cotswolds.' I thought for a moment. 'In fact, I'm not sure they actually exist. I think we invented them to fool Americans. Someone cruel just drew a circle on a map, gave the area a funny name, and now every café and antique shop inside that circle can charge three times as much for everything they sell.'

'Sounds like the Blue Ridge Parkway,' said a voice from behind me. It was a woman's voice, a sharp, nasal, city voice: a New York accent, maybe. I turned and saw a slim, attractive, vivid woman a few years younger than me, with short dark hair and big dark eyes. She was wearing beautifully cut cropped trousers and a close-fitting dark orange polo shirt: the kind of woman who makes me feel inadequate about my size and dress sense. She smiled at me, and then looked at Trey. 'Hey,' she said.

'Hey, Jules,' he said, without much animation. 'Oh, this is my wife, by the way. Maeve, Julie. Julie, Maeve.'

'I like you,' she said to me. 'You're funny.'

'Thank you,' I said, surprised at how much that meant to me. Then I asked her, 'What did you mean by the Blue Ridge Parkway?'

She grinned, ruefully. 'It's a real tourist trap. This road that runs through the mountains. Very beautiful, boring as hell. Tourists like to drive the whole length of it, specially in the fall, and any town lucky enough to live within a couple of miles of the Parkway can hike up its prices – motels, restaurants, gift stores, the lot.'

'Julie's just p'ed off that it doesn't come close enough to Bodie's Holler to bring floods of vacationers into her little store.' Trey was smiling, as if he'd heard it all before.

'Well, it'd be nice. Is all I'm saying. Anyway, Trey, you've done well here,' and she tapped my arm. 'Maeve, come over and see my store soon, won't you? I think we're gonna get on real well.' Then she turned and left as suddenly as she'd arrived. I watched her as she went, and decided she was right: we were going to get on real well.

17

The view of Bodie's Hollow from the top of the field behind the old Ferguson homestead was almost – almost, but not quite – enough to take away the acute disappointment of the town itself. It almost made the town look beautiful. It was the view I'd seen in the photographs that Trey had brought to England, and a view I never got tired of seeing. I would stand at the top of the field and below me, beyond the house, all of Bodie's Hollow lay stretched out at my feet: the main street winding through the valley, the old church on the small rise, the river glinting in the sun, the overhanging trees seeming to block the route out of the valley. In the mornings, small cotton-wool balls of mist would float around the town, and it looked peaceful and idyllic.

Beyond Bodie's Hollow, in every direction, our house was surrounded by mountains. It felt as if we were on the top of the world, as if you could skim a stone and it would bounce on each tree-lined mountain top in turn; as if I was a bird and could fly to the horizon, touching every peak with a dip of my wings. In each gap of the mountains, mist would hang suspended in the sky, filling the spaces between the peaks like the lace modesty inserts in the V-shaped necklines of Edwardian girls' dresses. Each zigzag line of peaks had another, fainter, zigzag line beyond it, fading from dark green to blue, and I could never tell for certain where the furthest line of mountains stopped and the sky started; where the green ended and the blue began.

One day I told Trey that, and he said, 'Apparently the Native Americans who first lived in these mountains couldn't tell either. They used the same word for both green and blue.'

'Really?'

He nodded. Then he laughed and said, 'When I was a kid, before I started wearing glasses, I didn't stand a chance. I knew in theory that there were mountains all around, but all I could see was a big greeny-blue cloudy mass on the horizon. Same with the trees. I couldn't pick out separate leaves at all, just a big mass of green. Or orange and red and yellow during the fall.'

'How old were you when they discovered you needed glasses?'

'Oh, everyone always knew I needed glasses, from when I was very young. It was obvious. I was blind as a bat. It's just that I didn't start wearing them until I was a teenager and wanted to start driving, and then I had to. By law. You could say that my entire childhood was spent in a blur.'

'Why? Did you not want to wear them? Did you get teased or something?' I could imagine that as a child Trey would have been the sort that bullies would pick on. There was still something very vulnerable about him, and children can always spot that kind of thing.

'No. My grand-daddy didn't hold with "eyeglasses", as

he called them. He thought if God meant you to be near-sighted, then that's the way you should stay.'

I felt my mouth fall open. 'Trey, this is the same grandfather who put Tabasco sauce on your tongue when you swore?'

He turned to me, grinning. 'Yep. He was a great man, my grand-daddy, but he had some old-fashioned ideas. Like something out of the last century.' He thought for a while. 'Well, of course, it *was* the last century. I mean, like something out of the century before that. He was firm but fair. He was very consistent, in fact. I always knew where I was, where the line was, but you could say he was very strict, very Victorian.'

'Trey, I'll apologise in advance for what I'm about to say, but – Jesus Christ almighty. I'm sorry, I can't think of anything else to say. Your poor thing. What did you do at school? How could you see the blackboard? How did you join in the games at break time?'

'I just sat in a corner with a book. Or with my penknife and a bit of wood. I got very good at whittling. That's how Jerry and I got to be friends. You know, Jerry the luthier who was my best man?' I nodded. 'We formed a woodworking club.'

I couldn't tell whether Trey was taking the piss or not, as he was now looking straight ahead. I reached out my left hand and smoothed the beautiful dark hair on his strong forearm. 'My poor baby,' I said. I turned his hand over and kissed the palm. I needed to ask him something. 'Trey, that scar on your back . . .'

I felt his hand stiffen.

'. . . Did your grandfather used to beat you?'

He took his hand away from me and studied the palm. He was silent for quite a while, and then he said, 'Maeve, I know you had an unhappy childhood. I did too. But I don't ask about your childhood because I know you'll tell me everything you want me to know. You'll tell me what you need to tell me. And I'll do the same for you.'

Don't ask, was what he was saying. I opened my mouth, closed it again. I looked at Trey. He was all hunched up, his shoulders almost up around his ears. As gently as I could, I asked, 'But Trey, if you were so unhappy here, why have you come back?'

'Because it's my home. I wanted to come home.'

I looked at him carefully. We had at that point been married less than a week but I was beginning to realise something: Trey's whole body could change shape at just the mention of his grandfather. His shoulders hunched and his body seemed to collapse in on itself, as if he was deliberately shrinking, making himself as small as possible. His face would close up, making it impossible to read. I'd seen it a couple of days earlier, when I'd tentatively suggested moving some of the photographs from the hallway; the same thing had happened when I'd asked him about opening up the front parlour. Trey's grandfather, that long-dead man, cast a long shadow.

CJ Ferguson wasn't the only shadow on our marriage. There was also my stupid unjustified insecurity, which centred on one person: Missy Ferguson. I knew

Trey loved me and I loved him. But I couldn't help myself. In public, among groups of people, I felt occasional stabs of something very much like jealousy; they actually felt like stabs, sharp physical pains high in my chest. Particularly in Bodie's Hollow: I could never let myself forget that Missy Ferguson grew up in this town. Almost everyone here must have known her. They would remember her well, with great affection – the town's most famous daughter, and Trey's childhood sweetheart.

People flocked around Trey. He was so popular, so well-loved and so completely charismatic that people would hang on his every word. He always seemed to be at the centre of every social circle. Sometimes I felt that when he introduced me to his friends I would be a grave disappointment to them. He had this phrase he used to describe me, which I didn't entirely like for reasons that took me some time to identify. 'My beautiful new wife' was what he habitually called me. When he introduced me to people around town – to Linda Sue and Kayla, to Ed who worked at the gas station on the edge of town, to Ginger, the girl who sat behind the checkout at our local supermarket down at the strip mall – that was what he'd say. 'This is my beautiful new wife,' and I'd almost always squirm.

It was the same when he took me to church. The old Presbyterian church at one end of the valley, the church his ancestors had attended for generations, was now abandoned; the Baptist church at the other end seemed, in contrast, almost exaggeratedly full of life, lit up every evening with its noticeboard showing details of events and meetings. So that was where he took me, our first Sunday morning together in Bodie's Hollow. We were sitting on the back porch having breakfast when Trey looked at his watch. 'Better get moving,' he said, 'We don't want to be late.'

'Late for what?'

He looked at me as if I should know exactly what he meant. 'It's Sunday,' he said. 'Church?'

I thought for a moment that he might be joking. 'What's up?' he said, and then: 'Oh, of course. I didn't even think. I guess you're a Catholic, aren't you? You know, I think there's a Catholic church in one of the towns over in the next valley, if you wanted to go to, like, Mass or confession or something.'

The way he said it made it sound like some kind of incredibly strange and exotic religion, possibly involving human sacrifice. I laughed. 'It's okay, Trey. I'm not really a Catholic. I'm not really an anything. I don't usually go to church.' From the expression on his face I realised I'd said entirely the wrong thing, so I quickly back-pedalled. 'But I'd love to come with you today, if that's okay,' I said.

I sat in the uncomfortable wooden seat and looked around me. It seemed as if every single one of the two hundred and seventy-nine people who lived in town was there. Most of the women were wearing bright floral dresses with big coloured straw hats that were decorated with artificial fruit and flowers. Most of the men were in smart trousers and shirts. The congregation, like the population of the town itself, was mostly white, but they responded to the preacher like I'd expect black people to do: loads of 'Yes, Lords,' and 'Hallelujahs'. Even my husband joined in. I looked at him out of the corner of my eye, trying to hide my surprise and disbelief.

The service lasted more than two hours. The singing was extraordinary. People sang harmonies and variations on the tunes, as if they'd rehearsed them. I could feel waves of something – emotion, passion – flowing like a river through the assembled congregation. The prayers went on for what seemed like hours – many more 'Yes, Lords,' and I noticed that people had their eyes clenched shut and were swaying backwards and forwards – even Trey. And as for the sermon, well, I couldn't tell you what it was about, but it was certainly scary. Almost enough to make me wish I had something to repent of. I was beginning to understand why CJ Ferguson was known as the Preacherman. The preacher at the Bodie's Hollow Baptist Church had the same fierce, righteous tone I'd heard in CJ Ferguson's music. There was hellfire and brimstone, and I thought to myself: any minute now, they're going to start speaking in tongues and handling snakes, like they habitually do in TV documentaries about the Appalachian Mountains.

When we came to the Mass – or whatever they call it in Baptist churches – the whole congregation milled around, hugging and kissing each other. I found myself caught up in dozens of sweaty embraces. Then Trey, smiling, held out his hand and led me to the front of the church. Now, I guess that technically speaking I *am* a Catholic. I was baptised as a baby, and I made my first communion in a frilly white dress when I was eleven. I don't think I'm supposed to take Mass – communion – at Baptist churches. But I knelt down beside Trey, and ate the chunk of bread and swallowed the thimbleful of grape juice that was offered me, and then the preacher put the heel of his hand hard on my forehead and said, 'Lord, bless this woman and make your face to shine upon her,' and I wondered how I was supposed to react.

Trey steered me around the church hall after the service, introducing me to family after family as 'my beautiful new wife, Maeve,' and that was when I realised why I found the phrase so annoying. It wasn't the word 'new' that irritated me, even though it carried with it a sense of temporariness, a constant reminder of Missy. No, it was the word 'beautiful', and particularly the precise stress that he put on the word. It was as if he was saying to everyone we met, 'I'm going to tell you up front that I think Maeve is beautiful, and there'll be no further argument on the issue.'

I wondered if he'd ever felt the need to describe Missy as beautiful.

18

B ut all in all I was happy.

I decided that I was happy when I woke on my third or fourth morning in Bodie's Hollow with Trey's arms wrapped around me as usual. Through the gap in the curtains I could see the final flush of dawn still tinting the blue sky. I smoothed the dark hair on Trey's forearms and wrapped them tighter around me. I could feel him snuggling up to me and I couldn't stop myself smiling. Yes, I was happy, although I made the diagnosis tentatively. It was something I hadn't felt in a long time.

I never thought I'd become the kind of woman who wants to be held all night. For someone like me, who's used to love being displayed in the form of an affectionate punch on the arm (my father, my brothers) or a raw, rough onslaught that would leave me sore (Martin), it felt like a surrender. Trey's tenderness was a new and unexpectedly lovely experience. I hadn't expected to enjoy being adored, but I did enjoy it and it made me very happy.

In spite of the state of the house, the unfamiliarity of the town and the forbidding, lingering presence of Trey's grandfather; in spite of Missy Ferguson, the sheer culture shock of moving from London to Bodie's Hollow – in spite of it all, I think I was happier during those first couple of weeks of marriage than I've ever been in my life. It was if we'd consciously decided we were on our honeymoon. Trey had said he wanted to get back to Bodie's Hollow quickly, to get back to work on his album, to get back into the studio. But in fact we became a pair of lotus-eaters. We'd wake early, full of plans, but then one of us would touch the other, and a casual gesture would almost inevitably lead to slow, languorous, luxurious sex that could use up whole hours of the morning. We were the only two people in the world and we were trying to learn each other's body by heart.

My head was buzzing with ideas for the house. I was itching to rip up the yellow lino from the hallway, to dismantle the old kitchen cabinets, to sand all the floorboards. I did manage to get quite a lot of cleaning done during that first week or so. I opened all the windows and doors and sprayed air freshener around the place, which did at least mask the worst of the fustiness. I did my best to ignore the closed door of the front parlour; to pretend that it wasn't there. I bought a new vacuum cleaner at a big home-improvement store down in our nearby courthouse town, Buchanansville, and lots of cleaning products. I pulled on some rubber gloves, tied my hair up in a scarf, and scrubbed the kitchen and bathroom from top to bottom. I was a whirlwind of energy, and Trey was co-opted as my assistant. He didn't seem to mind. But whenever I broached the idea of doing some more substantial redecoration he'd smile, take my hand and say, 'Maeve, we're on our honeymoon. Relax.'

We went on day trips, and I couldn't help wondering if they were just a way of preventing me ripping off the dark green wallpaper from our bedroom walls. We drove up and down the Blue Ridge Parkway, which was, as Julie had put it so precisely, 'very beautiful, boring as hell'. Miles of road with a tight speed limit; trees and mountains in every direction. You can have too much of a good thing. We went to Grandfather Mountain, too, and I tried to make out the profile that had given the peak its name. It was supposed to look like a bearded old man, but it was so foggy that day that I couldn't see a thing.

And then there was the river. My secret place. My bolt-hole.

I discovered it on the Sunday morning after Trey took me to church for the first time. We went to the café afterwards for brunch, along with what seemed to be the entire population of Bodie's Hollow. It was hot, smelly and crowded, and I could feel my back sticking to the cracked red vinyl of the booth we were sitting in. Conversations were swirling around my head as people greeted Trey and shook his hand, hugged him and asked him questions about me, as if I couldn't speak for myself. I stopped concentrating and the twangy mountain accent began to sound like a foreign language. I felt sick, sweaty and disoriented and suddenly I had to leave. I tapped Trey on the leg, said, 'I'm just popping out for a breath of fresh air,' and rushed outside.

I strolled down an alleyway beside the café and noticed

a wooden building I hadn't seen before, with a small shopfront full of guitars and violins and mandolins. I guessed it must be Jerry the luthier's workshop. The alleyway was unpaved, just wide enough for a car, and was lined with a few small one-storey wooden houses. Some of the houses were freshly decorated, with tidy front yards full of flowers and pots. Most were shabby and looked empty or otherwise unkempt.

The alleyway petered out into a narrow pathway that veered to the left as it made its way down the hill. It was lined by trees, and I could hear the faint gurgle of a stream. About a hundred yards further down I suddenly found myself on the river bank. I gasped with delight. It was beautiful. The sunlight dappled through the leaves and cast patterns on the smooth water. The river was calm, and the surface was broken here and there by large, flat rocks. I took off my trusty Birkenstocks and rolled up my trouser legs. I paddled through the clear stream and found a warm rock to sit on. I splashed my forehead with the cool water. A few yards from where I was sitting, the river bed fell sharply and there was a gentle cascade of water that, together with the birdsong, made a relaxing soundtrack for a beautiful day. It was peaceful and lovely and unexpected, and I wondered why Trey hadn't yet brought me here himself.

'Hey, Mizz Ferguson!'

I looked over to the river bank and saw Kayla, the teenage girl I'd met in the café that first morning. She was wearing cut-off shorts and a bikini top. I smiled and beckoned her over. 'Call me Maeve,' I told her. She was carrying some bottles of beer and gave me one. She was only about fourteen, but I figured that in a town where people marry at sixteen, drinking beer at fourteen was more than acceptable, even if it was only midday.

'So, how do you like Bodie's Holler?'

I thought for a moment, trying to think of the best answer. 'It's very pretty.'

'Yeah, really.' She had all the sarcasm of a typical teenage girl. 'Is it true you come from London, England?'

'That's right.'

'And you left London to come here?' Disbelief was etched in the curl of her top lip.

I nodded.

'Why?'

I laughed. I'd been asking myself that. 'Because I married Trey.'

'That must be love, right? To leave London and carry yourself here to Bodie's Holler.'

She made it sound like the action of a madwoman. I didn't really want to answer her question so I asked her one instead. 'Do *you* like Bodie's Hollow?'

She shook her head. 'Uh-uh.'

'Why not?'

'Because this place is dead. There's nothing to do but go to church. My mom and dad, they have this place and they grow Christmas trees? Like, what's that about?' She shrugged her skinny shoulders expressively. 'I'm gonna get out as soon as I can. Maybe I'll go to Nashville, like

Missy Ferguson did. Go and be a big superstar. Do you know Missy Ferguson?'

'Well . . .'

'She's so pretty,' said Kayla wistfully, with all the tactlessness of a true teenager.

We sat in silence for a while, and then I said, 'Anyway, this river's lovely. What a great place to come when the weather's good.'

Kayla looked at me with a conspiratorial expression in her eyes. 'I'm not supposed to be here. Don't tell my mom, will you?'

'Why not?'

'Because it's dangerous.' She made her eyes into saucers.

'Dangerous?' I looked around me at the shallow water, bubbling gently over the stony river bed.

'People die here, in this river.'

'Really? Who?'

She nodded gravely and just said, mysteriously, 'People. I dunno. My mom told me. She says she knew someone who died here. Someone she knew at school, or something.' She gave a mock shudder, and then laughed.

After Kayla left I sat there for a while on my own. I felt the sunshine on my shoulders. I looked around me at the green-leaved trees that crowded together on the river bank. Above the foliage I could see the blue ridge of the mountains. I wiggled my feet, enjoying the coolness of the stream. The whole scene seemed so benign, so beautiful, that I couldn't quite believe what Kayla had told me.

There's something about running water – rivers and the sea, I mean – that makes everything else seem very insignificant. I fell into a kind of reverie, musing on how far I'd come in the last few weeks. I thought about all the sadness I'd left behind. I thought about Trey, and how he made me feel. I thought about the beauty of the mountains around us. All will be well, I thought. All will be well.

Trey had gone. I went back to the café to find him and he wasn't there. The interior seemed very dark in contrast to the bright sunshine, and I stood hesitantly in the doorway scanning the seats and booths. People's faces loomed out of the darkness at me and I couldn't tell whether I knew them or not. I felt sick and disoriented again, and I wondered how long I'd been sitting by the river. Maybe I had sunstroke. Patsy came out of the kitchen and saw me. 'You lookin' for Trey, hon?' she called. 'He's gone back up to the old house.'

The hill seemed steeper than I remembered. What an ugly sight I must have looked, all red-faced and sweaty, as I approached the house. Nonetheless Trey smiled at me as he sat on the front porch strumming his guitar. He held up his hand in greeting. 'Hey, I thought I'd lost you.'

'Sorry, babes. I just needed some air.'

'Where did you get to?'

'I went down to the river,' I said, sitting down next to him. 'It's beautiful down there, so peaceful.' I babbled on, oblivious to the fact that Trey's shoulders were hunched up in that characteristic shrinking gesture until I turned to look at him. 'Babes, what is it?'

Trey took hold of my hand and squeezed it really tightly. He said nothing for a while, and then, quietly: 'Be careful. It's dangerous down there.'

19

A couple of days later Trey took me down to Asheville and that was when I heard the murder ballad again: the old song with its beautiful, mournful melody that I remembered from my schooldays;

Trey took me on a day trip to Biltmore House, a great monstrosity of a place that you have to pay forty dollars a head just to visit. It's a concrete French chateau plonked down in the middle of the beautiful mountains by one of the robber barons at the end of the nineteenth century. We wandered among the plundered European artwork and the overweight tourists, looking like a pair of hippie freaks. Trey was wearing faded holey jeans, a bright blue T-shirt that asserted 'Chesapeake Bay is for Lovers' and Jesus sandals. He looked very sexy, in a gangly, grungy, loose-limbed way. As for me, the heat and humidity had turned my hair into something approaching an Afro and I was wearing a crumpled linen shirt over cropped combat trousers, my feet in my favourite Birkenstocks.

I felt like we were a proper couple. We held hands, or constantly made some other physical contact. Trey had a range of gentle, understated gestures: his fingers stroking the palm of my hand, his arm flung around my waist or shoulders. People stared at us, I guess because of how we were dressed, and so we acted up. We wandered through the big, showy rooms pointing at paintings and pieces of furniture and loudly talked rubbish about them. I'd stand in front of pictures and, in the most cut-glass accent I could manage, spew forth convincing-sounding art critic bullshit as Trey stood and nodded, straight-faced, his hand clutching his jaw in intellectual fashion, his eyes behind his glasses glimmering with suppressed laughter. Tourists gathered to listen, and I realised that certain Americans automatically believe everything that's told to them in an English accent. What can I say? It was fun. We were like a pair of naughty schoolkids.

After we'd toured Biltmore we went into the centre of Asheville, and I realised what a lovely place it was. The city centre was full of unspoilt art-deco buildings from the 1920s and 1930s, as if it'd been caught in a time capsule. Most of the buildings housed either antique shops or hippie stores, selling scented candles and ethnic knick-knacks. Asheville was a city for relaxed strolling, with funky coffee houses and restaurants on every street corner. Trey had brought his mandolin with him and I asked him why.

'Because it's Wednesday.'

'Wednesday?'

'Jam night,' he said in a manner that suggested I should know exactly what he meant, so I didn't ask any more questions.

He took me to what he said was his favourite thrift store, where he'd bought the orange couch he was so fond of, the one in the kitchen. A long-haired young guy in a faded Hawaiian shirt was sitting behind the cash register. He greeted Trey enthusiastically, and Trey introduced me. 'This is my beautiful new wife, Maeve,' he said as I inwardly cringed. Afterwards he told me, 'Elias is a great harp-player'.

I was surprised. 'Harp?' I asked, and mimed someone playing the classical harp. Trey laughed, shook his head and did his own mime, fluttering his hands near his mouth so I realised that he meant the harmonica.

Trey was in heaven among the vintage clothes. He had a magpie eye for seventies T-shirts and shirts, and gathered together an armful of gaudy fabric. Then he spotted something in deep emerald green. He pulled it off the rail. It was a beautiful full-skirted 1950s cocktail frock. He held it up against me and his eyes shone. 'Maeve, you have to have this. It is the perfect colour for you. You should try it on.'

'Are you kidding?'

'What do you mean?'

'Trey, I'm not going to get in that. Look at the size of it.'

He did, and then looked at me. 'Are you sure?'

'Trey, it's vintage. There's no way I'll ever get into a vintage frock. Olden-days women were tiny. I'm built on a modern scale.'

He didn't demur, but then I suppose I wasn't actually angling for a compliment.

We walked through town, hand in hand, Trey's spare hand swinging his plastic bag full of second-hand shirts. It seemed we couldn't go more than a few steps without meeting someone he knew. The usual process went like this: some kind of hippie or arty-type person would be coming towards us, see Trey and do a tremendous double take. Trey would let go of my hand and greet the person in a huge embrace, his carrier bag still clutched in his other hand. Then, almost as an after-thought, he'd introduce me – 'This is my beautiful new wife, Maeve,' he'd say, the precise wording only barely changing.

We ended the day in a bar, and I realised why Trey had brought his mandolin. Jam night turned out to be a bunch of musicians in a place that was almost an English-style pub. I sat at the bar drinking excellent draught beer and watched my husband and a whole load of musicians playing old-fashioned traditional music, fast and furious. Every so often someone would leave and another musician would arrive, an almost seamless transition, the music continuing in a constant stream. I watched Trey, bent over his mandolin, his foot tapping, his glance darting from one musician to another, totally in the zone. I loved watching him play.

There was a fair-haired woman about my age playing stand-up bass and after a while, when another bass player arrived, she leaned her instrument against the wall and came over to the bar to order a round. As she waited for her drinks she turned to me and said, 'Hot damn.'

I smiled at her, assuming that 'hot damn' was an overture of friendship.

'Hot damn,' she said again, and pointed at Trey. 'Do you know who that is?' And before I could answer she said, 'Trey Ferguson. Trey fuckin' Ferguson. I never imagined that I would ever get to play with Trey Ferguson. That man is a legend. He is doing so much for our kind of music, that guy.'

I smiled again and said something like, 'So I've heard,' and she looked at me sharply and said, 'You're British.'

I nodded. 'Yep.'

She took a sip from her pint of Guinness. 'You on vacation?'

'No, I live here. Well, up in Bodie's Hollow, anyway.'

'Well, that's real Ferguson country up that way. What brought you to our part of the world?'

I began to tell her, but when she heard the word 'married' it started her on another tack. 'You know, when Trey and Missy Ferguson got divorced, I thought, oh goodie,' and she rubbed her hands together, 'he's back on the market. But apparently he's already got married.'

I blushed. 'Yes, I know. Um, I'm his wife?' I heard myself giving my intonation an interrogative twist upwards at the end, as if I wasn't convinced I was telling the truth.

She gave me a startled look. 'Fuck me!' Then she covered her mouth with her hand, giggled and said, 'Sorry, but you're not what I expected.'

I opened my mouth to say something but as I started to speak I heard a spontaneous burst of applause from the musicians and saw Trey blush and drop his head modestly. There was a short pause, and then a bearded grey-haired fiddle player (see, I was already learning the correct terms: fiddle, not violin) called out, 'Lily-white Maiden?'

There seemed to be general agreement among the musicians. There was murmuring, and even a couple of whoops. I watched as the fiddle player lifted the instrument to his chin and began to bow. And then I smiled to myself as I heard the first few notes. I knew this song. I didn't know how, I just knew that I knew it. I closed my eyes and listened as the mournful tune twisted up and down in what I knew enough to recognise as a minor key. So beautiful. And so familiar. I opened my eyes, squinting, and focused on the fiddle player. What was this tune? Was it 'Pretty Polly' under another name, that song I'd heard Trey sing on stage in London? That I'd heard his grandfather sing on the CD I'd bought? And then someone started singing, a woman I thought, with a deep, strong voice. 'My lily-white maiden, with eyes that shine like diamonds . . .'

I smiled in recognition, remembering with a sudden piercing stab of nostalgia the song that my music teacher had been obsessed with. The boys sniggering at the word 'bosom'. Me and my friend Lizzie singing it together in the playground at lunchtime, memorising all the words. A song I hadn't sung in years. I wondered about the etiquette of the jam session. Was I allowed to join in the singing? I opened my mouth and began, tentatively, to half-sing, half-hum. And then I nearly jumped out of my skin as I felt a hand on my elbow. It was Trey, mandolin in his other hand. He kissed me. 'We should go,' he said. 'The fog's coming down and it's a long drive back.' He led me out, his hand under my elbow, just as he'd steered me out of the Borderline back at the start of all of this.

'I know that song,' I said, with a certain amount of pride in my voice, as the truck wended its way up into the mountains.

'Which song?'

'That last one – "Lily-white Maiden"?'

There was a pause as Trey concentrated on negotiating a tight bend. Then, 'Well, it's a very old song. A lot of people know it.'

He had his stare fixed on the road. So I tried a different tack. 'So, that was bluegrass,' I said with enthusiasm.

Trey laughed. 'Actually, no. The bluegrass jam's on Thursday. That was old time.'

'What's the difference?'

'Well, that depends how purist and pedantic you want to be,' he said patiently. Then he began to explain in some purist and pedantic detail about different guitar and banjo styles, and the last thing I remember he was making a claw shape with his right hand, before I succumbed to the effect of the three pints of English-style bitter I'd drunk and fell asleep in the passenger seat.

Looking back now, trying to make sense of it all in hindsight, I wonder about the undercurrents of this particular conversation. At the time I didn't think much of it. 'It's a very old song,' he'd said. Just an old song, I thought to myself the next morning when I wondered, briefly, about his odd behaviour. An old hackneyed song that he's fed up with playing. And it had been a foggy night; he was right about that. By the time I'd woken up, as Trey drew the truck to a halt outside the house, the fog was so thick that Bodie's Hollow had completely disappeared.

20

Then, suddenly, the honeymoon was over and real life began. It really was as abrupt as that. Our second Sunday evening in Bodie's Hollow, not quite two weeks after our wedding, we were sitting on the back-porch swing sharing a bottle of wine and watching the sun set below the mountains. We'd been down to Asheville again for the day. Perhaps sensitive to my reaction the previous week, Trey hadn't even suggested that we should go to church. Instead, we'd spent a lazy day moseying around thrift stores and art galleries hand in hand. We'd had a long relaxed lunch at a table outside a busy noodle restaurant, and friends and acquaintances of Trey's had greeted us as they'd wandered past. It had felt to me something like a London Sunday, the kind of summer Sundays Martin and I had occasionally spent; the sort of day when you wander aimlessly along the South Bank or through Camden Market, buying second-hand books and bootleg tapes. Of course the air in Asheville was much cleaner, and Trey was so much more tactile than Martin had ever been, always keeping some part of his body in contact with mine. But my point is that it was one of those days that I understood, knew the script to; the kind of lazy summer Sunday that affluent, childless, vaguely alternative couples in their thirties were spending the world over.

So there we were, tired and content, gently pushing ourselves back and forth on the creaky porch swing, soaking up the glory of that early September sunset, when Trey cleared his throat and said, 'I need to start work again tomorrow morning.'

'Oh,' I said, and momentarily stopped the swing. 'Yeah, of course you do.' That was why he'd wanted to come straight back to Bodie's Hollow: to get back to work. The problem was, I had very little concept of what Trey actually meant by work. 'So you'll be . . .'

'. . . Down in the studio,' he said quickly. 'I really need to get my second album written.'

'Great,' I said. 'I've been meaning to get started on the house, anyway. Plus I've got other stuff to do. You know, pieces to research, features to write, that kind of thing . . .'

As if I'd actually been commissioned to write anything. I'd already e-mailed a few editors with proposals, trying to generate interest in a story about my huge life-change and my plans to do up the old house. I'd figured on a *Year in Provence* or *Driving Over Lemons* approach but I was beginning to realise that I'd have had more luck if I'd fallen in love with a guy who lived in Tuscany or Cornwall or Northern California or anywhere rather than backwoods Appalachia. I'd had one small bite for a piece about transforming the house, but only if I could work in a triumph-over-tragedy angle and

I wasn't sure I was ready to sell my grief about Martin so cheaply. But there'd be something, I was sure: all I had to do was absorb myself in my new life and something would occur to me. After all, I was a journalist. It was what I did.

So while Trey laboured in the studio – disappearing downstairs each morning around ten or eleven; reappearing, blinking in the daylight, for some lunch, then returning to his burrow – I started work on the house. I spent two or three happy days ripping out the old kitchen cabinets, setting the marble tops to one side and chucking the rubbish into the back of Trey's truck. It was joined there by the yellow lino from the hallway and the threadbare stair carpet. Then I drove down to Buchanansville, found the local tip, and dumped everything. I was in my element. Big, strong, capable Maeve was back.

I measured the kitchen and sketched out plans for some new units. I showed Trey my ideas and he seemed to like them. We had a fairly stilted conversation about money: I had no idea how much he earned, or how much it would be okay for me to spend on the house. Until I got some income myself I was pretty much dependent on him. 'I should get some rental income from my flat fairly soon,' I said hopefully. 'I'd put it up for sale, Trey, but it doesn't seem worth it because the market's so flat at the moment . . .' That was what I was telling myself, anyway.

'I'll be getting some more session work in the fall,' he assured me, 'so go ahead and get Brett in to do the work. He and Lonnie will do a great job. I want you to be happy here.'

Brett was a short, bulky man in his late thirties with a shock of straw-coloured hair and bright blue eyes. He came complete with a tool belt and a stub of carpenter's pencil tucked behind his ear and I warmed to him instantly: he was the kind of guy who'd worked for my dad, the sort who took pride in his handiwork. He looked at my roughly sketched plans, double-checked the measurements I'd taken and seemed to approve of what I'd suggested and the schedule of work I'd drawn up. His son Lonnie, Kayla's brother, just back from Bible camp, must have been eighteen. In contrast to his sharp-featured sister he had an unfinished look about him. He was lanky and bare-chested in his jeans, but still with a hint of puppy fat that hadn't turned to muscle. He liked to call me 'Ma'am', and he had a sweet, goofy, willing smile. He had a habit of dedicating each day's work 'to the good Lord' but otherwise he seemed like a good worker.

Brett seemed happy to be working on the old Ferguson homestead again. 'I'm real glad you 'uns all are doing something to the place,' he told me. 'God knows it needs it. I remember when the old man died, and I reckoned either Trey or his aunts would take the house and turn it around. But instead the old girl has fallen to rack and ruin. The kids in town used to say it was haunted, the way it stood empty up here on the hill, all by itself.'

I noticed Lonnie fidgeting. 'Haunted by who?' I asked him.

'Ma'am, I don't believe in ghosts. 'Cept the Holy Ghost.'

Okay. So I was definitely living in the Bible belt.

'Anyway,' said Brett quickly, perhaps noticing my incredulous expression, 'it's real good to see her coming back to life. I'm glad y'all are planning to use the old range again. I thought it was a tragedy when Nancy and Jean stopped using it.'

'Nancy and Jean?'

'Trey's aunts. They're to blame for the fireplaces, too.'

'What do you mean?'

Brett rubbed his nose, remembering. 'I reckon it must have been the mid-seventies when they first got electricity up here. Anyway, Nancy and Jean decided it was time to move into the modern era. I guess the old man was too old to be chopping wood, so instead those good women blocked up all the fireplaces with particle board and started using electric fires instead.' He shook his head in what looked like disgust. 'Anyway, we'll bring the old girl back to life for y'all. It'll be our pleasure.'

I've always loved the smell of wood, so I enjoyed standing with a mug of coffee in my hand watching Brett and Lonnie work, listening them talk to me in their chewy mountain accents. I got to like the two of them. I enjoyed the way Lonnie would blush deep red if I had to brush past him to get to the fridge. I enjoyed the way Brett would reminisce about the changes the town had seen. He was a real craftsman and I told him so. 'It's what this town was built on,' he said. 'Timber. My daddy used to tell me tales about when Bodie's Holler had a timber industry. He remembered the days when they sent the logs downriver. Dangerous work. Some good men died in that river.'

'And now you grow Christmas trees?'

He grimaced. 'It's a living,' he said. 'Folks always want Christmas trees.'

With the work under way in the house and Trey busy in his studio, I decided to immerse myself in the life of Bodie's Hollow, such as it was. I got into the habit of wandering down the hill into town every morning and stopping at the café for coffee and a chat with Patsy. Sometimes Ben, the old man who'd had half his lung removed and seemed a fixture in the café, would join in. Our conversations were necessarily stilted as we really only had two subjects of conversation: Trey as a child, and how well Trey was looking since our marriage. The latter subject was mostly a question of me politely deflecting compliments, as it seemed to be Patsy and Ben's view that I had wrought wonders, insofar as I could understand what they were saying. Ben in particular used a rich vein of vernacular. 'Trey's a-lookin' plum stout,' he said one day. 'Not so tuckered out.'

Patsy translated, sort of. 'He 'pears so much better since he met you. Less peaked. I reckon you're feeding him good.'

I blushed and thought about microwave meals, or the thing I did with pasta and tins of tomatoes that was what we mostly lived on. Another time Patsy told me how much happier I'd made Trey and the question I wanted to ask (but didn't) was: happier than ever, or just happier than since he got divorced from Missy? I supposed it was the latter, since Trey had only moved back to Bodie's Hollow since his divorce.

As for Trey's childhood, all Patsy's stories centred on herself as a kind of surrogate mother figure. 'The poor motherless mite,' she called Trey, conjuring up a picture of a skinny little waif who would have been starving and friendless but for the food she fed him at the café. I forbore to tell her that I too was motherless, and it wasn't the worst thing in the world; or, indeed, to remind her that Trey had had a grandfather and two aunts looking after him and presumably feeding him, but that would have ruined her narrative flow. 'Sarah 'n me sure fed him good,' she told me, wistfully.

'Sarah? Who's Sarah?'

Patsy's face clouded over. 'Sarah. Sarah Swigert. She used to work here. She took Trey under her wing. She was good to that poor boy.'

That was the first time I heard Sarah Swigert's name. It wouldn't be the last.

I spent a lot of time down by the river, reading, relaxing, dozing in the shade of the trees. I got to know Bodie's Hollow better, exploring the town on foot, walking all the streets and alleyways until I had a rough sense of where everything was. I tried to make some friends of roughly my own age. One day I went across to the internet café, wanting a change of scene for my morning coffee. The guy behind the counter was in his late twenties, with a pierced eyebrow, a surf-dude T-shirt and a crocheted beanie hat over his long, fair, dreadlocked hair. As he was making my latte he said, 'You must be Trey's new wife. May?'

'Maeve. Yes, I am. Pleased to meet you.'

We shook hands over the counter.

'I'm Cornell,' he told me, with a pronounced emphasis on the second syllable. 'I play the fiddle. What do you play?'

I didn't know how to answer. It seemed an odd thing to ask someone on a first meeting. Was I supposed to be able to play an instrument? Was I somehow sub-human if I didn't? I was beginning to wonder if everyone in Bodie's Hollow defined themselves by which musical instrument they played. I thought for a while, and then said, 'Kazoo?'

Cornell assumed that I was joking, and laughed. 'No, really,' I said. 'I don't play anything. I'm not musical. Sorry. I know that makes me some kind of freaky outsider up here but, hey, what can I do?'

'Don't worry about it,' he said. 'My old lady's not musical either.'

Old lady? I'd found myself in some kind of counter-culture time warp, a perception that increased when I got to know both Cornell and his wife Gretchen better. It was as if they'd been recruited to keep the hippie dream alive. They lived in one of the few remaining cabins up in the woods with their two barefoot dirty-nosed children, where – like the early settlers – they grew their own crops. Only in the case of Cornell and Gretchen the crop was mostly marijuana. They were sweet people, but not exactly stimulating acquaintances.

21

In some ways, Kayla was my first real friend in Bodie's Hollow. I felt sorry for her. Being a teenage girl sucks wherever you live, and being a teenage girl in Bodie's Hollow must have been really grim. It was the long summer vacation and her school friends all lived down in Buchanansville, our local county seat and court-house town. She was too young to drive and there was no public transport, so she'd taken to hanging around the café looking miserable and aimless and we got into the habit of chatting from time to time. I offered to take her down to Buchanansville with me next time I went down to shop or to go to the farmers' market that seemed to be the centre of Campbell County life. She perked up a bit at that idea, but then decided that her mom would probably, 'I dunno, freak out or something, if I, like, go down to Buchanansville just to hang out. Seriously, she weirds me out sometimes.'

I ran into Kayla one day at the local supermarket. She was hanging around near the checkout, thumbing through the paltry selection of paperback romances and thrillers that they sold. 'Hey, Kayla, what's up?' That seemed to be the correct form of address to use to an American teenager.

'Not much.' The standard reply, I'd learned, although the way Kayla said it, it sounded particularly poignant.

'Looking for a book?'

She twisted her shoulders, embarrassed. 'Yeah, I guess.'

'Do you like reading?' I don't know why I was surprised.

'Yeah, you know, 'cause it's like something to do.'

'What do you like reading?'

'Mysteries. Crime. Shit like that. I reckon.'

I thought of my collection of dog-eared Agatha Christies that I'd had sent over from England, the books I'd fallen in love with when I was about Kayla's age. 'You should come up to the house. I've got loads of books. You could borrow some.'

She gave me what I can only describe as a horrified look.

'What?' I asked.

'You mean come up to your house, the house on the hill?'

'Yeah, why not?'

She shuddered. 'Because it's really creepy up there. It's, like, haunted or something. So everyone says.'

'Haunted by who?'

'I don't know. The old man, I guess.'

That theme – the haunting of the old Ferguson homestead – came up again in conversation with my second friend in Bodie's Hollow: Julie, Julie D'Agostini, the sharp-tongued vivid dark-haired woman who'd told me I was funny.

One morning I decided to accept her invitation to check out her store. It was opposite the café, in one of the cute wooden shops lining the boardwalk, a few doors down from Cornell's internet café. Either side, the shops were boarded up, but hers was bright and attractive and freshly painted. A bell rang as I pushed the door open and walked into an overpowering smell of scented candles. I was the only customer. Julie was sitting behind the counter reading a magazine, and she smiled when she saw me. 'Hey, Maeve,' she said. 'Glad you could stop by.'

'I followed my heart to the mountains,' she said as we sat drinking cans of iced tea that she'd produced from a tiny fridge under the counter. 'Just like you, I guess. I'm from Jersey – New Jersey – originally, but I met this artist guy in New York and we decided to come up here to live, and maybe raise a family. We had this idea that we'd run weekend retreats, art courses, aromatherapy, something like that, or maybe just bed-and-breakfast. Anyway, it didn't last. He went back to New York but I decided to stay.'

'Why?'

'Because I still think I can make it work. I really do.'

I looked around the shop. It was full of beautiful products: wind chimes, antiqued mirrors, kitchen clocks made from old tin advertising plaques, elaborate greetings cards, aromatherapy oils. I couldn't imagine the Bodie's Hollow residents I'd met so far wanting or needing any of it. 'Who are your customers?'

'It does get busy in the fall. Honestly.' Then, 'Who am I kidding? Oh well, I guess something will turn up.' Julie scuffed the toe of her sandal against the raised edge of a floor tile and asked me, 'Do you know who holds this town's future in his hands?'

I shook my head, although I thought I knew what she was about to say.

'Your husband.'

'What do you mean, exactly?'

'We're all just wondering what's going to happen now that he's back in town. I mean, is Trey going to help us take advantage of the whole *O Brother* thing?'

'*O Brother*? What do you mean?'

Julie looked at me as if I was a child who hadn't been keeping up in class. 'The *O Brother* phenomenon.' She gave it inverted commas with her fingers. 'You know, the soundtrack of the film?'

'Oh. *O Brother Where Art Thou?*' I'd seen the film, but hadn't much liked it. I'd thought it was a major disappointment from the Coen Brothers after *Fargo* and *The Big Lebowski*, two of my all-time favourites. But I still didn't know what Julie meant.

'The soundtrack from the movie was all bluegrass stuff. Gospel. Old-timey. Whatever they're calling it these days.' She waved her hands vaguely. 'Anyway, it's sold millions of copies. I mean, *millions*. It's suddenly very hip, all that kind of music. Anyway, my point is this: we've got this cruddy little museum in the old schoolhouse here in town that no one ever goes to see. Trey should donate some stuff to it; maybe help them do it up. You wouldn't need much. Just a few old photographs, some instruments in glass cases. You could even have some kind of interactive thing, with computer screens. You could press a button and hear some of his grandfather's music.' Julie's eyes were alight: she'd thought a lot about this plan. 'You know, Bodie's Hollow is only about twenty miles from the Blue Ridge Parkway. Trey could really put it on the tourist map if he wanted to. Like Grandfather Mountain or something.' She paused. 'Hey, I've just thought of something.'

'What?'

'The house. You should turn the whole house into a museum. It's so old and atmospheric up there on the hill. It'd be great.'

'Julie, we live there.'

'Yeah, but you could build somewhere new, couldn't you? There's plenty of land around the house.' Obviously she hadn't just thought of it. It sounded like a plan she'd been hatching for ages. 'You can't tell me you actually like living in that old wreck of a place.'

'It's not old. It's 1930s. That's modern. Well, it would be in England, anyway. It's going to be great, once I've finished doing it up.'

She frowned at me, presumably puzzled at the concept of a 1930s house being modern. 'But it's so creepy. People say it's haunted. And what about that locked room – you know, the room of death?' She said those last three words in a kind of a horror-movie voice-over way, widening her eyes as she did so. Then she repeated them, in case I'd missed the point. 'The room of death.'

'What do you mean?'

Julie smiled. 'Hasn't Trey told you? It's where his grandfather died. He dropped dead in that front parlour. That's why he never goes in there. That's why he keeps the door locked. It was very traumatic. Apparently.' That final word was said dismissively.

'Oh.' And that was all I could think of to say.

22

People often talk about how the eyes in a photo or a painting can follow you around. It's the sort of thing that people who believe in ghosts tend to say. 'It was so scary,' they'll say with a shudder. 'The eyes followed me all the way around the room.' It always irritates me. There's such a simple explanation. If the subject is looking straight at the camera or the artist when the picture is made, the eyes will always follow you, whatever you do, wherever you go. But if they're looking away at the time, then you will never be able to get their eyes to meet you, no matter what you do. CJ Ferguson, I realised, liked to look straight at the camera. And in spite of myself I felt his eyes boring into me from every picture on the hallway wall as I fumbled with the lock on the door of the front parlour: the room of death.

I've never believed in ghosts. I don't believe in unquiet spirits. I truly, honestly don't believe that past sadness and unresolved trauma can somehow permeate the fabric of a building or a room and leave an echo. Even now, after everything that happened later. I'm as down-to-earth and commonsensical as they come. People die in houses. Old people die in old houses. It happens all the time, and the only way to deal with it is to air the room and carry on as

if nothing bad had ever happened there. I thought of
Trey, and how his shoulders hunched and his face closed
up every time we talked about his grandfather. It's
ridiculous, I told myself. It can't go on. A grown man
freaked out by a room. We can't go on living in a house
with a locked door.

I should have spoken to Trey about it, of course. Why
didn't I? Perhaps because I didn't want him to know that
I'd been discussing the subject with anyone else, particularly Julie: Trey had seemed so curt and unfriendly
when he'd introduced her to me. Perhaps because I was
afraid of upsetting him, of causing a scene. Perhaps I just
didn't know him well enough to be able to guess how he'd
react. Perhaps because I didn't want to make a big deal out
of the issue.

I'd found the key, you see. It had been there all the
time. I'd actually seen it on my first night in the house.
Upstairs in our bedroom, in the little cart pulled by the
boy with the donkey, nestling among the hairpins and the
buttons and the coins: a bunch of three rusty keys. I
figured that one of them had to be the right one. I chose a
day when Brett and Lonnie weren't in the house. They
were waiting for the plumber and electrician to come
before they could continue installing the kitchen. Trey
was downstairs in the studio. I even went down to check.
I tiptoed down the stairs to the basement and pushed the
door open quietly. He had his headphones on, his back to
me, and he was sitting with his feet up on the mixing desk,
strumming his guitar. He didn't notice me, so I closed the
door just as gently and went back up the stairs.

My hand shook as I turned the key. What was I afraid of? What was I expecting to find? I let my imagination wander to its wildest shores. The old man's skeleton, still dressed in a dark suit, would be sitting in a rocking chair, rocking backwards and forwards, the skull seeming to grin at me, white and spectral, out of the gloom of decades; one bony finger would be pointing straight at me. I shook my head to clear the picture and I laughed out loud – a sharp 'huh', a verbal slap around the face. Pull yourself together, Maeve. It's just a room where someone once died.

The lock was rusty and the door was stiff. The hinges squealed as I furtively pushed it open. I grimaced. It wasn't as if I was doing anything wrong, exactly; after all, this was my house now. But that didn't stop me feeling like I was trespassing. I pushed open the door of the front parlour, stepped inside and found myself again gagging on that smell, the smell I'd first noticed as I walked into the house that first night. It was much worse in this room.

Dust. Stale air. That's all, I told myself: the room's been shut up for nearly twenty years; it's pure superstition to imagine that it somehow smells of death itself. I pushed the door closed behind me and went over to the window. There were heavy curtains drawn across it, almost like a blackout in the Blitz. I pulled them open to let the light in, and was shocked by the thick layer of dust on the worn velvety fabric. The liberated dust motes danced crazily in the morning light that streamed, mottled, through the lace curtains hanging at the small window. I opened the window, with difficulty, and breathed in the fresh air.

I looked around me. And my first thought was: I have stepped back in time. You'd have thought Trey's grandfather had left the room just a few minutes before. It looked like something from a Depression-era domestic-life museum. The walls were covered with the same faded dark green floral-patterned wallpaper as the bedroom, and underfoot was a threadbare Paisley carpet.

While most of the other rooms in the house were empty, this one was fully furnished: a desk, chairs and even a harmonium – a small Victorian organ with pedals and stoppers. There actually was a rocking chair, next to the fireplace, and it looked as if it had just that instant stopped moving, as if CJ Ferguson had been sitting in it very recently. A tall wooden 1930s art-deco radio, a piece of furniture in its own right, stood to one side of the fireplace. A lace doily covered the top, and on the doily stood two china dogs, like the ones in the bedroom, and a picture in a decorated wooden frame. It was a wedding photo: Trey's grandparents, I assumed. I tried to get an impression of what his grandmother had looked like but I couldn't. CJ Ferguson was as imposing as usual, but next to him his bride was indistinct and blurry under a big hat.

There was a sampler on the wall with a verse from Proverbs. 'He that spareth his rod hateth his son.' I thought about Trey's grandfather 'hot-saucing' him when he took the Lord's name in vain. It had seemed absurd when he'd told me about it over dinner in my familiar London flat. But here, in this room, it was completely believable.

The fireplace was, like all the others in the house,

blocked up with a piece of chipboard. Above the mantel-piece was another picture, a black and white Victorian engraving on damp-spotted sepia paper in a heavy dark wooden frame. It showed a Biblical scene: Adam and Eve being expelled from Paradise. Huge ragged mountain peaks stood guard around the landscape, with the Garden of Eden, to the right of the picture, an oasis of lush, extravagant vegetation. Adam and Eve, two tiny figures dwarfed by the mountains, were hunched over, clutching their fig leaves to them, cowed and miserable under massed dark clouds in the sky.

In one corner of the room stood an old-fashioned roll-top wooden desk. The desk was open and a dusty leather-bound family Bible lay on the green leather writing surface. Next to the Bible there was a cane – a switch. I picked it up and flexed it between my hands, imagining the thwacking sound it'd make, the stinging pain across the palm of a hand or a backside. I could imagine CJ Ferguson, the Preacherman, gaunt and imposing, reading the Ten Commandments out loud and then reaching for the switch, beating the sin out of his son and his daughters, and his scared, skinny little grandson. I bit my bottom lip and felt myself shaking.

To the right of the door was the harmonium. It was made of dark wood, elaborately carved and decorated in high Victorian style. I noticed that the green baize on the pedals was worn through to the wood in places. I lifted the lid and ran my fingers affectionately over the cracked, yellowing keys.

We'd had a harmonium at home. An unlikely

instrument, I know, but someone had been sorting out the storeroom at our local church and found it, and remembered those poor motherless O'Mara kids. So instead of dumping it, two strong men from the church arrived on our doorstep one Saturday afternoon lugging the unwieldy thing. I loved it from the very start, and taught myself to play from the *Easiest Tune Book of Hymns*. I liked the way you could pull out the stoppers and make it sound different, and the wheezing effect you got if you didn't pump the pedals hard enough. To start with, my legs could hardly reach, so sometimes Sean or my dad would let me sit on their lap and play the keys while they worked the pedals. I played it every day of my life until I turned ten and started having piano lessons, and one day I got home and my dad had swapped the harmonium for a brand new upright piano. I gave up playing soon afterwards because it was no fun any more.

I sat down on the rocking chair, gently pushing myself to and fro. I looked at the harmonium, smiling to myself and itching to play it. I got up carefully, looked back outside the door just in case, then lifted the lid on the stool and found what I expected: hymn books and a pile of old sheet music. I sat back in the chair and flicked through the sheet music. What evocative titles those old songs had. 'I Wonder how the Old Folks are at Home?' 'Footmarks in the Snow'. 'Bury Me Beneath the Willow'. And then I found a song I actually recognised: 'Pretty Polly', the murder ballad that Trey had sung at the Borderline on the night we'd met, the song that made me cry.

I read through the words again, marvelling at how a

song about such a brutal killing could have been so popular. It seemed strange to me that a man like CJ Ferguson – a man known as the Preacherman, a man who had sung songs about God and about family and home life – would have been drawn to this: a song about a vicious, motiveless killing. Not much different from us singing those old folk songs at school, particularly enjoying the parts about tragedy and death. I thought about the human impulse that makes us love those songs so much, the impulse to tell each other gory stories. A few minutes ticked by, the house silent except for the gentle rhythmic sound of the chair, rocking. Somewhere, a fly was buzzing. I studied the music for 'Pretty Polly' and thought about trying to play it on the harmonium, but there were lots of quavers and semi-quavers and three flats in the key signature, so I decided against it. Still the harmonium beckoned. There was only one thing to do and sure enough, there it was in one of the hymn books: 'Amazing Grace', a hymn I knew almost by heart, a hymn designed to be played slowly enough so that even the worst musician has a fair shot; a hymn whose tune goes so relentlessly up and down the scale that even I could manage it, even after all these years. I propped the hymn book on the harmonium's music stand and – imagining Trey downstairs in the studio, headphones on – I began to pump the pedals and started to play. Bit by bit the tune came back to me and, filled with pride and a huge sense of achievement, I forgot everything else. I was caught up in the music, in the mechanism of the harmonium, and in a delightful sense of nostalgia. I guess I must have heard

Trey's footsteps running down the hallway but the first thing I noticed was when he pushed the door open suddenly and, breathlessly, said, 'It's you!'

He sounded relieved. No, beyond relieved. I laughed and said, 'Duh! Who else would it be?' And then I looked up at him as he stood in the doorway and suddenly stopped playing. He was as white as a sheet. 'Jesus, Trey, what's the matter? You look like you've seen a ghost.'

'It's you,' he said again. 'Thank God it's you,' and he slumped against the doorpost. I tried to read his face. It seemed to be a kaleidoscope of different emotions. Angry, upset, relieved, shocked. Or something else: I couldn't work out what, exactly.

I took my hands off the keyboard, embarrassed, a little guilty. 'Sorry,' I said. 'I found the key. It was upstairs. I just wanted to have a look at the room, that's all. I hate locked doors.' I gave a little laugh, hoping to lighten the mood.

Trey didn't say anything. He stood in the doorway, one hand on the lintel. He scanned the room as if he'd never seen it before. His face was still white and there were beads of sweat on his forehead. I noticed that he was panting.

'Trey, I'm so sorry,' I said again. 'I didn't mean to upset you. I was curious, that's all. Please don't be angry.'

'Angry?' He turned to me, a surprised look on his face. 'Why would I be angry?' He wiped his forehead with a tissue he pulled from his jeans pocket. He took a deep breath and gave me a shaky smile. 'It's okay,' he said.

'You took me by surprise, is all. I had no idea you could play the harmonium.'

Thank God. I smiled back at him and his smile widened. 'I can't, not really. I mean, I haven't touched one in years.'

'It sounded good to me.'

'Well, it was "Amazing Grace". It is officially the world's easiest hymn to play. Between you and me, it's the only tune I can play both hands together. I got Grade One piano and then gave up.'

Trey smiled again, and a tiny bit of colour returned to his cheeks. 'Grade One. I don't know about these British grades. Is that quite advanced?' Deadpan Trey had returned.

'God, no. Any fool can pass Grade One. I did.'

This time Trey laughed. I thought he'd come over and sit on the stool next to me. I thought he'd wrap his arms around me and kiss me: a lovely long relaxed married couple's kiss. But he didn't. He stood there in the doorway, leaning against the doorpost, looking hard at me as if trying to make a decision. Then, without moving from the spot, he reached out his right hand to me. 'Come and have some lunch,' he said.

23

Here's a bit of pop psychology for you. I opened the locked door, and suddenly Trey seemed much more willing to talk about his grand-father. We sat on the back-porch swing that evening watching the sunset, my feet in Trey's lap; and as he massaged them with his strong, rough hands, he stared dreamily at the sky and started to reminisce. 'I learned to play mandolin on this porch,' he said. 'I guess I must have been about six or seven. My grand-daddy decided it was time for me to learn. So after supper he'd bring me out here and make me play until my fingers bled.'

'Poor baby.'

'No, no, it was good. It made me feel special. It was like he'd singled me out. He never taught my aunts to play. I mean, they sang and they could play the piano and the harmonium, of course.'

'Of course.' Because everyone in Bodie's Hollow played at least one instrument.

'But the mandolin, and then the dulcimer. That was something special between my grand-daddy and me. He made me feel as if I was going to be the one to carry on the heritage. The chosen one, if you know what I mean. My aunts would be bustling around in the kitchen doing the dishes and we'd be out here making music.'

'I bet they were thrilled.'

Trey looked at me quickly and realised I was being facetious. He laughed. 'I'll tell you what it reminded me of. You know the Bible story about Martha and Mary?'

I muttered something, hoping Trey would hear it as yes but would not expect me to recite the story to him.

'Jesus comes to visit them, and Martha's busy in the kitchen preparing food while Mary sits at Jesus' feet and listens to him talking. Martha gets to fretting, because she's so busy and she resents Mary taking it easy. So she asks Mary to help her, but Jesus tells her that Mary's doing the right thing, just sitting at his feet listening and learning.'

He left it there, assuming I'd know what he meant. 'So in that analogy you're Mary and your grandfather is Jesus Christ?' I asked, as straight-faced as I could.

Trey opened his mouth to say something, and then shook his head and laughed. He slapped me hard on the soles of my feet and then grabbed me around the waist. He kissed me hard and I kissed him back. 'You see,' he said, 'that's just one of the things I love about you. The way you help me keep my feet on the ground.'

I seized the moment. 'Trey, I've been thinking. How would you feel if I wrote something about your grandfather? About his music, I mean. Looking at the heritage of the old-time stuff, maybe. And maybe tracing your grandfather's influence on other artists – like Johnny Cash, perhaps.'

Trey pulled away from me. His face was unreadable. 'Why?'

'Because I'm a journalist. It's what I do. I write stuff. It's my job. I write magazine articles. I just thought, you know, what with the increased interest in your type of music . . .'

He wrinkled up his forehead. 'Just the music?'

'Pretty much.'

'Just about the old time? Not family stuff?' He was thinking hard. He rubbed his hand over his mouth. He had his lips pressed hard together, making his bottom lip stick out. 'Okay,' he said finally, giving me a tentative smile.

It was Julie who'd given me the idea, of course, with her mention of *O Brother Where Art Thou?* The house project was going well, but I needed to keep my hand in with some writing. And after my failed attempts to sell an article about my new life in the Appalachians it had suddenly struck me as obvious. I remembered Nick's enthusiasm for the music of CJ Ferguson. I was sure he'd be interested in a piece.

I rang him the next morning, guessing he'd be in the office. 'You want to write about CJ Ferguson?' He sounded surprised, and not as excited as I'd hoped.

'Yeah. Well, maybe. I thought there'd be a market for it, what with this whole *O Brother* phenomenon.'

I could hear Nick laugh. 'Maeve, to be honest you're a few years too late. And I know I'm a big CJ Ferguson fan, but I'm not sure there are enough others out there . . .'

He petered out, and I couldn't think of anything to say.

'But it's nice to hear from you, Maeve. Everything okay?' He sounded so genuinely interested that I felt my throat start to tighten. For God's sake, Maeve, don't start crying.

'I'm fine, Nick. It's beautiful out here, Trey's great, everything's cool. But I'm bored. I need something to do. I just thought, you know, I'm here in the heartland of bluegrass music. Old time. Mountain music. Anyway, whatever.' Shit, he'd realise I didn't know what I was talking about. 'And I thought perhaps I could write something about it.'

'Hmmm,' he said, and I could imagine him there at his desk in the office he used to share with Martin: the tiny, untidy office that was full of dusty piles of CDs and freebies from record companies. I could see him running his hands through his hair, deep in thought. 'Okay. I'll tell you what, Maeve, why don't you write a short piece on spec for me? I can't promise we'll use it.'

'Nick, you don't have to do this.'

'Seriously, it could be good. A couple of thousand words, putting CJ Ferguson in context, tracing his influence on country music. Maybe a bit of social history, some geographical context? Use some grisly murder ballads to give it a bit of oomph?' Nick was obviously making this up as he went along. 'I'll tell you what would be really good,' he said, a surge of genuine enthusiasm coming into his voice, 'can you get hold of some old photos of CJ Ferguson to illustrate this piece?'

My turn to laugh. 'Photos, yeah. Loads of them. No

problem at all. Nick, are you sure about this? I know I'm not a music journalist, so I understand if . . .'

'Maeve, you're a good writer. So, okay, you've never written about music before. But maybe that will be an advantage. A fresh voice, a fresh angle. Why don't you get me something by this time next month and I'll see if we can use it.'

O kay. Now I was fired up. I told Julie about my project next time I saw her, and she said, 'You need to talk to my friend Chuck. He's this professor. He teaches, I don't know, sociology or something. Anyway, he knows all about the old traditions. I bet he can help you.'

24

My chance to meet Chuck came a couple of days later when we went for a barbecue at Cornell and Gretchen's cabin in the woods. Trey and I walked hand-in-hand through the almost silent town and up the hill at the side of the valley. It was a warm evening, with the sky just beginning to turn a delicate pink; and Gretchen's garden with its orange and yellow Californian poppies stood out defiantly in contrast to the scrappy, unloved front yards in the rest of the town.

They were round the side of the cabin drinking beer while Cornell tended the barbecue – Gretchen and their two barefoot kids, Julie and a bearded guy she introduced as Chuck. 'Charles, actually,' he said blushing, before telling us he taught social anthropology at the university up in Boone. He was fortyish, awkwardly dressed in a short-sleeved shirt and tie, and seemed stunned to find himself at that particular time and place with that particular woman.

Julie seemed thrilled with him. She'd met him at the craft fair down in Buchanansville and told us that he was doing research into mountain communities. 'He's divorced, no kids, good job – an actual, single, well-educated, non-redneck guy living right here in the mountains,' she'd confided to me earlier that week. 'Who'd have thought it?'

My chance to ask Charles about old-time music, murder ballads and mountain myths came later in the evening. The sun had gone down and we were sitting around on garden chairs feeling pleasantly mellow. We'd eaten barbecued lentil and tofu burgers and, while I would have preferred meat, the food had been good. Some of us had partaken of Gretchen and Cornell's marijuana crop. This is the life, I thought, letting the conversation drift around me. I felt as if I could be back home in London. Martin and I had spent many evenings like this in Nick and Fiona's back garden, eating burnt sausages and talking about everything and anything. The main difference was that by this point of the evening Martin would be arguing loudly with someone about something: Joy Division's place in rock history, for example, or whether *Big Brother* was the greatest television show ever made, whereas Trey, in contrast, was sitting on the back porch with Cornell as they quietly played their respective instruments.

Charles was talking to the other two women. 'Actually, I'm doing research into how Appalay—' He caught himself just in time. 'Appalatchun communities deal with death. I've been looking at mountain legends and myths, ghost stories, and also at the old murder ballads. Maeve . . .' I snapped out of my reverie. 'Julie tells me you're interested in murder ballads, too.'

'Well, kind of. I'm writing a piece about CJ Ferguson and his music for a magazine back in London. Maybe I could come and see you sometime and pick your brains?'

He looked at me with interest. 'Wouldn't you be better off talking to your husband about it? After all, isn't he a world expert on this kind of music? I've been wanting to pick his brains on the subject myself.'

I looked across at Trey, over on the porch with Cornell. I imagined trying to get the information out of him. It'd be like the time I'd asked him about the difference between old time and bluegrass. He'd go into such intricate detail that I'd probably fall asleep again. 'I thought it'd be good to get an outside perspective on the subject,' was all I said.

Julie chipped in. 'Chuck, you should definitely do some of your research up at Trey and Maeve's house. They have a ghost.'

I sighed, and gave her a pointed look. When would people shut up about that stupid story?

Charles looked interested. 'They have?'

'Yes,' said Julie. 'Everyone says that the old house is haunted.'

'Who by?' he asked.

'The old man, of course. CJ Ferguson.'

'Yeah. Like, really,' I said, trying to bring the subject to a close.

'No, really,' Julie said, and it seemed as if she truly believed it. 'Haven't you heard him yet? He walks around the front parlour at night, apparently, flicking through the pages of the old family Bible.'

'Who told you this?' I asked as brusquely as I could.

'Oh, people,' she said dismissively. 'Everybody knows about it.'

'And why is he said to haunt the house?' It was Charles who asked the question, sounding as if he was genuinely interested. I wondered if Julie was making up the whole story just to keep him in her grasp. I must admit that I felt a shuddery sensation as I imagined old CJ there with his dusty Bible, looking up more verses to justify whacking his grandson with that cane.

Julie widened her eyes as far as they could go and said, in a stage whisper that could be heard right across the yard, 'Because he didn't die a peaceful death . . .' and I jumped out of my skin when I suddenly felt a hand on my shoulder.

It was Trey. 'Julie, that's BS and you know it,' he said curtly, and then he turned to me. 'Come on, Maeve, let's go home.'

It was a dark night with just a sliver of moon, and the path up to our house was suddenly scary. The silence was broken by the occasional owl hooting and the crunch of the dirt road under our feet, but Trey said nothing. He was walking ahead of me, and I could just make out through the gloom that he had his shoulders in that characteristic hunch. 'Trey, what's up?' I asked breathlessly as I struggled to keep up with him. I knew he was annoyed by Julie's ghost story, but I wanted him to tell me that.

'Nothing.'

'Yes, there is. Tell me.'

Silence.

'It's Julie's ghost story, isn't it?'

He must have stopped because I nearly collided with him. He turned round to face me, and in the dark his face seemed all cheekbones and glasses. 'Yes, it is.'

'Why are you so annoyed? It was just a bit of fun. She was just making it up.'

He loomed over me in the darkness.

'That's my grand-daddy she was talking about,' said Trey eventually, his voice trembling with emotion. 'She was talking about my grand-daddy as if he was some kind of . . . freak show.'

'I'm sure she didn't mean it like that.' Then something struck me, and I figured it was now or never. 'Are you cross because what she said is sort of true?'

Trey drew in his breath sharply and seemed about to say something. I held up my hand to stop him.

'I don't mean literally true. But your grandfather *does* haunt that house, doesn't he? Metaphorically, I mean. And I think he haunts you as well.' There, I'd said it. 'You know what I said to you when you found me playing the harmonium? I said you looked like you'd seen a ghost. It was just a figure of speech, really, but I sort of meant it. Trey, what's the big deal?'

He said nothing, but grabbed my wrist and virtually dragged me back to the house. He pushed open the door to the front parlour and pulled me in. He turned on the light and looked around the room, his gaze resting for a while on the picture of Adam and Eve. He stood still for a few seconds, as if soaking up the atmosphere. Then he turned to me and said, 'I was sixteen years old. I stood here and watched my grand-daddy die.'

'Oh.' Shit. I'd really put my foot in it. I hadn't realised he'd been there. 'How did he die?'

'He had a stroke. The strongest, most upright man I will ever know in my life, and he crumbled in front of me. It was my sixteenth birthday and I watched him die.' He gave me a pleading look and I could see that he had tears in his eyes. I reached out to touch his face but he pulled away from me. 'Please, don't ever ask me about it again.'

I could have told Trey that I'd watched my father die. I sat by his hospital bed after he'd had his fourth and final stroke and I watched him die. I know what strokes can do: how they can take a strong man and wither him, make him crumble, take away his pride and his faculties bit by bit or all at once. I didn't need Trey to tell me how awful it could be. And, although technically I wasn't there right at the last moment, I watched Martin die too. Just over a year ago. And yes, it still hurt. And yes, I wouldn't particularly choose to go back into that same hospital room if I didn't have to. And yes, thinking about Martin still made me cry. It was early days, but I was getting over it. It's what you do when someone dies.

Get over it. I could have just said that to Trey. Get over it. It was nearly twenty years ago and you're a grown man. I could have been big bold blunderbuss Maeve, the woman who keeps her husband's feet on the ground. So you saw your grandfather die on your sixteenth birthday? That must have been tough. But so what? Big deal. Grow up. Get real. But part of the reason I'd fallen in love with Trey was the way he wore his heart on his sleeve. The first time I'd seen him I'd thrilled to the naked emotion in his voice, his face, as he sang. He was a musician. He was an artist. His emotions were close to the surface; that was what made him so good at what he did. He seemed to have one less layer of skin than most people. He was emotional and vulnerable and I loved him for it. So I didn't tell him to grow up and get real. Instead, that night, I held him close in bed and made myself soft and loving and caring.

25

It was a notice in a newspaper that began it all, back in 1928. It invited 'old-timey' and 'hillbilly' musicians to go to Knoxville, Tennessee, where a man from a record company was waiting to record them. Clyde James Ferguson, a lanky, sickly-looking eighteen-year-old with a widowed mother to support, read the article and saw a way to make money. Up till then his family had survived – by farming their patch of land, keeping chickens and a goat, growing small crops of tobacco and corn: virtually subsistence farming. So young, ambitious, driven CJ Ferguson borrowed a truck, went over the mountains to Knoxville with his guitar and recorded some old songs he knew onto wax cylinders. Something about his music proved popular not just to mountain folk like him but to America at large. Perhaps it was the stern preacher's tones coming from one so young, or the way he sang those desperately sad, dark songs about young lovers – always culminating in death – that touched a nation as it plunged into the darkest depression the country had ever known. Who knows? But by the end of the 1930s there was scarcely a radio station in the poor agricultural South or Midwest that hadn't featured a live performance from CJ Ferguson. He was, in his own way, a superstar.

Julie was wrong. This place wasn't a cruddy museum. Yes, it was a tatty old building with primitive displays, mostly just old curling photographs of Bodie's Hollow and its people, with typed cards explaining what each one was. There was a small display of oil lamps that was of strictly limited interest. There was a glass cabinet of old handmade tools, the kind of thing that my father would have adored and which I found moderately diverting. But the old photographs, and the information about the town's most famous son, CJ Ferguson, captured the spirit of the town and the man in an intensely moving way.

Of course, I'd seen these kinds of photographs before. I'd always admired that famous Dorothea Lange picture of the Okie mother and her two children, her face a mix of pride and desperation. But the difference here was that these were people I had a tangible connection with. Three children and their father, all in ragged dungarees, all with the hollow-chested, hollow-cheeked look that denotes real hunger, were lined up on the porch of a house that I thought I recognised. There was what looked like pride and defiance in their eyes. CJ Ferguson's achievement – and my husband's deep attachment to his heritage – made sense to me for the first time.

The museum was deserted. There'd been no one on the front desk when I pushed my way tentatively through the wooden door into the old schoolhouse, so I dropped a dollar bill into the jam jar on the desk and picked up a yellowed leaflet. My footsteps echoed around the building and I found myself walking on tiptoe. I came to the final display, and laughed out loud:

I never thought I'd see a picture of my own husband on display in a museum.

Actually, it was of Trey and Missy together, dating from the late 1980s, judging by Missy's extraordinarily large hair and Trey's pushed-up jacket sleeves. Neither of them could have been much older than nineteen. They were smiling and Missy was holding a trophy – the Country Music Association Horizon Award, apparently, whatever that was. Trey looked so young and vulnerable, with his big, blue-framed children's-TV-presenter glasses and his hair in a limp mullet, that I wanted to reach out and touch the picture, to stroke his face. The typed text on the index card told me that 'The musical heritage of Bodie's Hollow has now come full circle, as CJ Ferguson's granddaughter-in-law, Missy Ferguson, takes Nashville by storm with the help of her husband Trey (CJ Ferguson III).'

'I need to update that display.' The booming, deep voice cut into my reverie and made me jump. I turned, to see a short, broad woman with cropped grey hair and a sweatshirt covered with a design of appliquéd tartan cats. 'I'm sorry,' she said, realising that she'd taken me by surprise. 'I was in the back room. Anyway, I was saying I need to bring this display into the twenty-first century, now that our golden couple have got divorced. I'm Valerie, by the way. Valerie McLoughlin.'

She held out her hand and I shook it. 'Maeve O'Mara,' I said.

'Oh my goodness.' She covered her mouth with her hand and blushed. 'Well, I know who you are.' She looked me up and down, then reached up and, to my great surprise, pinched my cheek affectionately and said, 'I am so pleased to make your acquaintance.'

Valerie McLoughlin had taught Trey and Missy at school, in the very building in which we were now sitting. She made me a mug of what she called 'hot tea' and moved some paperwork from an old garden chair in the back room so that I could sit on it. Then she began reminiscing. 'He was such a strange, solemn little boy, your husband. Beautiful, too, with those huge blue eyes and that pale skin. He would sit very quietly in a corner of the schoolroom, poring over his books. Of course, it turned out that he was half-blind, that's why he never joined in with the rest of children. Can you believe that a man would refuse to let his grandson have his eyes tested? But then, that was CJ Ferguson for you.'

I thought about Julie's suggestion. 'Do you think the museum would benefit from having more stuff about CJ Ferguson? Do you think it would attract more visitors?'

'You've been talking to Julie, haven't you?'

I smiled. 'Yes. But maybe she's got a point?'

'Oh yes, she's definitely got a point. But you see, my dear, I find it very difficult even to have as much about CJ Ferguson in this museum as I already do. The man may have been this town's most influential figure, but frankly he was a monster.'

I raised my eyebrows.

'Oh yes, I know I'm being indiscreet. But it's true.'

'Because he wouldn't let Trey wear glasses?'

'It was more than that, my dear.' Valerie took a deep breath, as if deciding what she could trust me with. 'All children are naughty sometimes, but I can't believe that that scared little boy was naughty enough to deserve the beatings his grandfather gave him.'

Well, here was confirmation of what Trey wouldn't tell me. 'How did you know?'

'I saw the blood on his shirt.'

I couldn't think what to say. I was thinking of the small, faint, puckered scar, the ridge of hard skin that ran across Trey's lower back; a scar that I'd once asked him about and he'd shrugged off with an 'Oh, that's nothing'.

Valerie continued. 'Of course, this was twenty-five, thirty years ago. You didn't interfere in those days.' She shook her head. 'It was so sad about Trey's parents dying like that. Because, you know, I think he might have had a happier life with them, even if they were living in some commune in California.'

'Didn't they abandon him?'

She looked at me, with an amused, quizzical look on her face. 'Well, that's the story. In fact, I believe heavy emotional blackmail was used. CJ Ferguson was a formidable man. He would not allow his grandson to be brought up by unmarried parents. In the end, Junior just gave in to his father and handed the child over. I think he told himself that it would be for the best.'

'How do you know all this?'

She smiled. 'I was great friends with Trey's aunts. Those girls had a hell of an upbringing themselves.' She shook her head, as if at a rueful memory. 'Of course, I shouldn't have told you all this. That husband of yours still idolises his grandfather, in spite of everything. You know, of course, that he still blames himself for his death?'

I thought of what Trey had told me; how he'd watched his grandfather crumble in front of him. I wondered if Valerie would give me more insight. 'What actually happened?'

'Nothing particularly mysterious,' she said. 'According to Nancy and Jean, old CJ collapsed with a massive stroke on the day his sixteen-year-old grandson told him he was getting married. I don't think Trey has ever forgiven himself.'

That went some way to explaining Trey's reaction. If he blamed himself for his grandfather's death, no wonder he hadn't got over it yet. Maybe he was still trying to make amends. 'I guess he and Missy were childhood sweethearts, then?'

'Missy?' Valerie seemed surprised, as if I'd suddenly changed the subject. I suppose I had, in a way, but I was thinking of Trey telling his grandfather that he was getting married. 'Childhood sweethearts? Oh no, no. We were all very surprised when those two got married. Pleased, because it seemed like a good match after everything that had happened, but surprised as well. They were always good friends but I don't think anyone would have guessed they'd get married.'

As I left to go home, my mind swirling with new ideas and impressions, Valerie called after me. 'You should talk to Nancy and Jean if you're really interested in all these old stories.'

I froze. 'Nancy and Jean?'

'Yes. Trey's aunts.'

'I thought they were dead.'

'Why?'

'I don't know. Because I haven't met them yet?'

'Oh, my dear, I'm afraid there's been a family rift. That's too bad. No, no, Nancy and Jean are very much alive and well. They live just up the road in Boone. You really should go and see them. It's high time that rift was healed.'

There was a lot I should have talked to Trey about. I wanted to ask him about what his grandfather was really like. I wanted to ask him about his aunts and why he didn't talk to them; and I wanted to ask him about why he decided to get married as soon as he turned sixteen to a girl who wasn't even his childhood sweetheart. I wish I had asked him. Even though I knew he'd simply clam up and refuse to tell me, I wish I'd walked straight back to the house, found Trey alone, and made him give me all the answers.

But when I got back, when I walked round to the back porch, Trey came up to meet me, full of the lolloping, Tiggerish enthusiasm that I hadn't seen for a while. 'Guess who's back?' he said, and grabbed my hand tightly.

There, sitting on the back-porch swing like he belonged was the wiry fair-haired taciturn guy from the wedding. He stood up and walked towards me awkwardly. He was clutching a large white cardboard envelope. 'Jerry,' I said. 'Welcome home. Did you have a nice time in the Cotswolds?'

I kissed him on the cheek and he blushed. 'I bought you a present,' he said and gave me the envelope. I opened it and pulled out a calendar, one of those big ones with glossy photographs. 'Picturesque Britain'. I felt a lump in my throat. 'Jerry, that's so thoughtful. Thank you.'

He looked embarrassed. 'I thought you might be homesick.'

And as I flicked through the photos of thatched cottages and Devon beaches and the London Eye, I realised that I was. I was touched. What a sweet man he was. I swallowed hard.

Trey looked from me to Jerry and back again. 'Maeve,' he said, as if unable to contain himself. 'Do you know what it means, now that Jerry's back?'

I shook my head.

'It means we can have one of our famous Foggy Holler musical nights!'

26

I've always envied musical people. It's a gift they have, like the ability to speak a foreign language. I love music. I love listening to music, but I can never explain why I love it. I lack the words, the understanding, the vocabulary – and, most importantly, the ability to play a musical instrument with any real skill. That first musical evening at Jerry's house was an ordeal for me. I felt as Linda McCartney must have felt when Paul first handed her a tambourine and told her she was now a member of Wings. The musicians were speaking a foreign language that I barely knew.

My older brother Sean lives in Naples, that most uncompromisingly Italian of Italian cities. His voluble wife is Italian; his brood of voluble children are Italian. I painstakingly learned Italian at evening classes for two years. I have an A-grade GCSE in Italian. I was one of the best in my class, with the best accent and the best vocabulary. I worked really hard at the language. And then I went to visit Sean and his family in Naples and I was struck dumb. I sat at the kitchen table and the conversation washed over me. I panicked. I couldn't think of anything to say. My entire knowledge of Italian – my hard graft, my long hours in the classroom

– fled from my head in the face of proper Italian speakers.

And that's how it was on my first musical night in Bodie's Hollow. It started on the front porch of Jerry's house and then, as more people arrived, we moved into the loft above his workshop, which was beautifully fitted out with pine benches and scatter cushions, like a Scandinavian ski lodge. Everyone was there: Jerry with his guitar, Cornell from the internet café with his fiddle, Brett and his banjo. Some guy I'd seen around town a few times turned up with a guitar-like instrument that was apparently called a Dobro, accompanied by a woman who looked slightly familiar; she'd brought a guitar and a tambourine. And of course there was Trey, with his guitar and his mandolin and even an Appalachian dulcimer from Jerry's workshop, that big, primitive, rough-hewn wooden instrument that looked like a stretched-out guitar and sounded like nothing I'd ever heard before.

And as they played, almost everything I knew about music emptied itself out of my head. My days in the school choir, my ability to play the descant recorder, my years of mastering the *Easiest Tune Book of Hymns* on the harmonium, my scraped pass at Grade One piano – all of them disappeared. It was as if all I had was a simple phrase book. I could say 'please' and 'thank you' but everyone else could speak the language fluently. I felt like an impostor.

I busied myself with the catering. I fetched beer and wine for all the participants. I poured chips and nuts into bowls, arranged cheese and cold meat and fruit on a wooden board, made sure everyone had a plate of food to hand. I dimmed the lights and lit candles, and then curled up on the floor, leaning my head against Trey's legs, hugging a cushion and hoping that no one would ask me to sing or play.

I listened to the phrases that were being passed around. 'This one's in open D,' someone would say, or words to that effect, and then there'd be a flurry of guitar tuning. Someone would ask for a 'capo' and someone else would throw something – presumably a capo – across the room at them.

Many of the songs sounded tantalisingly familiar. At primary school we'd had music lessons using a series of books called something like *Time and Tune*, which were heavily reliant on old British folk songs. And from time to time that evening I thought I heard tunes that I recognised. But just as I felt ready to join in, the tune would swerve off in a strange direction, or the words would do something I didn't expect them to do, and I never summoned up the confidence to open my mouth.

During a break, as I poured more wine for everyone, the tambourine woman – whose name seemed to be Jill – said, 'So what instrument do you play, Maeve?'

That question again. What instrument do I play? It really is presumptuous, isn't it? 'I don't really play anything,' I said, blushing like mad and looking to Trey for support.

'Maeve plays the harmonium beautifully,' he said, proudly.

I glared at him and shook my head. No, please no. I had

visions of the next jam session being back at our house, and me being forced to prove my prowess on the harmonium, when all I could actually play was that one hymn, 'Amazing Grace'. I can't even sight-read. Before I can tackle anything written in bass clef I have to remind myself what all the notes are by reciting 'All cows eat grass'. I certainly can't do what it is that most truly musical people can do, namely pick out a tune they've heard once or twice, without having the notes written out in front of them.

Trey looked at me, and probably saw the horror in my face. He said kindly, 'Maybe we should play some stuff you know, like Dylan or something, and you could put on a harmony?'

Oh God, harmonies. I can just about carry a tune in a bucket, but only if everyone else is singing or playing the same tune. Harmonies are a step too far for my limited abilities. 'Honestly, Trey, it's okay, I'm just happy listening.'

'Do you want to borrow my tambourine?' said Jill, I think meaning well.

'I know,' said Trey, as if having a bright idea, 'Jerry, why don't you go and get that box of percussion stuff from downstairs?'

I figured: okay, I can play percussion. I do at least have rhythm. There's no way I can go wrong by just tapping out the beat. So when Jerry came upstairs with the box I picked out a kind of egg-shaped shaky thing, and as the musicians launched into 'It's All Over Now, Baby Blue' I flung myself into my new role as percussion supremo.

I thought I was playing well, but then I could see Trey glancing at me out of the corner of his eye, and he seemed to be struggling to stop himself saying something. As the tune finished, Jerry reached across and said, 'You need a bit more wrist action on it,' and demonstrated, and he was about a hundred times better than I was.

'You should play it. I'm no good. Sorry,' I said, and curled back into my corner.

'Hey,' said Brett. 'Are there any newspapers? We could get Maeve playing paper percussion.'

Trey's eyes sparkled. 'Great idea,' he said. I looked at him with narrowed eyes. Why would he insist I keep humiliating myself in front of everyone? He put his mandolin down and stood up, knocking his knees on the underside of the table as he did so, and I had to make a quick grab for his wineglass to stop it spilling everywhere. He went over to the couch and picked up a copy of a local free sheet. Brett took one of the sheets and showed me what to do. It looked easy. You start a tear at the top of one of the sheets of newspaper, and then tear downwards rhythmically, jaggedly down the page in time to the music. Newspaper-tearing. How difficult could it be?

Very. I could just about hit the beat, but I think they were expecting a bit more, some kind of syncopated rhythm beyond the straightforward. I threw myself into it with gusto, leaving a pile of torn newspaper on the floor that would keep a hamster happy for months, but I could tell I was doing it badly. I knew from the look on Brett's face, the glances he threw at Jerry and Cornell and Jill and at the Dobro guy; and most of all from the expression on

Trey's face, which seemed torn between sympathy for me and stifled irritation at the way I was ruining their musical evening.

I fumbled my way to the end of the song, my face hot with embarrassment, and then mumbled something like, 'Well, perhaps newspaper's not really my instrument.'

Trey was looking impatient. 'Why didn't you bring your guitar with you from London?'

'My guitar?'

'Yes, your guitar. The one in your apartment.'

And then it all started to become clear. Trey had thought I was musical. 'Trey,' I said, as quietly as he had. 'I told you, I don't play guitar.'

'I understand that,' he said, 'but maybe it's time you started again?'

It became even clearer. 'Oh God, Trey, when I said I don't play guitar, I meant it.' My neck and chest were aflame with embarrassment. 'No, actually, no. I didn't mean it, exactly. What I meant was, I *can't* play guitar. Not, I *don't* play; I *can't*. You know, I've never learned. You thought I just didn't play, that I'd stopped playing because of . . .' I pressed my knuckles hard against the bottom of my nose.

Trey looked confused; maybe, if I was reading his expression correctly, even a little disappointed. I looked at him with a level gaze. 'It was Martin's guitar, not mine. Martin's.'

Suddenly I wanted everyone to go away. I wanted it to be just me and Trey, and for Trey to hold me, or to use his thumb to wipe away those pesky tears that still appeared at the corners of my eyes every time I mentioned Martin's name. And I think he was about to, except someone – the Dobro guy, I think – had half-heard what I'd said, and called out, 'You've got a Martin guitar? Hey, that's really cool!'

I pulled away, holding my hand over my face, and ran downstairs. I ran through the workshop and straight out of the front door, and I ran down the lane to the river. I sat on the river bank sobbing, and slapping away the midges that had congregated in the warm, humid evening air. I watched the river, swollen by a string of showers we'd had in the past few days, and watched it rush and swell around the rocks. The rocks seemed sharper in the faster-flowing water, more pointed, altogether more threatening. I sat there and sobbed and got bitten, and I waited for Trey to come and find me and comfort me. He didn't. Instead, eventually, I got up and walked back up the lane to Jerry's house. He was sitting on the bench on the porch outside his workshop with a bottle of beer. 'Trey's gone back to the old house,' he said with what might have been a faintly sympathetic smile. So I took a deep breath and started the walk home.

27

'Why did you marry me?' was the first thing I said to Trey when I finally got home. I knew I'd got myself upset about something that probably wasn't as bad as I thought it was, but nonetheless I felt slightly hysterical, panicky, my throat constricted and tight.

Trey was sprawled like a bachelor on the couch in the kitchen, watching television. I could tell it was *Law and Order* because I heard the distinctive, dramatic 'dum-dum' that always denotes a change of scene. I walked over to the sink and poured myself a glass of water. I wiped my face with a towel, then walked across to Trey, perched myself on the arm of the couch, picked up the remote control and turned the TV off. 'Why did you marry me?' I repeated. 'Who did you think I was? What did you expect from me? Who do you want me to be?'

Trey breathed in so sharply that I heard it as a little gasp or a surprised cry of pain, as if he'd stubbed his toe or pricked his finger. He looked wary and apprehensive and annoyed. And I was getting angry, trying to force myself to stop the half-sobs and wild thoughts. This was no longer about Martin's guitar; this was about Trey and his arrogance. Presumption. Effrontery. Whatever the right word is for a man who jumps to conclusions and imagines everyone's like he is. What did I ever do to give him the idea I shared his musical passion? How dare he ask me to marry him, thinking I was someone I wasn't?

Trey opened his mouth, closed it again. He got up, went to the fridge and got out a couple of bottles of beer. He handed me one, and then sat on the other arm of the couch so he was facing me. He was wearing one of the shirts he'd bought in Asheville, with a flyaway 1970s collar and an all-over chevron pattern; my brother Sean had had a similar one when he was a kid. His hair needed washing, and his usual pallor had taken on a sallow tone, as if it had soaked up the yellowy-cream colour of the distemper on the walls. 'Maeve,' he said finally, 'why does this feel like a confrontation?'

'Because we need to clear the air.'

'Okay.' He said it gently, his expression concerned as if he were talking to a sick patient. 'What's this all about?'

'You thought I could play the guitar, didn't you?' I flung it out like an accusation.

'Yes,' he said quietly. 'Yes, I did.'

'Well, I can't.'

'Yes, I know that now.' No change of expression.

'You thought I was musical.' Less accusatory. It's difficult to accuse someone who doesn't respond.

'Musical.' He simply repeated the word, and twitched his mouth as if he was going to smile but then changed his mind.

'Yes, musical.'

'What do you mean?'

'I mean you thought I could play the guitar and that I was like all your friends up here who know about chords and harmonies and stuff like that, and that I know the difference between bluegrass and . . . and . . .'

'Old time.'

I glared at him. 'Old time. And that I could sing.'

'You *can* sing.'

'I mean really sing. Properly. Like Missy can.' And I put my hand in front of my mouth, feeling as if I was about to start crying again.

Trey said nothing, just sat there, looking at me, frowning at me.

'Trey, say something. Do you regret marrying me?'

He narrowed his eyes. He stood up slowly, his knee joints creaking as he did so. He walked across to the window and looked out, into the darkness. 'Shall I tell you the truth, Maeve?'

'Yes.' I was shaking, wondering what he was about to say.

'Of course I'm upset you're not more "musical", as you put it. I thought you could play guitar. I shouldn't have done. I made assumptions. There you were, in the front row at my gig, loving the music, and then you take me back to your home and there's this amazing CD collection and a real good guitar in the corner of the room. I thought they were yours. I'm sorry. I should have realised. But you know what I'm really upset about? That you didn't enjoy yourself this evening. They're great people, great friends of mine, and I love those jam sessions. But you didn't enjoy yourself. Actually, no. Do you know what I really mean? You didn't *try* to enjoy yourself. You closed your mind. You said to yourself, "I'm not musical" and you wouldn't even make the effort to join in. *That*'s what upset me most. You closed your mind, and that's not the Maeve I married.'

I felt my cheeks flush bright red. I was angry, full of almost teenage levels of frustration at the unfairness of it all. 'For fuck's sake, Trey, I tried. I tried the percussion thing. I tore the newspaper. I tried, but you all made it so obvious that I was crap that . . . well, how do you think it made me feel?'

He didn't say anything. He just shrugged his shoulders and gave me that pursed-mouthed, petulant, spoilt-kid look of his.

'Trey, be fair, for God's sake. I've given up everything for you. I have left my home, my country, my work, my friends – everything. I've come here, to this godforsaken town in the middle of nowhere, just to be with you. Because I love you. I don't know how you can accuse me of not joining in. I am making every fucking effort I can. It's not my fault that I'm so scared.'

He widened his eyes. 'Scared? Of what?'

'Of all that musical stuff. Getting harmonies wrong, and not being able to play percussion instruments, and people looking down their noses at me because I'm so cack-handed I can't even tear newspaper in time to the music . . .' Tears were dribbling down my face.

Trey stared at me with his mouth open. 'But Maeve, you're not scared of anything.'

'Yeah, I am. Roller coasters and clowns and, as it turns

out, being expected to sing harmonies. Sorry. Oh, and your dulcimer scares me a bit too; don't know why. It gives me the creeps, for some reason. So: roller coasters, clowns, harmonies and dulcimers – that's what I'm scared of. It's official.'

Thank God. He was laughing. It would be all right.

Trey was sitting next to me on the couch now, his long legs gathered up into a kind of lotus position. His bony but beautifully shaped right knee was sticking out through a rip in his jeans; I wanted to touch it. He was staring steadily away from me, picking intently at a loose piece of rubber on the sole of his baseball sneakers, a look of concentration creasing his face. 'You asked me if I regretted marrying you. I don't. But I wonder if you regret marrying me. You don't like this house. Can't say I blame you, the state it's in, but I'm trying to get you to understand what it means to me and I'm not doing very well so far. My friends all think you're great, but every time I introduce you, you seem to be embarrassed.'

'Well, that's because you keep describing me as beautiful.'

He turned to me, surprised. 'You *are* beautiful.'

That made me laugh. 'Trey, you are the only man who has ever described me as beautiful. You also have the worst eyesight of anyone I've ever met. Hmm,' I said, drumming my fingers against my bottom lip in mock-thought, 'I wonder if there's a connection.'

He smiled wearily and sighed. 'Maeve, the truth is,

every time I tell you I love you, I feel like you're putting up some kind of barrier. You fold your arms – like that!' I looked down, and realised I was doing exactly what he'd said. I unwound my arms reluctantly. He continued: 'I think maybe I'm competing with a dead guy. I want to tell you that you mean the world to me, but I feel like someone else got there first.'

It took me a few seconds to work out what he meant, and when I did I snorted, with a really unattractive snot-filled laugh. 'Jesus, Trey, do you mean Martin?'

He nodded.

'No. No, God, no. You know, Martin was a really crap boyfriend. I loved him like mad and I know he loved me but he never told me that. He would have died a million deaths –' and as that phrase left my mouth I thought, ouch, I didn't mean to say that, but I ploughed on regardless '– rather than tell me that he loved me or that I was beautiful or any of that stuff. You know, he would have made a really shitty husband.'

In my head I asked Martin for forgiveness, but it was worth it because Trey kissed me, then kissed me again and then explored my mouth with his tongue. And then his tongue explored the rest of me as well.

Afterwards he said, 'You asked me why I married you.'

'Ye-es,' I said, wondering what he was about to say.

'Well, quite apart from the fact that I love you, I married you because I need you. I married you for your

199

beauty and your strength and your boldness and your —
what can I call it? Your directness, your frankness, your —
emotional openness.'

Emotional openness? What the hell did he mean by
that?

'Maeve, I've written a song for you.'

'For me?'

'Well, not for you to sing, obviously, since you have
such a terrible singing voice and can't hold a tune . . . I'm
joking,' he said as I opened my mouth indignantly. 'A
song about you, might be a better way to put it. Can I sing
it for you now?'

I nodded, speechless, as Trey cleared his throat.

He really does have the most extraordinarily beautiful
singing voice, my husband. He took me right back
to that first night at the Borderline, when I first fell for
him. It's the straightness, the plainness, the directness of
how he approaches the tune, combining his grandfather's
stringent, almost plainsong style with just the tiniest,
faintest hint of sweetness; as if holding one of those
wooden honey drippers very high up and allowing one
single drop to fall, very slowly, onto the gravel road
below.

But as he was singing, I felt shivery and uneasy. All this
beauty, just for me? It's too much, too much; it's too
heavy for me, more than I deserve. As I listened to the
lyrics — something about a girl with the sky in her eyes and
the wind in her hair, a girl with a fearless heart — I got the

weirdest sensation. It seemed almost as if he was looking through me, not singing to me but to another woman altogether: someone more beautiful, bolder, more fearless; someone much worthier of this intense, beautiful scary song than I would ever be.

28

I don't react very well to hot weather. Of course I don't: I'm half-Irish, half-English, with the fair freckly skin that inevitably entails. Let's face it, I'm genetically ginger. I burn at the slightest exposure to summer sun. Besides, while other women look good in skimpy tops and shorts, I'm too hefty to enjoy that look. Summer was entirely the wrong season for me to marry a desirable man and move to the southern United States. I managed to get through August in Bodie's Hollow thanks to the cool breezes that blew across our mountain-top land, but I couldn't wait for the autumn – the fall. Everyone told me how beautiful the mountains would be then. Even Julie was forced to admit that the Blue Ridge Parkway was probably worth driving along at least once when the foliage was at its full glory in October. So as September went by, and the weather started to turn cooler, I began to feel a little better about life. I felt more confident about myself, about my marriage, about life in this small town; until the weather turned weird, and everything else went a bit strange as well. And that is the understatement of all time.

I suppose you could call it an Indian summer, except normally you expect a pleasant nip in the air during Indian summers, at least in the mornings and the evenings. Instead, the day would start with a heavy fog that took its time to lift and felt warm and oppressive. When I woke each morning, the first thing I wanted to do was to disentangle myself from Trey's arms. I felt sticky and lethargic. Stepping out of the house felt like stepping into a steam room. The sky stayed grey and heavy all day, as if it had been exhausted by the efforts of the summer. Temperatures weren't quite as high as they'd been in August, but the humidity sapped my energy and all I wanted to do was lie on the back porch with a jug of iced tea or a can of cold Coke. As Trey and I lay on the couch watching the TV news in the evenings we saw pictures of hurricanes sweeping the coast: the Gulf coast, the Florida coast and even the flat, frayed fringes of the North Carolina coast. It seemed strange: it was so still and eerie up here in the mountains, and yet so wild and wet along the coast.

The air was so heavy that I constantly felt headachy and bad-tempered and fat. And so maybe it was the weather that really was to blame for the way both Trey and I seemed to start worrying at the fault lines in our marriage, as if we were picking at a scab.

I suppose it started with Julie. I was in her shop, glad to be somewhere cool, and I was telling her about the musical night that I'd been forced to endure just a few days earlier. Julie was standing on a stepladder stocking shelves in her store, reducing prices on her summer merchandise and putting out the autumn stock: tea towels with pictures of falling leaves on them, Hallowe'en masks, that kind of thing. She rolled her eyes, then smiled broadly and pulled up a chair next to me. 'Oh my God, those jam sessions. Did you notice how they all do that special musician face, the one that makes it look as if they're constipated?' and she pulled exactly the same facial expression that I'd noticed on Brett and Cornell and the Dobro guy, and even on Trey. I felt guilty, but I had to laugh.

'Julie, you don't play any instruments, do you?'

'God, no.'

'So how come you've been to the jam sessions?'

She tilted her head on one side and gave me a puzzled look. 'You do know, don't you?'

'Know what?'

'About me and Trey?'

'What about you and Trey?'

'Well, we had a . . . "thing".'

I could virtually hear the inverted commas she gave that word. 'A "thing"?'

'Yeah, you know, a thing.'

A 'thing'. Shit. I tried to work out what I thought about it. It made sense, I suppose. Of course it did. She knew so much about Trey and his house. How else would she know about 'the room of death'? And his grandfather's ghost, apparently haunting the room? Plus, she was the only single woman in the town of about the right age. She was the person I liked most in Bodie's Hollow, the person I got on with best. Of course she and Trey would have gone out before he met me. It made perfect sense, but it didn't make me feel any better. I'd been planning to tell her about how the musical evening had made me feel, and the weird way Trey had sung me that song; I'd wanted to get her views on it, on who was in the right during that bizarre argument that Trey and I had had. But now, of course, I couldn't. Suddenly there was a barrier between us.

Julie seemed surprised that I didn't know. 'I figured Trey would have told you.'

'No, he didn't.' I thought for a moment. 'But then, to be honest, he's not exactly the world's most communicative person, is he? I don't really know much about Trey at all. We only just met. I didn't even know his real name until just before we got married. So, when was your "thing"?'

'I dunno. A while ago now. We were dating, then he went over to Europe on tour, then we dated for a while when he got back to town. He went back to London again and then he came back and told me he was getting married.'

So Julie was the loose end that Trey had had to tie up. 'Jesus. You mean he was still dating you when he proposed to me?'

She looked a bit embarrassed. 'Dating might be too strong a word for it. We were – you know – hanging out together. That's all. No big deal. Don't worry about it. It was nothing. That's probably why Trey hasn't mentioned it. I hope it doesn't affect anything, 'cause I really like you.'

But of course it affected things. How could it not? My now-husband was sleeping with something else just a few weeks before he proposed to me. As I walked home I tried to decide what I was most annoyed about: Trey proposing to me while he was still seeing Julie? The fact that my friendship with Julie would inevitably have to change? Or simply that Trey hadn't told me about it, and made me look stupid in front of Julie?

When I got back to the house, already hot, bad-tempered and out of sorts, Trey was slouched on the couch in the kitchen, all the doors open, a John Grisham paperback lying open across his lap. I was surprised he wasn't in the studio as usual. 'Hey, what's up?' he said as I walked in.

'Not much. You?'

'Blocked,' he said. 'Couldn't write.'

I rubbed my forehead with a tissue, trying to wipe away the sweat. 'Trey,' I said, 'I didn't know you used to go out with Julie.' I kept my voice light. I wasn't trying to pick a fight. I suppose I was telling him just to let him know that I knew.

He looked away from me and picked up the book, riffling through a few pages with his thumb. Then, 'Yeah. You know, just for a while. It was kind of a casual thing for a few weeks.'

No, that wasn't good enough. I needed him to be looking at me when he told me about it. 'She says you were dating at about the time you and I first met?' My voice was less light now.

This time he did look at me, with a frown. 'Um, I guess.

Yeah, I guess you could call it dating. We were keeping each other company sometimes.'

'So when you and I first slept together, you were also sleeping with Julie?'

He stared at me. 'Maeve, what exactly do you want me to say?'

'I don't know, Trey. Something. Anything.' And then, well, I suppose I could blame the heat and the humidity and the sudden sense of claustrophobia I had, the sense of being in a small town where everyone knew something I didn't, because I did that really annoying thing that women tend to do: I turned the row from specific to general with baffling speed. 'Trey, talk to me, for God's sake. You never talk to me.'

'I talk to you,' he said. He looked hurt. 'I talked to you the other night, you know, when you got upset during the jam session. And anyway, why don't you talk to me about what's really bothering you? If you've got something bottled up, tell me about it.'

Stupid American psychotherapy speak. 'Bottled up?' I repeated. Me? Talk about the pot calling the kettle black, or whatever the expression is. This was a man who'd told me nothing important about his past, this house, his grandfather's death. A man so 'bottled up' that I could actually see his body and his face close up – almost literally – when I asked him about something that touched a nerve. It made me even angrier. 'For fuck's sake,' I said, and I started hurling abuse at him. Phrases like 'this bloody town' and 'this fucking house' and 'your precious grandfather', and other stuff along similar lines, and there sat Trey looking first hurt, then baffled and finally amused. As I was ranting, the phone rang and – almost unbelievably – Trey picked it up, holding his finger in front of his mouth as he did so, to tell me to be quiet.

It was Missy. I could tell from his body language, the coy way he started fiddling with the laces of his sneakers; and from his voice, which became soft and sweet and reassuring. I listened for a while, stunned at first, and then because he hadn't dismissed me from the room and because we hadn't, as far as I was concerned, finished with our argument. 'Of course I will,' he kept saying. 'Of course I will, honey. Don't you worry about a thing. I'll be there. Of course I will.'

I went over to the fridge and pulled out an ice-cold beer. Just one for me: that was how petty I was feeling. I stood with my back to Trey as I drank it, trying to calm myself down, trying not to feel bad about the phone conversation he was having. He was promising Missy that he'd come to Nashville to do some work with her. Work on her new album, I guessed, the one she'd been working on with him in this very house.

'I've got this great song that'd be wonderful for you,' he was saying – crooning, almost. 'I wrote it as a guy's song, but it's no problem to change it. It could be just what you need.' There was a pause, but I knew what was coming. The next words he said felt like a kick in the teeth: 'It's called "Fearless Heart".'

I strode out of the kitchen, slamming the back door behind me, and started stomping up towards the top of the field behind the house.

29

'Maeve, stop.' Trey was panting as he ran to catch up with me. I stopped where I was but, childishly, refused to turn around. Trey put a hand on my shoulder and tried to make me turn round to face him but I wouldn't, so instead he walked around me so that he was facing me. 'Maeve,' he said. 'What's this all about?'

'You know perfectly well.' I scowled at him.

'Actually, I don't. Are you cross with me about Julie?'

I shook my head. I wasn't, really, not any more; in the same way that a sharp new pain can make you forget an old dull ache.

'So what's the matter?' He looked as if he genuinely didn't know.

'Missy.'

He shrugged his shoulders, as if he didn't know what I meant.

'Missy,' I said again. 'You're going to Nashville to work with your ex-wife.'

Trey reached out one hand and touched my shoulder. 'Maeve, she needs me. She's . . .' He paused. 'She needs a friend. She's emotionally needy right now.'

'And I'm not?' I could not believe what I was hearing.

He just smiled at me. 'Of course you're not. That's one of the things I love about you.'

How could a man be so blind? How could he misunderstand me so badly? At that moment I needed him to put his arms around me and hug me to him, as if I was the most precious thing in the world to him. I wanted him to tell me that I was more important to him than his grandfather, his ex-wife and even his music: that I was the centre of his world, not just some tough, hard-as-nails sidekick. Maybe I should have found the words to say that. But instead: 'You're giving Missy my song' was all I managed to splutter out in my anger.

I looked at Trey's face and expected his expression to be apologetic, conciliatory, loving: the way it was, eventually, when we'd had our heart-to-heart after the jam session incident. But it wasn't. He looked hard-faced and serious— angry, even. He looked upwards, as if trying to find an answer there, in the grey, overcast sky, and then he took a deep breath. 'Okay,' he said, through clenched teeth, 'You wanted me to talk to you? I'm going to talk to you.'

'Okay,' I said, trying to avoid looking him in the eye. 'So talk.'

'Not here,' he said, and steered me back down the hill to the back porch, his hand clasping my elbow, as he had that first night.

'Maeve, what do I do for a living?'

'You're a musician. You make records and go on tour.'

Trey laughed. 'Oh yeah, that's right. My best-selling album and my sell-out tour.' Sarcasm wasn't one of his usual notes, and it surprised me. 'Maeve, do you really think that being the opening act on a tour of tiny venues in Europe will actually pay for the studio I've just built? Not to mention remodelling the kitchen and the rest of the house?'

I looked across the field, stuck my bottom lip out like a small child – like Trey himself, in fact – and shrugged my shoulders. 'I don't know. How should I know? You never talk to me about your music.'

'Only because you don't seem interested.'

'Of course I'm interested. I married you, didn't I?' I flicked a sideways glance at Trey and saw that he was staring at the ground, twisting his hands together. He didn't reply for a while, so I said, 'Go on, then. Tell me about your music.'

'I'm a session musician and a producer. That's how I make a living. You know that perfectly well. I remember you e-mailing me, telling me you'd Googled me, saying you were really impressed by all the people I'd worked with. And, Maeve, that's what I do. People hire me to play mandolin and acoustic guitar on their records. Sometimes they hire me to produce tracks for them. Even whole albums. I'm quite good at it, you know. I've won Grammies and everything.' His voice was dry, almost droll. 'Anyway,' he continued, 'the other thing I do is, I write songs. I record some of them myself, and a tiny handful of people buy my CDs or come and see me perform, and that's great. But what is really great is when some big-name artist decides to record my song, and they play it on the radio. That's when I can make a living from my songwriting.'

I said nothing. I was still sulking.

'So when Missy Ferguson, who is one of the biggest stars in country music right now, tells me she needs one more song to complete her album, it seems a perfect opportunity to get her to record one of mine.'

'You wrote that song for *me*.' I spat the words out.

Trey seemed taken aback by the venom in my words. 'Maeve,' he said, and his voice was much gentler now, 'I wrote it *about* you. And I'm going to record it on my next CD, and in the sleeve notes it'll say that the song's about you, and I'm going to dedicate the whole CD to you, and maybe twenty people will buy it and listen to it. If I'm lucky. Oh yeah, and Missy will also record the song, and maybe it'll be a single, and every country-music radio station in the world will play it, and every time you hear the song, even though the words are a bit different, you'll still know it's your song. And you can think of the money we'll earn, money to spend on remodelling the house. But anyway, most of all . . .' And he reached out and took hold of my hand; 'Most of all, every time you hear the song, even if it's Missy singing it, you'll know how much I love you.'

That night I lay in the bath and thought about the row we'd had. I tried to work out who was in the right, who was in the wrong. Then I wondered if it was childish and simplistic to look at things that way. I have never been a woman who's prey to insecurity. But then, I'd never been married before, least of all to a man who was idolised by everyone who knew him. I'd never been a second wife before. I dried myself and shook out my hair so it was huge and frizzy – the way Trey told me he liked it. Lucky, really, given how humid the weather was. It would have taken me hours to straighten it. I smoothed cocoa butter into my skin and looked at myself in the mirror. Okay, so Trey thought I was beautiful? In that case, I suppose I should act like *I* thought I was beautiful too.

I walked naked into the bedroom. He was already in bed, curled up with his back to me. I ran a finger down his spine and over the faint ridged scar in the small of his back. He tensed, then relaxed, turned over and smiled at me, a smile that made my heart leap. I kissed him, he kissed me back, and very soon our argument was all but forgotten.

Next morning, Trey got up early and packed a few things to take to Nashville with him. 'I'm going to be there a few days,' he said. 'I'll come back at the weekend, and then maybe I'll need to go down again.' He thought for a moment. 'Maeve, I hate to think of you alone in this house; I know you don't like it much. Why don't you come with me? I've got this little studio apartment I stay in. You could come too. Nashville's a cool town. There's lots to see there. You'll have a great time. Please?'

I looked at him, all cute and puppyish, and nearly said yes. But it was so clearly an afterthought. He hadn't thought of asking me to come with him until that very moment. I thought about hanging around in Nashville, sitting in the control room of the studio watching Missy Ferguson sing while Trey twiddled mysterious knobs on the mixing desk; and of all the hundreds of people Trey would want to introduce me to, people who'd ask me what instrument I played. I shook my head. I thought I'd rather face a few days alone in Bodie's Hollow than put myself through that. 'No, you go,' I said. 'I'd only get in your way.'

And besides, I had other plans.

31

I don't hold with family feuds. I have no patience with families that fall out and refuse to speak to each other. This is why: I only have a few memories of my mother. I had just turned five when she died. I remember her picking me up from nursery school one day when it was snowing, the first time I'd seen snow, and she was holding a brand new pair of Wellington boots in one hand. I remember her taking me to feed the ducks in our local park, and a swan came and pecked my hand and my mother kissed it better. And there's a memory that only came back to me when I saw Martin in hospital that last time. I remember my father holding me up, tightly around the waist; holding me up to a window so that I could wave at my mother. But my mother was asleep in a strange white bed and she didn't wave back.

There were photographs, of course. My parents at a dinner dance, as they used to call them: my mother, tall and slim with big dark eyes and elegantly tousled hair; my father, slightly shorter than her, flushed in the face, his tight curly hair obviously red, even in a black and white photo. My parents, arm in arm in front of the Eiffel Tower on their honeymoon, a shot taken, one assumes, by a passer-by. My mother, Sean on her knee, sitting in front of a Christmas tree in our front room. My father showed us the photos regularly, and told us the story of the great romance. The way he told it, it was a real Romeo and Juliet scenario. The rough-handed Irish labourer made good; the elegant daughter of his boss. No one approved of the marriage. Her parents were furious, he told us. He got the sack; we never saw our grandparents.

Except once, at my mother's funeral. Another early memory. I know I was wearing a dark blue flowered dress from the Ladybird shop. My father's secretary Miss Stacy had taken me out shopping and I remember being puzzled by that. So there I was in my smart new dress, and Sean was in his school uniform for some reason, except without his cap. I don't know where Mickey was. Perhaps Miss Stacy was looking after him for the day. I remember two tall old people, a man and a woman, both wearing black. The woman leaned over and kissed my cheek and the man shook Sean's hand. Then the woman sat down between the two of us and put her arms around us, and even at that age I remember thinking that she was stiff and awkward. I looked for my father, and then I could see him talking to the tall old man. I think they were arguing.

Of course now I know what was going on. My grand-parents – my mother's parents – wanted to raise us. They wanted my father to give us up to them. That was what the argument was about. 'Come on, man, see reason' was the kind of thing I guess my grandfather would have been saying, and my father, who loved us desperately, who did such a fantastic job bringing us up alone, was shaking his head and standing his ground.

You'll probably understand now why I've got no patience with family rifts. Your family is the only one you've got; it makes sense to keep them on your side. I wish I had more family. My brother Mickey thinks we've probably got cousins galore in some Irish backwater, and he is determined to find them. Sean's simply created his own big family by having five children over in Naples. I wanted to do my bit to make peace in Trey's family. I was intrigued by the feud that meant he no longer talked to the two aunts who'd brought him up, his only living relatives. Or maybe I was just nosy.

Boone passes in these parts for a big town. It's got a university and everything, even a Museum of Appalachian Life. Trey had taken the car – his ten-year-old Chevy something – down to Nashville, leaving me with the truck, and it took me more than an hour to get there. All the way I told myself that I was going to Boone purely to see Julie's friend Chuck. Charles. I was going to pick his brain about murder ballads and find an angle for the magazine article I was supposedly writing for Nick. I found him in his comfortable office on the campus, surrounded by books and files. He seemed pleased to see me. I guess I offered him a diversion from his real work.

Charles was a nice guy, but I soon realised that he was as dull as ditchwater. He pulled down a heavy book from one of his shelves and started talking in great detail about murder ballads while I pretended to take notes. 'You could speculate that they have their roots in the deep-seated feuds and border skirmishes of seventeenth-century Scotland,' he said, rather pompously. 'Alternatively, I have a theory that we might be able to trace their origins to old tales of honour killings. You see, the victims in these ballads are almost invariably women. Many of the killings are motiveless, but in others women are killed for rejecting proposals, or to conceal a pregnancy. Another interesting aspect of their survival is to note the correspondences of landscape between Scotland and the Appalachians. It's striking to note how many of the murders in these songs take place either on mountainsides or on river banks . . .'

I fidgeted and looked at my watch. Any more of this and I would lose my nerve. I would find myself driving back to Bodie's Hollow without visiting Trey's aunts. I cleared my throat to stop him. 'Chuck – Charles, sorry – this is great. This is so interesting. So useful for the piece I'm writing. But I realise I'm taking up too much of your time . . .'

He blushed, presumably guessing that he was boring me. 'Well,' he said, 'do come and see me again. But in the meantime, take this with you. It has the words and music to many of the most famous murder ballads. You'll find it fascinating.'

So I walked out of his office with the heavy book under my arm and set off to find a street map of Boone. I was more nervous than I could possibly say. What on earth could have caused Trey to fall out with his aunts? And what would they think of me?

I needn't have worried. When I introduced myself, they greeted me at the door with squeals of delight. 'Trey's new wife!' exclaimed one of them, and held me at arms' length to have a good look at me. I found myself smothered in kisses. They led me inside and made me sit down in their most comfortable armchair. They fetched me iced tea and I looked around their welcoming, modern, cluttered house, so different from the old Ferguson homestead. I tried to trace resemblances to Trey. Jean was tall and thin, like him; Nancy was shorter and stouter. Both were spry, lively women in their late sixties or early seventies, with bright blue eyes and deep tans. Both were wearing the same kind of clothes as Valerie McLoughlin at the museum wore: 'leisure wear' – sweatshirts with gaudy appliquéd patterns, worn over polyester trousers. It seemed as if it was a uniform for a certain kind of elderly spinster.

I hadn't really planned exactly what to ask them. I suppose I wanted to know about their father and about how he died, and about why Trey had fallen out with them. I guess I also wanted to know something about what Missy was like. But they were frustratingly difficult women to pin down. They were conversationally skittish. Direct questions got parried with offers to fetch more iced tea, or random reminiscences. For example, I actually managed to ask them this: 'Why doesn't Trey keep in touch with you any more?' and the answer I got was something like, 'That dear boy. He never did fully get over . . . now, Nancy, where did we put that photograph, you know, the one of Trey with his first guitar?'

Or, another of my bold questions: 'Did you know that Trey blames himself for his grandfather's death?'

There was a sharp intake of breath by both aunts, and then I think it was Nancy who answered. 'Well, the thing you must remember is, it was nearly twenty years ago, and of course in those days we didn't have . . . Jean, when did we have the telephone installed at the old house?'

'I heard that your father had a stroke because Trey told him he was getting married.' As I asked it, I realised I was crossing the line into rudeness. 'I'm sorry,' I added, 'it must be very difficult for you to talk about that day.'

It was Jean who gave me the long, shrewd look. She shook her head. 'Not really,' she said. 'You see . . .' and she cleared her throat and took a sip of iced tea. She seemed to have made a decision to talk. 'What you need to realise is that our father was not an easy man to live with.'

Nancy made a strange choking sound. Possibly it was a suppressed laugh.

'Anyway,' Jean continued. 'You could say that it was a blessing that the old man died so quickly. He didn't suffer. But poor Trey did. He's never forgiven himself. He suffered so much tragedy that day and he's always felt responsible. Do you remember that day, Nancy? There was that big storm, and Trey was pacing around the house?'

'Oh yes. He had something on his mind he needed to talk to the old man about, but he wouldn't tell us what it was.'

'And then Trey went into the front parlour to speak to

our father. We could hear some shouting and then Trey came running out in tears. 'I've killed him,' he was saying. 'I've killed my grand-daddy.' The poor boy. So much tragedy in one day for one so young to cope with.'

As I drove back home to Bodie's Hollow that phrase kept repeating in my mind. So much tragedy in one day. It seemed an overdramatic way to describe Trey's grand-father's death from what were, after all, purely natural causes. So much tragedy. Was there was something more to this, something that no one was telling me?

Trey rang me that night from Nashville. What is it about cordless and mobile phones that makes us walk around when we're talking on them? Anyway, as Trey told me about his journey, and about how he'd managed to get a couple of hours in the studio that evening, I found myself walking around the kitchen, running my fingers along the beautiful new worktops and the gleamingly clean wood-fired range that I planned to start using soon. I wandered out into the hallway, feeling the naked floorboards under my bare feet. I'd hoped to sand them down and wax them, but I was beginning – reluctantly – to admit to myself that the quality of the wood wasn't good enough. Maybe carpet would be better – warmer and more homely. I made automatic responses to Trey's news, sounding like a standard-issue stay-at-home wife. 'I miss you,' he said.

'I miss you, too.' I was getting good at this lovey-dovey stuff.

'So, did you do anything interesting today?' he asked.

And because I'm honest to a fault and find it difficult to lie in reply to a direct question, especially one from my husband; and because at that moment I looked up at the wall and saw CJ Ferguson staring fiercely back at me, many times over, I told the truth. 'Um, yes. I went to see your aunts?' I voiced it like a question, bracing myself for his response.

There was a silence. For a moment I thought he might have put the phone down. Then he repeated, very calmly and quietly, 'You went to see my aunts.'

'Yes.' There was another long silence. Was he cross? Upset? I didn't know him well enough to guess. I sat down on the staircase. 'Trey, say something. Please, you're worrying me.'

'I'm worrying you and you want me to say something.' There was a muffled noise that might have been a laugh. 'You want me to say something.' His voice was still very calm and controlled. I ran my fingers over a protruding nail in the woodwork. I waited to hear what he was going to say. 'Okay, here goes. Here's my something. Why in God's name did you take it upon yourself to go and see my aunts?'

I had barely ever heard Trey curse before, and perhaps that was my cue to apologise meekly for whatever it was I'd done to upset him. But when people get snippy with me I don't apologise: I answer back. It's automatic. 'Why the hell shouldn't I go to see your aunts? I'm your wife, for God's sake. You do know it's usual to introduce your wife to your relatives, don't you? I mean, it's not like you've got a lot of family. Those two women are all you've got. I have no idea what happened between you, babes, but I wanted to meet the two women who helped bring you up.' There were no photographs of his aunts on the hallway wall, I realised for the first time. There was nothing in the house to show that they had ever lived there; nothing apart from the chipboard blocking off all the fireplaces.

'Don't call me babes.' His voice was barely above a mutter.

'What do you mean?' I always called him babes. It was a word I used a lot for people I loved. I'd borrowed it from Martin, one of his mock-cockney affectations, and it had stuck. 'Why not?'

'Because it . . . it diminishes me.'

'What?' I couldn't believe my ears. Here's a man who chooses to go by a name that basically means 'the third', and he doesn't like being called babes, I thought. He had to be kidding. I swallowed hard and stifled my laugh. 'Trey, I'm so sorry I upset you. Can you please explain to me why going to see your aunts was so wrong?'

It was his grandfather's will that did it. It seemed that Trey had fallen out of favour with his grandfather shortly before his death. 'Because you were planning to marry Missy and run off to Nashville? Is that why?' I thought about the story of the stroke: Trey watching his grandfather drop dead after telling him he was getting married.

'Kinda,' was what he replied, after a pause.

So my husband, who loved his grandfather with all his heart, was left just the house, while his aunts got everything in the house, all the money and the rights to CJ Ferguson's entire back catalogue.

'It's not their fault. You can't blame them.'

'They sold the rights before he was even cold in the ground. They took almost everything out of the house. All they left were the photos in the hallway and the furniture in the bedroom and . . . and the parlour. They bought a condo in Florida and that house in Boone and got rid of everything they had that reminded them of my grand-daddy.'

'Is it the money you're upset about?' Oh shit, what a crap question. Even before it was out of my mouth I regretted it.

'Of course it's not the money.'

I suddenly realised exactly what it was. 'It's the heritage, isn't it?'

'Uh-huh.' Then after a while he said, 'I sometimes feel as if I'm the only one who cares about my grand-daddy's legacy. Oh sure, there are hundreds of musicians and fans out there who say they care about CJ Ferguson, and how much he meant to them. But it feels like an uphill struggle to get people to see behind the image, to get people to understand that my grand-daddy was perhaps the single most important figure in this kind of music. Maeve, you do understand, don't you?'

I wasn't at all sure that I did.

31

I sat sideways on the third stair up, staring at the photograph of Trey clutching his grandfather. His grandfather's legacy: what was it? Some scary old songs and this scary old house, if you wanted to be really reductive. I realised it was important to Trey. I got that. But I didn't entirely understand why. I put my head in my hands to try to think. What I was trying to work out was this: his grandfather's legacy was important to him; helping his 'emotionally needy' ex-wife Missy was important to him; coming back to his home town and getting back in touch with his roots was important to him. So whereabouts on the list of Trey's priorities did I come? How important was I to him? The woman who kept his feet on the ground, sure. The woman who was surprisingly good at ripping out old kitchen units: that, too. Those were the good things, the things he loved me for. Then there was the woman who couldn't – or wouldn't – tear newspaper in time to music, and the woman who kept blundering her way into bits of Trey's past that he didn't want to talk about. He wasn't so keen on that Maeve O'Mara.

And then I felt disgusted with myself for the way I was thinking; as if my happiness, my state of mind, depended

entirely on what Trey thought of me. What had happened
to me? Where had I gone? Had I succumbed? Had I
melted into Trey and somehow become a non-person, the
kind of woman who's defined only by her husband's
opinion of her?

Here was the more important question: what did I think
about Trey? We seemed to have done nothing but argue
and snipe at each other in the last few days. I looked
around me, at the dark hallway, at the photographs of CJ
Ferguson, at this old house sitting alone on the top of a hill
at the head of a remote crease in the Appalachian
Mountains. Here I was, all alone, and for what? What the
hell was I doing here? I remembered Julie's expression: 'I
followed my heart to the mountains.' I guess that was
what I'd done. I'd followed my heart. I'd fallen in love and
found myself here. But if it turned out that I wasn't
actually in love, then there was no point in me being here.
That thought sent a chill down my spine.

I walked out to the kitchen to put the phone back. I
looked around me, and realised that I was actually
beginning to like the house. It was responding to the work
and care I'd put into it; blossoming as a result of being
nurtured. Yes, I could see myself ultimately loving this
house.

I walked back down the hallway and out onto the front
porch. I stood there in the warm night air. I listened to the
chirping of birds, or insects, or whatever it was that made
the chirping sound. Don't ask me; I'm a London girl. The
kind of night-time sounds I was used to were police sirens
and the dull thump-thump bass-line of the music from the

local pub. Over the tops of the trees I could see the lights of Bodie's Hollow, such as they were. It really was a dump, an armpit of a place. And yet I was becoming curiously fond of Bodie's Hollow, now that I knew more about its history. I understood the pride of the town; I respected its survival. I loved the river, the way it would either dawdle or rush over the rocky bed, depending on the weather; and I loved the way the mountain tops faded into the sky, almost as if they were infinite. But did I love Trey?

That was a big question. I'd nearly forgotten what it was like being alone, the way your brain dwells on profundities that would never cross your mind in a million years when you're with someone else. I remembered the days after Martin died, and the thoughts that passed through my mind on all those lonely evenings; the way I'd re-examine every aspect of our life together. Had he loved me? Had I loved him? Had we loved each other enough? Was there anything I would have done differently?

And now here I was again, over-analysing, picking holes in a relationship. Did I love Trey? I thought about him physically to start with: the way his limbs seemed slightly too long for him; the way he stooped and lolloped when he walked; the way he would sit down in a chair, collapsing suddenly, all arms and legs, like a daddy-long-legs or a wrongly erected deckchair. And then those sudden moments of grace, when he leaned over his guitar or mandolin; when he gestured at the landscape; when he stood naked in front of me and ran his fingers down my body. Oh yes, the sex was wonderful. He could turn me to liquid with a look, a touch, a kiss. Ardent: that's a word you don't hear very often these days, do you? But that was Trey: the way he could smile and his eyes, his whole face would suddenly come alive, catch alight. I wrapped my arms around myself and shivered, although the air was warm. Oh yes, I loved Trey.

I sat on the front-porch swing, put my feet up on the low fence and swung myself backwards and forwards. I loved Trey. But, but. For every time he was ardent and graceful and open; for every time he adored me and loved me and liquefied me; as many times as he did all that, he could also be petulant and thoughtless and closed-off. A little boy sulking; a scared little boy refusing to talk; a cold, thoughtless man who didn't trust me enough to share his past with me. Haunted by something that he wouldn't talk about.

I took a deep breath. Fuck it, I thought. Here I am. I'm married to Trey, for better or worse. Better make this better, not worse. And the only way I could think of was to go through, not round: to find out exactly what it was about his grandfather's death that haunted him so much.

The single light bulb in its heavy, fusty, fussy shade did very little to illuminate the front parlour. It cast a faint sheen on the glass that covered the picture of Adam and Eve, and on the varnished case of the art-deco radio. I ran my finger over the radio's walnut veneer. For just a moment I had a wild idea about the radio witnessing what had happened, as if I'd be able to turn it on and somehow hear that last argument Trey and his grandfather had had, imprinted on the airwaves like a ghost. I knew I was being stupid. Nevertheless I touched the chunky radio knob. It turned with a satisfying click but no sound came out of the speaker. Of course it didn't. When I looked down at the skirting board I could see that the cord from the radio had no plug on the end.

I sat down in the rocking chair by the fireplace and began to rock it backwards and forwards, as if somehow I'd be able to conjure Trey's grandfather. I closed my eyes; tried to imagine what must have happened on that day. I could almost see it: Trey standing there, all skinny and nervous and white-faced. The old man, glaring at him from under his eyebrows, hearing what Trey had to say and then standing up, maybe hanging on to the mantelpiece – like this – to haul himself up to his full height. And as he opened his mouth to speak, to shout at Trey, to forbid him to throw his life, his future away, instead he collapsed in on himself, like an industrial brick chimney with a fire lit at its base. And as I stood there, almost acting out the encounter, one hand clasping the mantelpiece as if my life depended on it, that was when I heard footsteps. Light footsteps across the kitchen floor and then creaking on the bare floorboards in the hallway, approaching me. I froze. The door started to creak open. I could feel my heart beating as if it would burst out of my ribcage. A pale face appeared in the narrow crack between the door and the doorpost; a pale face that looked almost as scared as mine must have done.

'You in there, Mizz Ferguson?'

'Oh, Jesus Christ almighty, Kayla. You gave me the fright of my life.'

32

'I had, like, this big fight with my mom. I didn't know where else to go.' Kayla was sitting on the orange couch in the kitchen, her hands wrapped around a mug of coffee I'd poured for her, and she was looking around the room with saucer eyes. She was obviously desperate. She must have been, to make her way up to the old haunted house in the dark. She still looked white as a sheet, and she was visibly shaking.

'What was the fight about?'

'Oh, you know. Whatever. You know what moms are like.'

I shook my head. 'No, I don't. I didn't have one.'

'How can you not have a mom?'

'She died when I was five.'

'I wish mine had.'

'No, you don't.'

'Yeah, I do.'

I looked hard at Kayla. Her eyes were, as usual, rimmed with heavy black eyeliner, but it had smudged into the papery violet skin around her eyes. There were red blotches around her mouth and nose, making her usually hard face seem much softer and younger than usual. She was an attractive girl. She'd probably be beautiful soon. I smiled at her, trying to get her to smile back. 'So, come on, Kayla, spill the beans. What were you really fighting about?'

She twisted her fingers together and looked at them. 'Mom went through my stuff. She found some rubbers I had in my drawer.'

Rubbers. Condoms. 'How old are you, Kayla?'

She threw me a sharp look of teenage disdain. 'Don't *you* start, Mizz Ferguson.'

'Maeve.'

'Maeve.' She said it back to me with distinct and sarcastic inverted commas round it. 'You're not my mom.'

'No, but you have to remember I'm probably about the same age as her.'

'Yeah, but you're, like, younger, 'cause you're from London and you don't have kids and you're cool.'

'Thanks.' I was flattered. I opened my mouth again, trying to think what I should say to Kayla next. Did she want advice or approbation? Should I be on her side or her mum's?

She cut in. 'I'm fifteen. Virtually, anyway. Next month.'

'Okay. And are you sleeping with someone?'

She shrugged, and blushed. She looked down at her hands again. 'Yeah. No. I dunno. Maybe. There's this guy at school I like, and, you know, I figured that maybe I would. So I thought I'd better be prepared. I don't wanna get pregnant, I know that. This girl in my class? She got pregnant last year and now she's living in a trailer with her boyfriend and her baby and her life is over. She's never gonna leave this place.'

I stifled a laugh. It wasn't funny, but the way Kayla rolled her eyes at the thought of the trailer was so emphatic I couldn't help myself.

'What's his name – this guy you like?'

She squirmed, and blushed again. 'Eric.'

'And he likes you?'

'I think.'

'Kayla, you're ever so young. You do know you don't have to sleep with him to prove you like him, don't you?'

That disdainful look again.

'Sweetheart, you're a clever girl. You're got so much potential. Promise me you won't do anything stupid, will you?'

She shrugged again. 'Can I stay here tonight?'

'No, Kayla. Your mum will be worried sick. You need to go back home and make it up with her. Talk to her. She was young once. It'll be fine, I'm sure.'

I took Kayla home in the truck. I drove her out through Bodie's Hollow, on to the main road, up further into the mountains and then down a narrow track to the Christmas-tree plantation that Brett owned. The house was low, one-storey, with a steeply pitched white roof. I took Kayla to the front door, my arm around her shoulders. Linda Sue opened the door just a crack, and looked at me suspiciously. I went to kiss Kayla's cheek but Linda Sue grabbed her daughter's arm and pulled her away from me. Then she hit Kayla round the face with her open hand, so hard that I could hear the cracking sound.

I drove away into the darkness, creeping through the narrow wooded lane at no more than ten miles an hour. I was mentally kicking myself for not handling the situation better. But what else could I have done? The last thing I needed was to get between a troubled teenager and her mother. Deep in thought, I missed the turning from the main road back into Bodie's Hollow, and I had to pull a U-turn in the parking lot of a breeze-block roadhouse that was full of big black motorbikes. As I eventually nosed the truck up the hill to our house I realised I'd left the light on in the front parlour. It glowed faintly in the darkness. I let myself in by the front door. I stood for a few moments in the doorway of the parlour. Then I turned off the light, closed the door, locked it, and took the key upstairs to the bedroom and put it back in the little china donkey cart where I'd first found it.

I thought I'd find it difficult to sleep on my first night alone in the house. But maybe because I was so tired from the whole Kayla incident, or maybe because of the luxury of having the whole double bed to myself, I fell asleep almost immediately: a deep, dreamless sleep.

33

The phone woke me. I looked at the clock and saw that it was gone ten in the morning. I fumbled for the receiver and grunted a hello.

'Hey, Maeve, there's something I forgot to ask you last night.'

It was Trey. His voice sounded soft and gentle. I sat up in bed and tried to gather my thoughts. 'What do you mean?'

'I should have asked you how my aunts are doing.'

'What?'

'You did a good thing. Going to see my aunts, I mean. How are they doing?'

'They seemed fine. What is this, Trey? I thought you were cross with me for going.'

He cleared his throat. 'Yeah, okay, what I'm trying to do is to say sorry. In a way. Without, you know, actually saying the words.'

I smiled. 'What did you say? You're what? I didn't quite hear you.'

'Okay. Listen, my beautiful, wonderful wife, who I love more than anything in the world: I'm sorry. I'm sorry. Oh, and did I say I'm sorry?'

It was raining, hard. I was glad. The air felt much fresher. I stood on the back porch in bare feet, my mug of coffee in my hand, and looked across at where I knew the mountains were. The peaks were swathed in dramatic grey clouds, moving swiftly across the windy sky. It was a beautiful day. This was a beautiful house. And I had three more days on my own here: three days in which I could invest more love and care in the house. I was planning to make a start on the upstairs.

I drove down to Buchanansville and went to the big hardware store. I filled a trolley with everything I thought I'd need. Then I dressed myself in overalls, piled my hair under one of Trey's baseball caps and rolled up my sleeves. I started on the bathroom. I scoured the bath, the basin and the chrome taps. I gouged out the old sealant, got rid of the mould, cleaned the tiles and re-grouted them. I fixed a new chrome towel-rail to one wall, and put down new vinyl tiles on the grotty floor. While I worked I listened to the radio, a hot country station that Trey would probably have hated, blasting out slick, shiny, sing-along pop country from the likes of Shania Twain, Faith Hill and even Missy Ferguson herself: more synthesisers than steel guitars.

I spent my second evening alone in the old house curled up on the orange couch watching TV detective shows while eating a huge bag of some kind of cheesy corn snacks, washed down with three cans of beer. I was exhausted and pleased with myself. I went straight to sleep and didn't wake up until the birds started singing outside the bedroom window.

The next day I moved on to the smallest of the bedrooms, Trey's old room. I guess I had an idea that it would make a good guest room, if I ever got the house to a decent enough state to invite friends to stay. It would certainly serve as a study for me. Maybe in the back of my mind it was even a future nursery. I opened the built-in cupboard next to the fireplace and found boxes of old books and toys. There was a train set and boxes of educational jigsaw puzzles. There were piles of yellowing books. I picked one up: *My Friend Flicka*. I opened it and was surprised to see the name 'Melissa Hann' in childish handwriting on the inside of the cover. It was only as I gave the room a thorough clean, vacuuming up decades-old cobwebs from the ceiling and the skirting board, and found a child's red plastic hair-slide being sucked up by the cleaner that I realised who Melissa Hann must have been. A little girl who'd no doubt played in this room as a child. Missy Ferguson herself.

I took a good look around the room. Decent floor-boards: maybe I'd hire a sander and give them a good going-over. The walls and woodwork simply needed a coat or two of fresh paint. Apple white, I thought, for the walls. The small cast-iron fireplace had – like all the others in the house – been blocked up with a sheet of chipboard. I knelt on the floor by the fireplace, took hold of the top of the board and wobbled it. It wasn't fastened; it had just been put in place. I reached my arm into the gap between the top of the chipboard and the fireplace surround, grazing the underside of my wrist in the process. I moved the board from side to side and eventually managed to manoeuvre it out of place. There, in the fireplace, in the rusty fire basket, was an empty Jack Daniels bottle and three stiff, faded copies of *Playboy*, dating back nearly twenty years.

I laughed. Teenage boys are all alike. I remember finding Sean's porn stash under his bed when I nosed around his bedroom after he'd gone away to university. I held the *Playboy*s by one corner and started to carry them downstairs to the dustbin. But as I did, something fell out of one of the magazines and plopped to the floor: an exercise book with a fawn cover.

'Clyde James Ferguson III: My Diary' it said, in spidery handwriting on the front cover. The date, eighteen years ago. I traced the handwriting with my fingertips and then, feeling furtive and sneaky, I curled up on the couch in the kitchen and began to flick through the pages, reading – with difficulty – the loopy writing in faded blue ink.

34

July 2nd: We smiled at each other in the café. I thought again that she is the most beautiful person of the female species I have ever seen. I don't know why she likes me.

I smiled ruefully to myself. Typical Trey, with his hyperbolic compliments: he hasn't changed a bit, I thought. I flicked over a couple more pages.

July 23rd: Today she was wearing a bright green sweater and she looked even more beautiful than ever.

I remembered the green dress he'd wanted me to try on in the thrift store. I felt uncomfortable reading this. It wasn't good for me. All I was going to find was stuff about how much he loved Missy, and I would start comparing myself unfavourably to her. It would do me no good at all. I should put the book back where I found it. But I didn't have the will-power. Instead, I let my gaze run further down the page and I found this entry:

August 2nd: I can't believe how lucky I am. I get to kiss the most beautiful woman in the world. We met down by the river and we sang some old songs together. She has a beautiful voice. Afterwards she let me kiss her. Her mouth tasted of strawberries. I stroked her stomach and we talked about the baby.

I went cold all over. The baby? What baby? Missy was pregnant? I read on, hungrily, as if I was reading a suspense novel. I needed to know what happened next:

August 10th: My grand-daddy doesn't know about me and her, even though we've been seeing each other for months. He mustn't know. He calls her 'trailer trash'. Today Aunt Jean and Aunt Nancy were talking about her. They think the clothes she wears are 'low class'. I don't care. I smiled to myself. It's the best secret in the world. I love her and she loves me.

Trailer trash? Missy? I smiled in spite of myself.

August 15th: I got into trouble today because of her, but I don't care. Jerry and I went down to Buchanansville to the movies and then we drove home late. We had a bottle of JD so we went down to the river to drink it because it was so warm. It got really late and I knew I'd be in trouble when I got home, but I didn't care. Jerry went home but I stayed there for a while because it was so beautiful with the river running by. That's when she came out to me. We sang our favourite song together. Then we kissed again, and we used our tongues, and then we 'did it', although I had to be careful because of the baby. She seemed to like it. When I got back home,

Grand-daddy heard me come in. He made me come into the front parlour and he read to me from the Bible. Then he thrashed me, but I didn't care because I was so happy.

I swallowed hard. I could feel tears forming. Trey at — what, fifteen? Sixteen? Sitting by the river because it was so beautiful. Making love to Missy. And then getting thrashed by his grandfather. I shouldn't be reading this, I told myself. Imagining Trey at that age, so vulnerable and so in love, actually made my stomach hurt. But I couldn't put the diary down.

August 26th: The most exciting day of my life so far. We've decided what to do about the baby. We're going to get married. I'm so happy. I told her I'll marry her as soon as I turn 16, in October. We'll get married and move to Nashville. I can't wait. My grand-daddy won't like it, of course, but I don't care. It's the right thing to do.

Oh shit. So now I knew. Now I knew what killed his grandfather. I thought of Trey, bravely going into the front parlour to tell his grandfather about Missy, telling him that he'd got her pregnant and was going to marry her, knowing he'd get a thrashing, and instead having to watch the old man die.

I thought about Kayla, telling me how she didn't want to waste her life by getting pregnant. I thought of the way Linda Sue had slapped her around the face. I wondered if Linda Sue and Brett had got married as teenagers because their son Lonnie was on the way. I wondered if it was the way things happened here in the mountains. It explained why Trey and Missy had married so young.

But what it didn't explain was this: what had happened to the baby? I remembered the one conversation Trey and I had had about children, back in London, what seemed like a lifetime ago. He'd seemed evasive. How was it he'd put it? 'We were never blessed': that's what he said. Now I realised what he'd meant; why he'd answered like that. He wasn't evasive, he was sad. They'd lost a baby. Missy must have miscarried, or maybe the baby had died. So much tragedy, his aunts had said. Was this what they meant? His grandfather's death and the loss of their baby?

There were no more diary entries after that one, nothing to clear up the mystery. I closed the exercise book, running my fingers again over Trey's full name on the cover. Those poor kids. Just children, dealing with that kind of tragedy. I even felt a rush of warm goodwill towards Missy. I got up from the couch and stretched. I went to the fridge to get a Diet Coke. I slammed the fridge door shut and that was when an evil thought came into my mind. Missy Ferguson. I'd never met her; I had no reason to think ill of her. But I remembered the picture of her on the website, all prim and perfect, and I remembered how the website copy had failed to mention her divorce. Just a glimmer of suspicion came into my head: had she really been pregnant back then? Trey was fifteen years old and, judging from the way he wrote, he was a naive, sweet-natured fifteen-year-old. I knew Missy was about the same age as Trey, but girls are so often manipulative and more experienced than boys of the same age. Was she really pregnant, or did she just want to force CJ Ferguson's grandson to marry her? 'Trailer trash' – that made me smile again. There she was now, all groomed and glamorous; and yet she'd been so easily dismissed as low-class trailer trash by Trey's family, who themselves lived in this rickety old house in the mountains.

I found Jerry in his workshop. He was planing a long, thin piece of wood with a craftsman's care, his mouth protected by a gauze mask. I stood in the doorway for a while, breathing in the seductive aroma of sawdust. He saw me, and waved. After he'd finished, he took off his mask, came out to the doorway and said, 'Hello, Maeve. What can I do for you?'

Call me nosy; inquisitive; a born journalist. Or you could call me hideously insecure. 'Jerry, you and Trey go back a long way, don't you?'

'Yup.' He sat down on the bench on the front porch and patted the space next to him.

'So I guess you remember when he and Missy were dating?'

He gave me a strange sideways look, which I interpreted as reluctance. Eventually he said 'Yup' again.

'Was Missy pregnant? I mean, is that why they got married?'

Jerry gave me an even odder look: narrowed eyes, furrowed forehead, as if he didn't understand a word that I said. Eventually he said, 'What are you talking about?'

'I just wondered, Jerry. That's all. I wondered if Missy was pregnant, and that maybe that's why they got married when they were so young.'

'Maeve, don't do this.'

'What do you mean?'

He patted my leg, somewhat awkwardly. 'There's no need to worry about her,' he said.

'I'm not worried about her, Jerry. I'm not jealous, if that's what you mean.'

'Good. That's good. Trey loves you, you know.'

'I know.'

I waited for Jerry to say something else; to answer the question I'd posed. But he didn't. We sat there for a while, and then he got up and said, 'Maeve, this was real nice. But I've got to get back to work.' It was clear that he had no intention of telling me whether Missy had been pregnant – if, indeed, he even knew the answer.

Instead I went up to the museum in the old schoolhouse and found Valerie McLoughlin. She was pleased to see me. 'I updated the exhibit,' she said, and showed me. She'd added a new index card right at the end of the display that read: 'Missy and Trey Ferguson are now divorced, but continue to work together.'

I guess that just about summed it up. 'Valerie, can I ask you a question?'

'Of course you can.'

'You knew both Trey and Missy . . .' I tailed off. I wanted to ask her what I'd asked Jerry, whether Missy had been pregnant when they got married, but I thought better of it. She'd think it was a really weird question to ask; the kind of question I should only ask my husband. Like Jerry, she'd assume I was asking her because I was so insecure about Trey's first wife. So instead I gestured at the photo of Trey and Missy together and asked her, 'Do you have any older photos? I mean, of Trey and Missy when they were younger than this?'

She gave me a surprised look, but told me to follow her. She went into the back room and began rummaging in the drawer of a filing cabinet. After a few moments she produced a tatty manila envelope and emptied a sheaf of photographs into her hand. She shuffled through them for a few seconds. Then, 'Here you are. This is their class graduation photograph.'

A faded colour photo showed just seven students – four boys, three girls – lined up in Sunday-best clothes. Trey was easy to spot: he was at least a head higher than everyone else and twice as skinny. He was wearing a checked shirt, a mismatched tie and a dark jacket that was too loose in the body and too short in the sleeves. His hair was short at the sides, revealing his slightly protruding ears, and hanging long over his forehead in what looked like a bid to be trendy. I wondered what his grandfather thought about that hairstyle. Next to him I vaguely recognised Jerry, a mop of fair hair almost obscuring his features. In the front row stood a very small, very neat girl with her red hair in pigtails. She was a foot or more shorter than Trey and was dressed in a drab knee-length skirt and a white blouse. 'There you are,' said Valerie, pointing. 'There's Trey. And that's Missy.'

She looked neat and clean and cared-for. She did not look like low-class trailer trash, whatever Trey's diary had said. I figured she must have made a special effort for the graduation photograph.

35

It was late in the evening and I was painting Trey's old bedroom, putting the final touches to the white gloss woodwork. I heard Trey's car pull up. The car door slammed, and then I heard him run into the house. Before I even had a chance to put the paintbrush down Trey had bounded upstairs and found me, grabbed me around the waist and planted a huge kiss on my lips. I responded to the kiss, awkwardly holding the paintbrush out to one side to avoid dripping paint on him. When I eventually managed to pull away, I noticed he was wearing the blue floral-print shirt he'd worn for our wedding, and he looked well and happy. I rested the paintbrush carefully on top of the paint tin and gestured around the room. 'What do you think?'

His eyes were sparkling. 'It looks wonderful. And so do you.'

Nonsense: I was wearing overalls and a baseball cap, and I had paint all over my face. But – hey – it was Trey: it was the kind of thing he said. I let him kiss me again. I kissed him back, and suddenly we were both hungry, grinding our mouths and our hips together, clashing teeth and bones. I clung on to his hair and kissed him harder. He pulled the baseball cap from my head and tried to run his fingers through my tangled frizz, pulling it so tightly that it hurt. I felt his erection rubbing against me, so I wrapped my legs around him and together we somehow stumbled out of the small bedroom and onto the landing, where we fell into a heap on the floor.

Trey pushed me against the wall so forcefully that I hit my head. I bit into his bottom lip in retaliation. He ripped my overalls open and pinched one of my nipples so hard that I cried out. I wriggled free of the overalls and then I grabbed Trey's balls through his jeans and squeezed them until he groaned. I unzipped his jeans and his dick leaped up to meet me. Trey gave me a wicked smile as he sucked the fingers of his right hand. Then he pulled the gusset of my knickers to one side and thrust three fingers up inside me with such force that I came immediately with a spasm that shook my whole body. Trey shoved his erection into me. We ground ourselves into each other as if trying to grind our hipbones into one. With each thrust I hit the back of my head against the wall, and I dug my fingernails into Trey's back, deliberately trying to draw blood. It was noisy and violent and painful, and possibly the best sex I've ever had. Afterwards, we lay exhausted in each other's arms, full-length along the upstairs landing, still semi-dressed. 'Well, that was nice,' I said. 'Welcome home.'

Trey gave a huge laugh. 'Nice. Yeah, you're right. It was very nice.' Then he kissed me gently on the end of my nose and said, 'I missed you.'

'I missed you too.'

A couple of days later, days we'd spent mostly in bed together, we went to church for Lonnie's baptism. I felt thoroughly sinful and depraved. I felt that everyone would be able to tell that we'd done almost nothing in the past two days except have rampant, frequently inventive sex. Trey's bottom lip made it look as if he'd been punched; I felt so sore and achy that I wasn't sure I'd be able to sit still for long enough. It didn't seem to be the right frame of mind to be in for such an important religious moment.

The Baptist church was full of people I didn't recognise. It seemed as if everyone Lonnie knew in the world was there. School friends, teachers, Bible Camp friends, I guessed. Relatives too. The parking lot was crammed with cars and trucks and you'd have thought it was a wedding, judging by the turnout and the way people were dressed. Thank goodness Trey had warned me. He was wearing his grandfather's dark suit, a white shirt and a tie, the first time I'd ever seen him wear one. He was even wearing shoes, not sneakers. I had on my favourite black wide-legged trousers and my orange wraparound cardigan, the same outfit I'd worn to meet Trey at the airport when he'd flown over to London to see me. On Trey's advice I was also wearing a hat, a black straw thing that I'd borrowed from Julie.

The service seemed to go on for hours. We were treated to testimonies, not just from Lonnie but from friends of his as well, about how they had found the Lord. 'Yes, Lord,' called the congregation at intervals. 'Hallelujah.'

Trey pressed his thigh against mine all through the service. He held my hand tightly and smiled at me from time to time. I was glad. I needed some sense of security. Exposure to this much religion made me feel dizzy. I started thinking about the kind of language they used to explain their experience. 'I found the Lord': did that mean they were actually looking, or did they simply stumble across Him? And if they were looking, what got them started on their quest? Did they have things in their life that had gone wrong, or did they simply have what my friend Helen once referred to as a 'God-shaped hole' that needed filling?

After Martin died, Helen came round to the flat and we held hands and she comforted me. She told me she'd been praying for me throughout Martin's illness, and that she would carry on praying for me, that I would be given the strength I needed. She said she hoped I didn't mind, but that it was something that she needed to do. I don't know whether it actually made any difference. Logically speaking, it can't have done. I don't suppose God sits up in Heaven and thinks, 'You know what? I wasn't planning to bother about Maeve O'Mara, but since Helen asked me so nicely perhaps I will look after her, after all.'

Maybe it's the simple fact of knowing that Helen cared enough about me to pray that actually gave me the strength I needed. But I suppose deep down I do sort of believe in God – or in some vaguely benign force – because of this: things gets better, eventually. When Martin died I thought my heart would break. But it didn't, quite, and eventually it healed.

I looked at Trey and saw the way he was semi-joining in, muttering 'Yes, Lord' and 'Praise be' under his breath, as naturally as breathing. I knew he'd been raised a Presbyterian, a faith I knew little about except that it was strict and dour and Scottish. How could he switch so easily to this boisterous, noisy, joyful, spontaneous kind of worship? I looked around me. I felt myself swaying with the rest of the congregation. In a weird way, it was a bit like being in the mosh pit at a really good gig. I was actually starting to enjoy myself. Soon I'd be shouting 'Hallelujah' myself.

The baptism itself took place in a pool hidden below the floor at the front of the church. Two sections of the floor pulled apart at the touch of a button on the preacher's pulpit, almost as if it was a booby trap, like a piranha-filled tank under the floor of a Bond villain's lair. Lonnie reappeared dressed in a white robe and stepped into the waist-deep pool with the preacher. The preacher said some words to him and then abruptly, almost violently, pushed him backwards so that Lonnie was completely underwater. I suddenly remembered something I'd seen, a scene in a film – possibly even *O Brother Where Art Thou?* – with people in white robes being baptised in a river. I said, slightly too loudly, 'They should do the baptism in the river.'

Trey said nothing, but I felt his hand clamp mine so tightly that I thought he'd break the bones.

As we milled around outside the church afterwards I saw Kayla standing on her own, looking ill at ease in a dark skirt suit. I went up to say hello and as she turned to me I saw she had an ugly bruise on her face where her mother had slapped her. 'How are you doing?' I asked.

She shrugged and wouldn't meet my eyes. I put out my hand to touch her shoulder but she shook it off. 'Kayla, what's up?'

I meant it as a genuinely concerned inquiry, but she took it as a standard greeting and gave me the standard reply. 'Not much,' she mumbled.

I felt a heavy hand on my own shoulder. 'Stay away from my daughter.' Linda Sue was almost shouting at me as she pushed me away with some force.

'Why? What have I done?'

'You need to ask?'

'Yes, I do.'

Trey was now standing by my side, one hand on my back. 'What is it?' he said to Linda Sue.

'It's your . . . wife. She's corrupting my family. First she flaunts herself nearly naked in front of my husband and son . . .'

I nearly laughed, thinking about the morning I'd stumbled down to breakfast in my ratty towelling dressing gown only to discover that Brett and Lonnie had started work earlier than usual. One look at Linda Sue's face stopped me.

'. . . And then she bought birth control for my daughter. My fourteen-year-old daughter.'

'What?' Trey and I said it in unison, except while I was

staring at Linda Sue in horror, Trey was looking at me with a puzzled look on his face.

'What do you mean, I bought Kayla birth control?'

'I found rubbers in her drawer. She says you gave them to her.'

I looked at Kayla. She was standing behind her mother with a pleading look on her face. She was asking me to cover for her.

'Yes,' I said, 'I did. I thought it would be better than her getting pregnant.'

Kayla gave me a shaky smile. Linda Sue loomed over me and looked as if she wanted to hit me. Trey got between us but instead of turning to Linda Sue he looked at me. 'Why?' he asked.

'I'll explain later,' I whispered.

'Because she's a whore,' said Linda Sue. 'Trey, we all love you. You know that. I hate to tell you this, but you've been had. Your wife is a hypocrite and a harlot. It makes me sick that you should give up a good, God-fearing woman like Missy Hann for this woman. She has turned your head. She is bad for you, Trey Ferguson. She has suckered you. She will lead you astray. She's like another Sarah Swigert.' And with that she turned and walked away, taking Kayla with her.

'Trey, were you planning to step in at some point and defend my honour? Obviously I can look after myself, but when some shrew starts calling me a whore and a harlot in the church parking lot on a Sunday morning so loudly that the whole town can hear, it would be nice for my husband to – I don't know – say something? Anything?'

Trey had his back to me and his shoulders were hunched. He turned around slowly, and I could see that he was even paler than usual. His hands were clenched into fists. He looked at me as if he was seeing me for the first time, and for just a moment I thought he believed everything Linda Sue had said. 'Before you ask, I didn't buy Kayla those condoms.'

He gave me a thin smile. 'Why did you say you did?'

'Because Kayla's my friend and I didn't want Linda Sue to hit her. Again. Trey, I know she's an old friend of yours but she's a bully. A big fat bully who enjoys hitting her daughter. And, yeah, I know you probably believe it's okay for parents to beat their children, I mean it happened to you and you'll probably tell me it made you a stronger, better person . . .'

I stopped there because Trey took one step towards me and wrapped his arms around me tightly. He buried his face in my neck and he rocked me from side to side. 'I'm so sorry,' he said. 'So, so sorry. I keep thinking you can fight all your own battles. You're so strong and so fierce and brave that sometimes I think you don't need me. Please forgive me.'

I pulled him even closer to me and we stood there in the middle of the church car park, wrapped in each other's arms. If we had been in a film, the camera would have pulled back while simultaneously spinning around us, making the two of us the still centre of the turning world.

I didn't want the moment to end, but it had to. 'Trey,' I said eventually. 'Who the hell is Sarah Swigert?'

'A friend of mine,' he muttered, his face still buried in my neck and my hair. 'She was someone I used to spend time with. A long time ago.'

36

I found Sarah Swigert almost by accident a couple of days later. You could say I stumbled over her. Trey had gone back to Nashville for a few days. I stayed in Bodie's Hollow. I had floors to sand, a feature to write; and besides, our reunion had been so sweet that we'd both decided a little bit of distance worked wonders for our relationship. It was another heavy, foggy, humid day. Needing some air, I walked aimlessly towards town around lunchtime. But as I wandered down the hill the old churchyard looked so atmospheric and eerie in the fog that I decided to take a look.

I found CJ Ferguson's gravestone right in the centre of the churchyard. It was a tall, straight, plain memorial stone with two names on it. My husband's grand-parents:Margaret Jean Yancey Ferguson, born 1912, died 1971; Clyde James Ferguson, born 1910, died almost exactly eighteen years ago. There were no angels or decoration of any sort on the stone; just this text, in plain unadorned letters: 'For not the hearers of the law are just before God, but the doers of the law shall be justified.'

Justified. I stood in front of the gravestone and thought about that word. It spoke to me of an uncomfortable uprightness, the kind of man who would be unbending in his allegiance to the law of God. The kind of man who wouldn't let his grandson be brought up by unmarried parents. The kind of man who thought you could thrash the sin out of a child. What exactly did happen on that day, the day he died? Trey blamed himself so much that he now dedicated his life to honouring his grandfather. He was still trying to make amends. For what? For getting his girlfriend pregnant and shocking his grandfather so much that the old man dropped dead of a stroke? Or did something else happen? Something more?

The room of death, Julie called it. Trey went into the room that day knowing he'd be getting a thrashing. He'd been pacing around for hours, plucking up the courage. CJ Ferguson's cane was lying on the table next to the Bible. Did something else happen? Did Trey, this time, pick up the cane himself? Was there a fight? A struggle? Maybe he was right in blaming himself for his grandfather's death. And now he was still desperately trying to atone.

The gravestone was well tended, with flowers that looked as if they'd been laid there just a few days earlier. I guessed Trey must have been down here. I stared and stared at that gravestone, as if it could tell me the true story. I reached out and traced the date with my index finger. The anniversary was coming soon.

I shook myself out of my reverie. It was lunchtime, and I could smell tempting food aromas from the café. I crunched along the gravel path towards the gate that led from the cemetery to the main street, but as I opened the gate my gaze fell on another gravestone, just inside the churchyard.

I probably wouldn't have noticed it had it not been so well tended, with a bunch of fresh wild flowers and leaves in a small jam jar. It was just a small stone, crammed against the wall, as if it was an afterthought. No Bible verses on this one, just these words: 'In loving memory of Sarah Swigert and her unborn child.'

Sarah Swigert. Trey's friend. 'Someone I used to spend time with a long time ago.' I looked at the dates on the gravestone. Two dates – her birth date and the date of her death. The latter was a date I recognised: the same date as I'd just seen on CJ Ferguson's gravestone.

Two people in this small town had died on the same day. Two people who meant something to Trey. I felt the hairs on the back of my neck stand up, and I couldn't tell you whether it was the coincidence of the date, the fact that Sarah Swigert was just nineteen when she died, or those heartbreaking words: 'and her unborn child'. I remembered what Trey's aunts had said: 'So much tragedy in one day for one so young to cope with.' Was this the other tragedy that his aunts were talking about?

I felt dizzy, and I put my hand on the church wall to support myself. Something was spinning around in my head. Things were falling into place. The girl in the diary. The girl who was pregnant. The girl Trey was planning to marry. I'd assumed it was Missy Ferguson. Had I been wrong?

'Who was Sarah Swigert?'

Patsy would know. She knew everyone. She'd taken care of Trey when he was little: hadn't she said so herself? But my question seemed to take her by surprise because she paused, midway through doling out my portion of meat loaf with sides of corn and green beans. She looked shocked; upset, maybe. 'Now, why are you asking that?'

'I was just in the churchyard. I saw her gravestone. It sounded like a sad story.'

Patsy nodded. Suddenly she seemed close to tears. She perched herself on the seat next to me. 'We all loved Sarah. She was such a sweet girl. Her father was a drunk. Poor Sarah didn't have much of a childhood. But after her father died she really pulled her life together. She got a job here in the café. All our customers loved her. She was the kind of girl who'd bring a real smile to your face. She was like a breath of fresh air – so honest and so direct. Funny, too. A real good girl.'

'What happened to her?'

Patsy sighed. She nodded her head towards the television in the corner of the café. It was showing pictures of the hurricane that was hitting the coast. A reporter was on the oceanfront somewhere in Florida or Georgia, dressed in waterproofs from top to toe, being blown sideways. 'Imogene,' she said.

'I'm sorry?' Who the hell was Imogene?

'Hurricane Imogene. It was one of the worst we've had in these parts. Not much wind left in it by the time it reached us, but the rain! I've never seen the like. It fell from the skies like Noah's flood. The river burst its banks. Sarah lived down in that old trailer on the river bank. She drowned. I guess she lost her footing on the river bank. She didn't stand a chance.'

'She was pregnant when she died . . .'

I had wanted to ask Patsy if she knew who the father was, and about how come Sarah had died on the same day as CJ Ferguson, but she just said quietly, 'Yes, she was,' and walked back behind the counter.

It was hotter down by the river than it had been in the churchyard, the close, humid kind of heat that makes my skin crawl. Soon my blouse was sticking to my back as I made my way along the river bank under the over-hanging trees. I was heading upstream, back towards the old church. I wanted to see Sarah Swigert's trailer. The thought was still whirring around in my head: she lived in a trailer, the daughter of the town drunk. Trailer trash? But half the people in this town lived in trailers. No doubt Missy had done, too. Sarah was pregnant when she died. But where did Missy come in? If she wasn't the girlfriend in the diary, how come Trey married her when he turned sixteen? I couldn't believe that short-sighted beanpole of a boy would have had two girlfriends on the go. Come to that, how could a runty teenager have attracted a nineteen-year-old woman of the world? It was just a strange coincidence, I told myself. But still, I needed to look further. No harm in finding out more.

Much of the time there was a detectable footpath along

the river bank, but at other times the river narrowed to pass through a rocky bottleneck, and then I had to take off my sandals and make my way through the stream itself, carefully stepping from one rock to the next. I was used to country rambles from my childhood holidays in Yorkshire, but it was years since I'd walked anywhere other than London pavements. After about fifteen minutes with no sign of the trailer I was breathing heavily and beginning to regret setting off this way. I wasn't panicking, but I was worried.

The river rounded a sharp right-hand bend, and the path narrowed so that I could only put one foot in front of the other. I thought about Sarah being washed away when the river burst its banks. I thought about Kayla's saucer eyes when she told me people had died in this river. I grabbed hold of the roots of a tree that grew out of the bank to my right, realising that however calm the river was I was now ten or more feet above it. The path had climbed without me noticing. I guess that's why I was breathing so heavily. As the bend straightened out I could see what looked like a building to my right. It was a trailer, almost hidden among the trees.

I left the path and walked up to the trailer. It was one of those that had sprouted roots and fixed itself into the landscape. In fact, the landscape had grown up around it, with tree branches and leaves obscuring some of the windows. Clearly someone had lived there once, but it was now a rusty old wreck, flecked with the remains of what looked like a dark green paint job. I stepped onto the makeshift wooden porch, which sagged damply under my weight. There was an old car seat sitting on the porch, with stuffing oozing out of the ripped cushions. The trailer's chrome door was open and maybe that was why I went inside. Sheer curiosity, I guess. I'd never set foot inside a trailer home before.

I was shocked to find that it wasn't empty. I don't mean there was someone in there, but that there were items of furniture and clothes and pieces of crockery scattered around, as if Sarah Swigert had left in a hurry and forgotten to close the door. At one end of the trailer, two stripy couches faced each other across a small table. On one of the couches there was a battered, cheap-looking suitcase, with clothes spilling out of it. I walked further in, holding the bottom of my blouse up over my nose and mouth to block out the overwhelming smell of damp that permeated the trailer and everything in it. I looked more closely at the clothes. Women's clothes. Sarah's, I assumed. Brightly coloured: something red, something else in a deep shade of green. It reminded me again of Trey in the thrift store, picking out the green dress for me to try on. I thought of that bit in his diary, about how she – Missy? Sarah? – was wearing a bright green sweater and looked beautiful in it. The suitcase looked as if Sarah had simply cleared out a drawer or a cupboard and crammed the whole lot anyhow into the case. I reached out a finger to touch the suitcase but pulled away quickly: the whole case and everything in it was covered with a creeping mould of some sort. I wiped my hand on my trousers to get the mould off, and I stood for a while, getting my breath back and trying to work out what might have happened.

Sarah had packed this suitcase, I was sure of it. Had she been planning to leave? To leave in a hurry, taking everything with her? I could picture this woman hurling her clothes in this case, perhaps looking behind her, over her shoulder. Perhaps she was scared of something. Or someone. And then, before she could finish packing, she went out to the river, lost her footing and drowned. What or who was she scared of? Was there someone there when she drowned?

I stood there in that trailer, which was cool and damp after the heat outside, and felt feverish runnels of sweat run cold down my arms and the back of my neck. I shuddered. I was scaring myself. Stop it, Maeve, I said. And at that point I jumped a mile in the air as I heard a faint scratching noise and the sound of something moving behind me. Then something scurried over my feet.

Just a rat, and of course I'm not scared of rats. I'm not scared of anything. But nonetheless I left pretty quickly after that, letting the door of the trailer crash closed behind me.

37

Trey had his glasses dangling from the neck of his blue Chesapeake Bay T-shirt. His eyes were closed and he had a huge pair of headphones clamped to his head. He sat behind a giant mixing desk, dozens of faders and knobs in front of him, and listened with his whole body. His long, elegant hands were making intricate shapes to the music that only he was hearing. Behind the glass was a tiny woman with beautiful collarbones and the lollipop-head look of women who keep themselves on a starvation diet. A beautiful face, almost perfectly triangular, with skin stretched tightly – too tightly – over sharply defined cheekbones. Her arms were almost too muscular, like Madonna's: she'd been toned and trained and dieted to within an inch of her life. Huge dark blue eyes, with make-up so perfectly applied that only another woman could tell she was wearing any. Her hair was the streaky dark red of Old English marmalade, glossily straight and curled under at the ends, framing her face with a heavy fringe. She was wearing perfectly cut jeans and a sapphire blue vest top that exactly matched her eyes. Missy Ferguson tapped her beautifully manicured nails on her microphone stand and waited for the verdict. I curled up in the corner of a leather sofa at the back of the control room and tried to be as inconspicuous as possible.

It was working. So far Trey had no idea I was there.

It was Trey's birthday. And, shamefully, it had taken Jerry to remind me, although in my defence I don't think that Trey had actually ever told me when his birthday was. Jerry had come up to the house to tell me, in his shy, taciturn way. 'I think you should go to Nashville. Trey's missing you, and I reckon it'd be good for y'all to get together in the studio.'

'Why?'

'Because Trey wants you there.'

'Did he tell you that?'

He fidgeted. 'Nope.'

'So how do you know he wants me there?'

'I know how important you are to him. You make him real happy. Now, I don't usually try to interfere in my friends' marriages, but you two are so great together and I hate to see you apart, and I think it'd be a real nice surprise for him to see you there.'

So I drove to Nashville, six hours or more by car, listening to country music radio stations the whole way, and I enjoyed feeling the freedom of the road. I thought hard about Trey and me. The way he'd stood by as Linda Sue had insulted me: I had to admit that still rankled. I knew he loved me, but he still seemed to be treating me as a mate, a pal, not the centre of his universe. There were so many secrets, so many things he wasn't sharing with me.

Or maybe it was me who wasn't sharing with him. Perhaps – as Jerry had suggested – it would be good for me to take more of an interest in his work.

Using Jerry's map, I pulled up outside a nondescript hangar-type building on an industrial estate just off the freeway. The beautifully made-up girl behind the reception desk greeted me suspiciously until I told her who I was. Then she smiled and led me down a long corridor lined with gold discs and into the control room. Various musicians and technicians just nodded at me, guessing, I suppose, that I must be a musician of some sort. And now I was sitting on the leather sofa waiting to say hello to my own husband, who looked as if he couldn't be disturbed.

Finally Trey seemed happy with what he was hearing. He pushed his headphones down around his neck; put his glasses back on and peered at Missy through the glass. He pressed a button on the desk and said, 'That was sweet, honey. That was so sweet. Now, shall we do that harmony vocal we spoke about?'

Missy smiled a huge toothpaste-ad smile and gave Trey the thumbs-up. He stood up and swung around, and then did a double take as he saw me sitting there. He stepped towards me, arms outstretched, and nearly throttled himself on the headphones that were still around his neck. One of the technicians leaped across and unplugged them from the mixing desk, and Trey gathered me into his arms in a huge bear hug. 'Hey, everyone,' he said. 'This is my beautiful new wife Maeve,' and of course I blushed right

across my face and neck. I caught sight of Missy through
the glass, and she didn't seem terribly happy to see me.

Trey lollopped across the control room and into the
studio with the same uncoordinated freedom I'd noticed
when I met him at the airport that first time. He's in his
element, I thought. He's perfectly happy right now, at this
moment. But I didn't know whether that was because of
me or despite me.

Then something happened that I can only describe as
an epiphanic moment. And if that seems like an extreme
way of describing two people singing then you've never
been lucky enough to hear two people singing old-time
mountain harmonies, their voices brushing so close to
each other that you think they're going to crash, swerving
away only at the last minute. I'd been hearing Missy's
voice on the radio while I'd been redecorating and in spite
of myself I'd been impressed. It had some of the same
sweet mountain purity as Dolly Parton's, but deeper and
less quivery. Trey's voice I knew, of course, and I
recognised the song as well. 'Fearless Heart', the song
he'd written for – about – me. But the vocal arrangement
was extraordinary. Missy mostly held the tune, while
Trey's voice, sometimes higher, sometimes lower, sometimes almost on the same note, darted around hers. The
harmonies were strict, harsh almost: Trey's stern,
unbending, uncompromising notes blended with Missy's
sweetness in a curious way, as if he were building a vocal
brick wall for her song to bounce off and echo around.
And – this will sound pretentious but I can't think of any
other way to describe it – for a moment it was as if a rip

had appeared in the modern world and I was seeing and hearing something from a very long time ago.

I sat transfixed as that lovely sound chimed around the control room. I looked at Missy, tiny and beautiful, singing her heart out. I looked at my husband, his eyes closed, his hands clenched into fists at his side, his whole body immersed in the music. I felt a thrill that was almost sexual but perhaps went deeper than that. It sent chills chasing through my whole body, down my neck and back, and along my arms, down my legs. I felt a spasm go through me, and I found myself with tears streaming down my face.

The song ended and, embarrassed, I rubbed my face on my sleeve to wipe away the tears. I looked up, and saw Missy with her arm around Trey's waist. The contrast in their heights was almost comical – a foot or more – and I realised that was why Trey had that strange way of walking, like a newborn foal, like a man who'd only just grown to his full height: he'd been married for seventeen years to someone who, in comparison with him, was virtually a midget. Missy reached up, pulled his face towards her, kissed him on the cheek, and said, 'How did I ever let this man go?'

Perhaps it was that moment that raised my hackles and got my competitive instinct working. Perhaps it was Missy's perfection, her fluttery sweetness, her body language with Trey, that got me thinking that I was in a fight to save my marriage. I prefer to think that it was simply the fact that I'd seen Trey in his element, with that same freedom of movement, the same blitheness, the same joy that I'd originally fallen in love with. All I know is that I said to myself: Maeve, this man is worth fighting for.

I was surprised what a big, vibrant city Nashville was. We found ourselves sitting around a table in a noisy, glitzy bar and grill, packed to the rafters with well-dressed diners and drinkers, far from the redneck cowboys I'd been expecting. I introduced myself to Missy: 'Maeve O'Mara,' I said, and she rolled her eyes in a gesture that seemed slightly disparaging. Then she kissed me on both cheeks and asked if I'd got her flowers.

'Yes. Thank you. It was very thoughtful of you.'

'And how are you liking Bodie's Holler?' Her manner was intimate, girlie, confiding; much like that of my friend Fiona. She put her hand on my arm while she waited for my answer, a gesture I hate.

'It's very . . . pretty,' I finally managed. 'Lovely countryside. Beautiful views.'

Again she rolled her eyes. I wondered what she'd expected me to say. I looked across the table to see Trey watching us, an amused look in his eyes.

Missy patted me on the arm. 'I'm so glad you're enjoying it. Maybe I'll see you up there one day soon?'

She kissed Trey on the cheek and drifted away, her duty obviously done. Trey was still looking at me, and he mouthed 'Well done.' I felt myself blush.

Later, in the little studio apartment that Trey was renting, I started trying to tell him what I felt about his music. I wanted to apologise for not taking any interest, for not realising how much the musical night had meant to him. I wanted to say sorry for not getting the point of his grandfather's legacy, and for not asking Trey anything about how his second album was going. I wanted to tell him that I understood, that I finally realised what it all meant to him; but all I kept saying was this: 'I get it. I finally get it.'

He seemed pleased but bemused.

I was bouncing on the bed, dressed in my bathrobe. 'I mean, I get it. I understand it. I had this . . . moment, there in the studio. I get why this music is so important to you. I've never heard anything so beautiful in my life.'

Trey laughed. He came over to the bed and kissed me, his hands on either side of my face. 'Oh Maeve, I do love you,' he said, and his beautiful hands found their way inside my bathrobe.

We made slow, deep, luxurious love that night. It was the kind of night when two people are completely in sync, drowning slowly in each other. I think I was perfectly happy that night.

38

nd then it all went wrong.

My fault, I guess, but with the best of intentions. I was still on a high as I drove all the way back to Bodie's Hollow the next day. 'I get it,' I said again and again to myself. 'I get it.'

I made a vow. I was going to make a real effort to find out all I could about Trey's music. I'd finish the feature I was writing for Nick, and make it something that Trey would be proud of. I would find out the difference between old time and bluegrass. I would learn to play the guitar. Okay, I would at least learn to play the newspaper properly. And first of all, I was going to learn a song. Here was my plan: when Trey came home, I would arrange a music night – a jam session – at our house. In our lovely new kitchen. And I was going to surprise Trey by singing. He had told me that I could sing, and I figured that if I sang the main tune I'd be okay; I'd let the others add the harmonies. My plan was, I was going to learn one of the old songs. It was about time I started taking a proper interest in Trey's music. It seemed the least I could do.

I sat at the harmonium in the front parlour with the pile of sheet music I'd found in the stool. I had to find a song to sing, something I knew – or could learn – the tune to. I thought about that old favourite 'Amazing Grace', but then dismissed it as too easy, too obvious, too religious. I looked at the song called 'I Wonder how the Old Folks are at Home' and tried to play the first couple of lines, but there were lots of quavers and some of the notes had dots after them, which I half-remembered was something to do with making the notes longer. There were also some random sharps scattered throughout the tune, which was more than my rudimentary keyboard skills could cope with. I found another old song called 'Wildwood Flower', which seemed a lot more straightforward to play. I thought I'd be able to learn it quite easily. The tune was quite simple, running up and down the scale, and it was in the key of C as well. It was a very sad song, about a woman mourning her lover. Except when I got to the last verse I realised the reason she was mourning him was not because he was dead, but because he'd left her for someone else. Not the ideal choice.

Sad songs: there were so many sad songs. But as I rummaged through the sheet music I realised that I'd probably end up singing a sad song, because most of the happy songs I found were too difficult for my limited ability: too fast, too many different notes. Sad songs were easier to sing, it seemed. And then I remembered the book that Chuck had lent me, about murder ballads. Of course! Perfect. It had been a murder ballad that had first made me fall in love with Trey. It would bring everything full circle.

I found the book on a shelf in the kitchen and carried it back into the parlour with me. I sat down in the rocking chair, flicked through a few pages and saw some of the songs I'd heard of, the ones Nick had mentioned to me: 'Pretty Polly', of course, 'Knoxville Girl', 'Banks of the Ohio'. And then I found 'The Lily-white Maiden.' The song they'd sung at the jam night in Asheville, the one that had brought back my memories of music lessons at school; the one I'd sung in the playground with my friend Lizzie. I thought hard. I remembered Trey being a bit dismissive of the song as he drove us back from Asheville that foggy night. 'It's an old song,' he said. 'Lots of people know it.'

But that was a good thing for my purposes, wasn't it? An old song was just what I wanted. A traditional song. A song that everyone knew. I wanted everyone to join in. I looked again at the words. Funny how you can suddenly remember something so clearly. The narrator takes his 'lily-white maiden' for a 'ramble' 'down by the river'. While she is kneeling, he puts his hands around her neck as if to strangle her. She pleads with him, her eyes shining like 'diamonds in the sky'. But her killer does not relent. Instead, he strangles her and throws her body into the river. That night, as he lies in his bed, he thinks about 'the hangman's noose' that is surely waiting for him. The crime seemed strangely motiveless, although I remembered what Chuck had said about honour killings. Had she perhaps been unfaithful? Or had the narrator simply been drinking? Was he actually her lover, or was he a brother or a father? I also wondered about why the song had meant so much to me as a young girl. Perhaps it was the heightened drama of the life-and-death struggle. Little girls are so often bloodthirsty.

I took the book to the harmonium and tried to play the tune, the pedals wheezing as I pumped them. It seemed that the key the tune was written in wouldn't suit me at all. It was either too low or too high. It needed – what was the word? I dredged my memory. It needed 'transposing': that was it. I decided to forget about it; to find another song, something more suitable for a fun night with friends.

But as I went into the kitchen to make myself some coffee I found myself humming snatches of it. As I sang it to myself in the echoey kitchen, tidying, drying the dishes, putting things away, it sounded almost beautiful. Mournful. Fairly tuneful. Trey was right: I did have a nice voice. It was deep and a bit husky around the edges, and quite dramatic-sounding. I also thought that it was mostly in tune. Okay, so 'The Lily-white Maiden' it was going to be.

Cornell was delighted to help. Of course, I could have asked Jerry, but I wanted this to be a secret, a surprise for Trey, something I'd managed to do by myself. And as Cornell was as much my friend as Trey's, he seemed to be the right person to ask. He got me to sing the song a couple of times, 'a cappella', as he put it. He worked out the best key for me, and then pointed out to me a couple of places where I'd got the tune slightly twisted. Then, seemingly without any effort at all, he worked out a violin part and got me to sing the song again, this time as he accompanied me on the fiddle. It sounded good. I thought so, Cornell said so, and so did Gretchen, as she drifted into the room where we were working, a pile of damp washing in her arms. And so we hatched our plan: when Trey got back from Nashville next week, we'd have a jam session and I'd surprise him with my sudden and hitherto unexpected musical ability.

There was no way I could have guessed what would happen.

39

I t was a hot night. It'd been another humid day, and most of the muggy heaviness remained in the air. We sat outside on the back porch in a rough semicircle, on kitchen chairs and folding garden chairs and a couple of stools that Brett had brought round in the back of his truck. I wondered if he'd defied Linda Sue to come; if she'd tried to ban him from seeing me. Moths were gathering around the porch light and although the air was mostly still, every so often a fierce, sudden warm gust of wind blew, strong enough to clatter beer bottles to the ground. I was sitting in the creaky porch swing, doing my best to rock it in time to the music.

I nearly didn't do it. I nearly wimped out. I nearly decided to sit and listen, just lie back in the swing with my bottle of beer and soak up the atmosphere. Being in my own home made me feel that there was less pressure than at the last jam session. Cornell rolled a couple of joints and we passed them around. I was mellow, I was relaxed. We were all relaxed. It all felt spontaneous and unplanned, just a group of friends sharing songs. I couldn't remember why I'd been so stressed out by the last musical evening. And I wouldn't have done anything if it had not been for Cornell who – after a few seconds' silence between songs

– picked up his fiddle, played a few notes, and said, 'Have you got a song for us, Maeve?'

Trey was leaning over his mandolin and I'd swear that he smiled then, just a little secret, knowing smile that I wasn't supposed to see. Then he looked across at Cornell and shook his head. 'Maeve's not musical,' he said, smiling, as if quoting me. 'Hadn't you noticed?'

'Well, that's where you're wrong,' I said, and sat forward in the porch swing, planting my feet firmly on the ground so that it would stop swinging. 'Cornell, can you give me a G?' I said, with a confidence I didn't feel, and I had to smile as I saw Trey's stunned expression.

I closed my eyes to sing. I found it easier to stay in tune that way. I screwed my eyes tight shut and heard my perfectly adequate singing voice ring out, true and mournful, into the warm night air. I held the tune, while Cornell wove in and out of my vocal line on his fiddle. Of course I'm musical, I thought. This sounds great. Trey will be so impressed.

When I got to the bit about the narrator's hands around the girl's 'lily-white throat', I heard a sharp intake of breath from Jerry, who was sitting next to me on the left, and then Cornell abruptly stopped playing in the middle of a line, his bow clattering clumsily across the strings. When I opened my eyes I saw Jerry's face first. Aghast is the word, I think. But he was staring at Trey, not at me. I followed his stare. If Jerry was aghast, I'm not sure how I can describe the look on Trey's face. He was looking at me with his mouth open. Utterly dumbfounded. Horrified. 'What?' I said. 'What is it?'

'You . . . You can't . . . You don't . . .' was all he said. Then his hands shot up to cover his face and he stood up so abruptly that his chair fell over backwards with a loud clatter. He stumbled off the porch, hands still clasped to his face, and then I watched him walk away from the house, towards the path to the river, walking hesitantly like a blind man, his white shirt ghostly in the moonlight.

I turned back to the circle of musicians. Cornell looked as surprised as me; the others were looking at the ground, their hands, their instruments, in embarrassment or something. I turned to Jerry and asked again, 'What? What have I done?'

'It's that song,' he said.

'What about that song?'

'Maeve, we don't play that song.'

I looked at Cornell, a look that said: you should have told me. He simply shook his head at me and shrugged his shoulders. He looked baffled.

'Cornell wouldn't have known,' said Jerry. 'He's not known Trey that long. You wouldn't have known either. Trey doesn't play that song any more, not since Sarah died.'

Oh Jesus. Sarah. Sarah Swigert, who drowned in the river. You stupid, stupid woman. Why didn't you just think? I looked around. The other musicians were packing up to go. If I hadn't been so upset I would have found it funny: have you heard about Trey Ferguson's new wife? She turns every musical night into a drama.

'Jerry,' I said, 'tell me about Sarah. Tell me what happened.'

He shook his head. 'Maeve, go and talk to Trey. This is really between the two of you.'

In the moonlight things become two-dimensional. It's a cold light that flattens perspectives, shortens distances and casts its own weird shadows. As I trudged down the path to the river, and then along the river bank, towards Sarah's trailer, the trees on the horizon looked like a stage set: arching beams framing an open space where a lone actor sat, stage left, as if preparing to deliver a monologue.

Trey was sitting down on the grass, his long limbs folded in around him. In the moonlight his glasses loomed dark on his deathly pale face. He seemed an ethereal, flimsy thing. I sat down heavily next to him, my knees creaking as I did so, and I mentally cursed my substantiality. I felt out of place: an earthbound, clumsy, red-faced woman intruding on a beautiful moonlit Victorian painting.

'Sorry,' I said in what was supposed to be a whisper but came out way too loud. Trey didn't say anything, just wrapped his arms tight around his body as if he was in pain. Something about the gesture reminded me of me, the way I'd felt when I left Martin in the hospital for the last time. I swallowed hard and actually felt a physical pain in my left side, near my armpit, like a stitch or the early warning sign of a heart attack. I looked at Trey's face and could see that he was crying.

'Trey,' I whispered, managing to modulate my voice this time. 'I'm so sorry. I don't know what I've done, exactly. I know this is about Sarah, but I don't know what she was to you. All I know is, I've made you sad and I'm really sorry. Please talk to me.'

There was a long silence. I looked at Trey, who was staring straight ahead, staring at the river. It glistened in the moonlight, running fast and shallow over the rocky bed. On the other side of the river was a fringe of tall trees and beyond the trees I could see the zigzag outline of the mountains in the distance. The wind had risen. It was now whipping through the trees around us, setting the branches whispering and calling to each other. Any moment now the rain that had been promised all day would start to fall.

I looked back at Trey. Eventually, after what seemed like an eternity, he reached out his hand and found mine, his long fingers cold on my warm, sweaty skin. He interlocked his fingers with mine, which he drew to his lips and kissed. With my free hand I brushed away a dark lock of hair that had fallen into his eyes, and he looked at me with a surprised expression that was almost a smile.

'I shouldn't have come back here,' he said, gesturing at the trailer. 'You tell yourself that time heals everything but it doesn't. Grief. That's the word, isn't it? It lurks in dark corners and leaps out at you and . . .' He paused, as if searching for the right word. 'And hijacks you when you least expect it to.'

I was silent for a moment, remembering how I'd cried that night at the Borderline when Trey and I had first met. 'Trey, tell me about Sarah.'

He took a deep breath, and then began.

'Sarah Swigert was my first true love.' He laughed, as if it was a ridiculous idea. 'She was four years older than me, she lived in this old trailer and my grand-daddy said she was poor white trash.'

'Why?'

'She wore make-up and bright clothes, and she didn't go to church.'

'How did you get together?'

Trey tilted his head back and closed his eyes, remembering. 'Her clothes.'

'What do you mean?'

'Remember I told you I couldn't see too good when I was a kid? Well, I always noticed Sarah. She was always a riot of colour – oranges and purples and greens and reds, all worn together anyhow.' As Trey was talking I thought about the suitcase full of mouldy clothes in the trailer, all bright red and green. 'I gravitated towards her and she took me under her wing. She worked in the café, and I'd go and sit there for hours, making one coffee last all evening. She had a car and we'd go off together, down to Buchanansville or Boone or even Asheville, and look for thrift stores. She'd try on old clothes and she'd buy stuff, the brighter the better. She loved colours.' He smiled to himself. 'She would wear this sparkly turquoise eye make-up. It was kinda tacky, I guess, but it was Sarah.

'Another thing was, she loved to sing. She didn't have a great voice, not like Missy had, but she sang out loud and clear, and I taught her songs – all my grand-daddy's songs. I took her up to the house a few times, before my grand-daddy put a stop to it. I tried to teach her to play the harmonium. I thought that must be why she liked me, because I could teach her music and songs.' Trey laughed ruefully and shook his head. 'When I started wearing glasses and suddenly I could see people properly, I thought she'd drop me, that she'd stop feeling sorry for me. But it all changed in a different way. Suddenly fifteen and nineteen wasn't that big a gap. We were in love. We were wild and free and we loved each other. I'd never known anything like that before. I thought I was the luckiest guy in the whole world. We were going to get married but then she died and . . .' He swallowed hard. So did I. 'Well, you know what that feels like,' he said, and he wrapped his arms tightly around himself again.

I should have taken Trey in my arms and hugged him. I don't know why I didn't. My sheer English awkwardness, I guess. I don't do hugs very well. But I wish; I wish. Instead, as the thunder came and the skies finally broke open, I said, 'Tell me about the song.'

40

Trey took a while to answer. The sky rumbled and the rain fell in heavy sheets. The river rushed and swelled, getting faster and fuller all the time. I was chilled and soaked to the skin. I waited, and shivered, and waited. Eventually, his voice no more than a whisper, he began. 'It was her favourite. I don't know why. Why is it that women always like the saddest, most mournful songs? Anyway, she loved to sing it, in that loud, heartbreaking, natural voice of hers – just like yours, you know. We'd meet up down here by the river . . .'

I heard a hiccup in his voice and looked hard at him. There were still tears in his eyes, I think, although it was difficult to tell as the rain had drenched his hair and it was dripping down his face. '. . . And we'd sing that old murder ballad, and we'd laugh about it. And then she died, just like in the song.'

'What do you mean?'

'That's how she died. Like in the song. Down by the river.' His voice had become very calm and cold. 'That fall, the tail end of Hurricane Imogene whipped around here in the mountains. I've never known storms like it. The river was – well, like something alive. Hungry. Ravenous. Part of the river bank crumbled away. You could see debris and mud in the river. It was flowing in a dark brown torrent. Sarah was washed up twenty miles downstream. Her body was . . .' Trey paused, gulped, and wiped his eyes, pushed his hair off his face. 'Her body was badly damaged. Jerry drove me down to Buchanansville to identify her. There wasn't anyone else to do it. I'll always remember it. She'd been beaten against the rocks in the river. It looked like someone had beaten her to death.'

I let him cry for a while, and then I reached out and took his hand in mine. Again I wanted to hug him but I felt too big, as if I would crush him. 'Oh babes,' I said. 'I'm so sorry. Why didn't you tell me?'

Trey took a deep breath. He stood up. He stood in front of me, facing me. He held out his hands to me in what looked like a gesture of surrender. The pale hairless underside of his forearms looked as white as paper in the moonlight. He closed his eyes. He swayed suddenly. I thought he was going to faint. I stood up too, prepared to catch him if he fell.

'Why didn't I tell you? You know, Maeve, that's almost funny.' His voice was once again calm and cold. I felt my stomach churn with apprehension. 'Maeve, you heard the words of the song. Why didn't I tell you? Because I killed her. Sarah Swigert, my lily-white girl. I killed her. Just like in the song.'

I looked hard at him to try to read his expression, but his heavy, dark-framed glasses made hollows of his eyes. His dark hair was plastered to his skull. 'I killed her,' he said again, and then he stepped towards me. 'The two people I loved most in the world. My grandfather and my Sarah. I killed them both. On one day, I killed them both.'

I shivered again: cold or scared, or both. Trey came closer, and took hold of my hands. Then he put his right hand up to my cheek, caressing it with his thumb. His hand moved down to my neck, and then both hands were on my neck, his thumbs resting in the hollow of my throat. I was too scared to move. I could feel the strength in his thumbs. I could feel them pressing against my windpipe. I could hardly breathe, let alone swallow. Half of my brain was telling me he was about to kill me. Defend yourself, Maeve: you're big, you're strong, you're fearless. Fight him. Knee him in the balls. Whack him around the face. Don't let him do this to you. The other half was telling me something else: don't move. Don't move. He loves you. Don't do anything. Surrender to the moment.

In fact, I didn't have a choice. I was frozen to the spot. I closed my eyes and tried to breathe, to take shallow, level breaths. I could feel the rain running from my hair and dripping on to my face. I could feel Trey's breath on my face. I concentrated on the here and now; on actual things. Trey's breath: it smelled of beer and the joint we'd passed around the circle earlier that evening. His fingers: the hard ridges at the tips, the nails slightly longer on his right hand, digging into my neck. A particular drop of water that had found its way down my back and was pooling against the strap of my bra. Again, I measured my breathing, and then I realised with relief that Trey had eased his pressure on my neck. Now his hands had moved, and were caressing my cheeks again. I wondered if I'd imagined the whole thing. Trey's head was against my right cheek. His hair was wet on my face. I could feel the rim of his ear rub against my cheekbone. Now he was kissing me. 'Oh Maeve,' he said in an exhausted voice. 'Oh Maeve, I'm sorry. Hold me. Please hold me.'

But I didn't. I couldn't. I couldn't move. I stood there, arms rigidly against my sides like some big dummy. I opened my eyes. The moon was still in the sky. The river was still flowing in a torrent of muddy water. Nothing had changed. Everything had changed. 'Why did you come back here?' I asked, my voice sounding as constricted as my body felt. 'Why did you marry me and come back here to live? Here, of all places?'

And that was when Trey pulled away from me. He looked at me sadly. 'I wanted to come home. I thought you'd understand,' he said, and then he turned and stumbled away from me, back along the river bank towards the house.

41

I should have gone after him. I should have gone after him; I should have grabbed him, shaken him, made him tell me exactly what he meant. He killed Sarah Swigert? Really? Just like in the song? My gentle, loving husband? The man who'd just put his hands around my own throat as if to strangle me?

But I didn't. Of course I didn't. I sat down on the soaking wet, muddy ground; sat down and wept. The wind was still blowing hard, gusting with freakish vigour, whipping my hair around my face and howling in my ears. And I was howling too: weeping and sobbing as the rain fell from the sky, as if the whole year's rainfall was bucketing down in one storm. I curled my knees to my chest, wrapped my arms around my legs, rested my chin on my knees and made myself as small as possible. I was sitting in the wind and the rain by a fast-flowing river in a narrow valley thousands of miles from home, and I felt a whole year's worth of doubt and anxiety and grief pour out of me.

I had tried so hard to understand Trey. I had tried so hard to find out his secrets, but when it came to the crunch I couldn't help him. I couldn't reach out to him. He was in his own private hell.

'I killed her,' he had said. Really? Did he really mean it? Did he actually put his hands around her lily-white throat and squeeze the life out of her? I thought of the way he'd had his hands around my neck and the strength in those fingers. He could have strangled me in a moment. But he hadn't. I put my hand to the hollow of my throat and felt it. I'd have bruises there tomorrow: thumb-shaped bruises that people would notice and talk about. I thought of what Trey had said about killing Sarah and killing his grandfather. He'd talked about the river. He'd talked about how wild and ravenous it had been back then in the storm, the storm like this one. That was right, that was what Patsy had told me. She'd said that Sarah had drowned. She'd lost her footing and drowned. It was an accident. It must have been. But was it an accident caused by Trey? He'd said that he'd killed his grandfather. But his grandfather had had a stroke: something perfectly natural for a man of his age. It was what my own father had died of. Yes, Trey had been there; he'd probably even sparked the stroke by making his grandfather angry. But that didn't make him a killer. He was sixteen years old, for God's sake. A weedy, skinny sixteen-year-old. I'd seen that photo of him in the museum aged nineteen or twenty, scarcely strong enough to hold his guitar. How could he have killed two people in one day?

I don't know how long I sat there, but when I eventually came to stand up my feet had gone numb, my soaked clothes clung to my skin and my hair was plastered against my face and neck. I didn't want to go back to the house. I was afraid of what I might find there. Trey, still angry with me: white-faced and thin-lipped, his hands fastening again around my neck, tighter this time. My husband the killer. Or, and this picture was even more vivid, I could actually see it right in front of my eyes: Trey hanging from the beam in our bedroom, the beam he habitually bumped his head on. Trey, all long and narrow, his shoulders slumped in on themselves, strung up by the neck from that beam; his feet in his faded red Converse sneakers dangling uselessly beneath him. A weird sound came out of my mouth when I saw that picture.

Nonsense, I said to myself. Pull yourself together. I slapped my hand against my thigh once, twice, so hard that it hurt. And then I made my way back to the house.

All the windows were still open and the back door was banging shut and blowing open with each gust of wind. There was rainwater sloshed onto the kitchen floor that I nearly skidded on; some of the chairs on the back porch had been knocked over – by the wind, or by Trey blundering in? I turned on the kitchen light. I turned on all the lights in the house. I closed every window and searched every room. Trey wasn't there. He was nowhere to be seen. But when I went back into the kitchen I realised that the keys to the truck were missing.

The light went on in Jerry's workshop as I banged frantically on the door. He was pulling his shirt over his head as he opened the door. 'Maeve,' he said. From his face it was clear that I was the last person he expected to see.

'Jerry, Trey's gone. He's taken the truck.'

He looked at me with a question in his eyes.

'And I'm worried. He's in such a state. And he's been drinking, and smoking, and he's so upset . . .' Upset. Scarcely the best word to describe it, but what else could I say? My husband who is also your best friend seems to have turned into a homicidal maniac who has just tried to throttle me? I felt my throat again and wondered if the bruises had started to show yet. 'And Jerry, I'm scared. I'm really worried what he might do.' I must have looked a sight, with my muddy sandaled feet, my hair drying into tightly coiled curls and my clothes so wet that they were virtually transparent. I took deep breaths and tried to calm down. Eventually I forced out the words I wanted to say. 'Trey says he killed Sarah and his grandfather. But he didn't, did he? Please tell me he didn't.'

'Of course he didn't,' said Jerry in his slow, calm way; his very taciturnity was somehow reassuring. 'Of course he didn't,' he said again.

He picked up his keys from his workbench, handed me a waterproof coat and steered me out to his truck.

Jerry drove slowly, in silence for a while. At every side turning he slowed even more, peering into the darkness, looking for Trey's truck. After a while, when I thought I had my emotions under control, I asked him: 'Please tell me. Please tell me what happened all those years ago.'

'Maeve, it was nearly twenty years ago. It's long forgotten.'

'No, it isn't. That's the problem. It's my fault, I know, but I didn't know. I just wanted to know about my husband, I wanted to get to know him better, and instead I've opened up this whole can of worms, and I'm so worried.' My words turned into sobs.

Jerry sighed. He rubbed his top lip and then his chin. He squared his shoulders. And he started to talk as he drove.

'It was a weird year, that year. Hormones, I guess. We were coming up on sixteen, Trey and Missy and me. Trey had this friend, Sarah. Well, I reckon she was my friend as well. I always thought she was like Trey's big sister or something. But that year it changed. He told me they were lovers. And that she was pregnant.'

'And Trey was the father . . .'

Jerry frowned. Not at me, but as if he was working out something in his memory. 'Well, I reckon so. No reason to think anything else. Anyway, that was when he and his grand-daddy started to fight. Trey was spending time with Sarah, and he should have been at home doing the chores. I think it was the first time I ever heard him say anything against his grandfather.

'So one day Trey tells me that he and Sarah are getting married. The plan is, they're going to elope.' He stopped, and smiled to himself. 'I know it seems real old-fashioned now. But that was the plan. They were going off to Nashville, just the two of them, to get married. They'd set a date and everything.'

'Did everyone know that Sarah was pregnant?'

'Well, now. Sarah was a big girl. Kind of heavy-set,' and he seemed to look at me as he said that. 'You couldn't really tell until quite late on. I reckon most people just thought she was putting on some extra weight. The day they'd set to elope, she was maybe a month or two short of giving birth. It was a hot, wet day. Like today. Very humid, very wet.

'Now, Trey has always been very respectful, very honourable. He wanted to do the right thing. So at the last minute he decided to tell his grand-daddy what he was fixin' to do. He went to see the old man who was sitting in that front parlour, and he told him he was going to Nashville to get married, that very day. So that's when ol' CJ had a massive stroke. Apparently he just fell to the ground, right in front of Trey.'

'And so Trey thought he'd killed him.'

'That's right. He was just a kid, remember? There was nothing Trey could do, but he blames himself. And of course, all this time Sarah was waiting down by the river, waiting for Trey to take her away. By the time he got down there to tell her about what had happened to his grand-daddy, she'd gone. They found her body a few days later. We reckon she killed herself. And of course Trey blames himself for her death too. She was waiting for him. And he never turned up.'

Oh God. Oh God. That poor boy. Sixteen years old, just. So much tragedy in one day, his aunts had said.

And how. I couldn't say anything. I was choked up. I leaned my head against the cool glass of the truck window. I was trying to think; trying to put myself in Trey's shoes. What must it have been like? I could imagine his white, shocked face as he ran out to his aunts shouting, 'I've killed my grand-daddy.'

Maybe Trey had tried to save CJ. Maybe he'd loosened his grandfather's collar, or tried mouth-to-mouth, or any of the things I could imagine myself doing in those circumstances – frantic, blundering, desperate; trying to stay calm. And then, after all that, after all that grief and panic and agony, to lose Sarah and the baby in that awful, awful way; and to blame himself. All these years he'd blamed himself. 'Oh God,' I said again, this time out loud. 'Why the hell didn't he tell me?'

Jerry looked quickly at me, shrugged, and turned his stare back to the road.

I leaned against the window again. I'd just thought of something. I remembered a moment when maybe Trey had nearly told me about Sarah. Just after he proposed to me, when I was telling him about Martin, he'd said something like: 'I know what it's like to lose someone.'

But I'd been curt; defensive. I hadn't let him speak. I'd assumed he'd meant Missy, and I'd been annoyed that he could even think of comparing his divorce with my bereavement. I couldn't remember what I'd done or said. It must have been some kind of gesture that made him stop; that made him decide not to tell me. I should have let him speak. I should have listened to him like he'd listened to me.

Except: why should I blame myself? He could have

told me at any time. I thought about Trey and his emotions. I thought about how open and enthusiastic he could be; the way his face would light up; how ready he was to tell me how much he loved me. But he'd never told me any bad stuff, had he? He'd always clam up, refuse to answer the question. He couldn't do it. He just couldn't share his grief with me. I wondered if he'd ever spoken to Missy about it.

There was one more question I needed answering. 'Jerry, if Trey was so much in love with Sarah, how come he married Missy that same year?'

Jerry gave me a quick, grim smile. 'Because she was sweet to him. That's what he always says. She was there, you see. There in the house when his grandfather died. She was his friend when he needed one. She latched right on to him. And after they buried Sarah and his grand-father, they got to thinking that there was nothing keeping them in Bodie's Hollow, so off they went together.'

She was sweet to him. She was his friend when he needed one. That's all. That's all it was. And there I was, being ridiculously jealous of Missy Ferguson when I should have been jealous of Sarah Swigert. 'Good luck!' Missy had said on the flowers she sent me. Now I knew what she'd meant. She'd tried to take on the ghost of Sarah Swigert and had lost. Now it was my turn.

'Jerry, where are you going?' We'd been driving for nearly twenty minutes, seemingly in circles around the twisty mountain roads.

'There's a place Trey and Sarah used to go and park. Up on Eagle Knob. I think he might have gone there.'

Jerry's mouth was set in a straight line across his face, and I think he was as worried as me. The road climbed in a switchback fashion, with sudden sharp turns. Trees overhung the road to our left, but to our right I could see that the mountainside fell away sharply: there was nothing to keep the car on the road. As we climbed higher the road swerved suddenly to the left but I could see a faint light below us on the right-hand side. A faint red light. Two faint red lights. 'Jerry,' I said, going cold all over. 'What's that down there?'

The truck had swerved off the road and come to a stop against a tree that was twenty feet or more down the side of the mountain. The bonnet was crumpled and concertina-like. I clambered down, my heart in my mouth. In the driver's seat was my husband, slumped over the steering-wheel, no air bag. Blood was flowing from cuts on his face; the windscreen was shattered into tiny pieces and his glasses were broken. I reached out and took hold of his cold hand and held it as if my life depended on it.

42

I have spent far too much of my life in hospital waiting rooms. Time spent in a waiting room isn't time, exactly: it's just a blank, something suspended. It doesn't follow time's usual rules. It goes faster or slower at will.

Moments I will always remember from hospital waiting rooms: after my father's third stroke, the one before the one that killed him, I sat and waited while Mickey paid one of his usual flying visits between gigs, parties, whatever. I wanted to give them some time alone together, so I sat in the waiting room and I waited and watched as a little girl of five or so rearranged all the seat cushions in the room. There were alternate brown and beige chairs in the waiting room, and she worked her way around the room singing to herself, moving the cushions so that every brown chair had a beige seat and vice versa. When she got to the chair I was sitting in, she stood there shyly until I stood up to let her change the cushion. And that's what I'll always remember about the day before my dad died: a little girl and some seat cushions. Mickey flew back into the room, didn't notice the cushions, kissed me, said, 'Thanks, Maeve, you're so good at this sort of thing,' and left in tears. The next day my father had a fourth stroke and died.

And then there were all the times I sat in waiting rooms, waiting for news about Martin, and feeling the awkwardness of being with his mother and his sister. I remember sitting with Karen one day and she was reading some gossip magazine, and she kept saying stuff like, 'I didn't know she was going out with him,' and 'That would be a good look for you, Maeve.'

I desperately wanted to respond to her overtures of friendship but I couldn't because I'd been crying so hard all night that I literally couldn't speak. And I sat there, my stomach all tied up in knots, almost forgetting about Martin because I desperately wanted to say something, anything, in response to his sister's comments so that she wouldn't think I was a snob.

And here I was again, watching the sun rise over downtown Buchanansville from the window of the hospital waiting room, drinking disgusting cups of vending-machine coffee that Jerry kept fetching for me, feeling the plastic of the cheap chair cut into my thighs, aimlessly flicking through an out-of-date business guide to Campbell County and instead of grief, instead of worry, all I seemed to be feeling was anger. I was getting crosser and crosser with Trey. I'd had no sleep and I felt dead inside: defeated. All I could think was: how dare he? How dare he put me through this again? He drives off into the rain and crashes his stupid truck, and here I am, all over again, in the waiting room of another fucking hospital, waiting for someone else to die.

I snapped at Jerry when he brought me the fifth cup of

coffee. I sent him home. 'Please, Jerry, just go. I'll be all right.'

It didn't occur to me that he had just as much right to be there as I did; that he loved Trey and cared for him, and was desperate to know if he was all right. I sent him home and he left.

And then, blame the sleepless night or the emotional switchback that I'd been riding, but I must have drifted into some kind of waking sleep. Because when the apparently teenaged doctor came out to see me with a broad smile on his face, I thought for one brief, shivery second that he was about to tell me that Martin had come back to life.

The doctor sat down next to me and said, 'Mrs Ferguson, I'm pleased to tell you your husband will be just fine.'

I blinked, woke up, and for a moment I felt absolutely nothing. Trey had concussion, a couple of broken ribs and a few cuts. That was all. My husband drives his truck off a mountainside while drunk, distraught and doped, and he escapes with not much more than a slight headache.

'Oh, okay,' I managed to say.

'We're going to keep him in for a couple of days, just to keep an eye on him.'

'Okay,' I said in the same flat voice.

The doctor gave me a strange look. 'I have to tell you, I'm delighted to meet you. I'm a great admirer of your husband and his music.' He looked at me expectantly, obviously expecting more emotion: pleasure, relief, gratitude maybe. But I didn't have any feelings left to offer him. I was too exhausted to feel anything. It was as if any emotion would have been too heavy for me to lift to the surface. He continued: 'Would you like to see your husband now?'

I shrugged, nodded and then followed the doctor down a medicinal-smelling corridor to a small room at the end.

Trey looked ridiculously young with his face all stitched and bruised. He smiled a weak smile as I sat next to him and held his hand. He squinted at me – no glasses – and then seemed to give up and closed his eyes instead. 'Sorry,' he whispered.

Sorry: probably the most-used word in our relationship. How many times can you apologise to each other? How many hurts, injuries, misunderstandings, secrets can one brief marriage sustain? 'That's okay,' I whispered back. Okay. As if. It was all very far from okay.

'I can't remember much,' he said. 'What happened? What did I do?'

I let go of Trey's hand. I wrapped my arms tightly around myself. What could I say? You tried to strangle me and then you drove your truck off a mountainside, and I don't know if either act was deliberate or not? I stared at Trey for a while. He opened his eyes and gazed at me, a puzzled look on his face. I shook my head slowly, and then I stared at the wall opposite me. There was a picture on the wall, a scenic photograph of the mountains, the kind of thing you'd get on a calendar. I bit my lip and then I buried my face in my hands. Oh God, what on earth was

I doing here, with this man? How come he was looking to me for answers, comfort, whatever? Who was he? How the hell did I get here? Finally I felt some emotions flood to the surface. I wanted to surrender to them. I wanted to let the waves of grief and hurt flood over me; I wanted to sob my heart out. But I didn't. I didn't, because Trey would have thought the emotions were for him, for him to share. And they weren't. They were mine alone. I knew I needed to be on my own.

I picked up his hand again, squeezed it lightly and said, 'It was a strange night.'

43

I sat on the orange couch in the kitchen, listening to the rain beat down on the roof of the old Ferguson homestead. I got myself a bowl of hot soapy water and a towel, and I washed my feet, still muddy from where I'd climbed down to the river bank in my sandals. I smoked the tail-end of a joint left in an ashtray on the kitchen table after the abortive jam session. I drank what was left in all the beer bottles. I finished off an opened bottle of red wine. I sat there while the sky got darker and the fierce downpours exhausted themselves and turned into grey evening drizzle, and I tried to put my thoughts and emotions in order.

Trey needed help. That was obvious. He needed to work through his past traumas before he could move on. That was what a therapist would say. That was what he needed: therapy. He needed to learn to talk about his feelings of grief and guilt. Okay. That was, if not simple, at least do-able. It was something practical he could achieve. But where did that leave me? Marriage counselling? Is that what we needed? Could it be as mundane as that? I felt my throat. It hurt when I swallowed. I could still feel Trey's hands around my neck. Had he meant to hurt me? If he had, I could just walk away. I *should* just walk away. Physical abuse: it's not something to work through; it's something to walk out on. It's a marriage-ender, no two ways about it. And yet, and yet: had Trey really meant to hurt me? He was the gentlest, most loving man I'd ever met. His hands had been around my throat for a matter of seconds, surely, and then they'd moved to my face. He'd kissed me. It had been a tender embrace.

Oh Jesus. I needed a friend. But who? Who on earth could I talk to about this? I looked at my watch. It was nearly nine o'clock. I thought about ringing Helen, but it'd be two in the morning back in England, and if I rang her now she'd assume it was something urgent and react accordingly. She'd misunderstand. No one can cope with subtleties when they're woken in the middle of the night. She'd hear me tell her about Trey's hands around my neck and she'd tell me to leave him. And anyway, there was something I was only just on the verge of admitting to myself: something that I wouldn't be able to admit to anyone else. In my heart of hearts, it wasn't Trey's hands around my throat that had upset me the most. What was really, truly upsetting me was a disturbing thought that kept popping up in my head: Trey had only married me because I reminded him of Sarah Swigert.

Look at the evidence: I had a singing voice like hers; I, too, was 'heavy-set' (in Jerry's delicate phrase). Patsy in the café had said that Sarah was direct and honest, and that's exactly what Trey had said he loved about me – my fearless heart, as he'd put it in the song he gave to Missy. Even the colours I wore: it was my lime-green shirt he had noticed that first night at the Borderline, and then the clashing orange and pink when I picked him up at the airport. Sarah always wore bright colours — that was one of the things he had loved about her.

I reminded Trey of his first love so he married me. Was that it? Was that all? If it was, it was a humiliating truth for me to have to face. If that was all I was to Trey then I should leave him. I should fly home, go back to my dear old grotty flat in South London and tell my friends it just hadn't worked out. But I felt a pain in my chest when I thought of doing that. I pictured Trey: the way he walked, the way he touched me, the way he laughed. Oh God, I loved him; and in a weird way that made me feel even worse about everything.

Enough; enough with the over-analysis. What good was it doing me? I uncorked another bottle of red wine and poured myself a glass. I opened the fridge door and stared at the contents for a while, as if they'd provide an answer to something. I pulled out some cheese and some ham and I made myself a sandwich. I turned on the television and forced myself to eat while I watched an episode of *CSI*. Gil Grissom and his team solved a multiple murder by measuring the trajectory of blood spatter, and they did it within the space of an hour. Life's so simple on TV, isn't it? I wondered what they'd make of Sarah Swigert's death.

Suicide, said Jerry. Accident, said the townsfolk. I wonder what the inquest verdict was. If there'd been one: I didn't know how these things worked in small-town backwoods America. Sarah was down at her trailer, packing her clothes in the suitcase, waiting for Trey to arrive. They were going to elope. They were going to go to Nashville together, that glittering, golden city full of opportunity; that Mecca of country music. And then she jumped or she fell. She lost her footing or she deliberately launched herself into the river, and the ravenous, dirty, muddy water swept her downstream, battering her against the rocks so that she was almost unrecognisable.

I sat on the edge of our bed. I looked at the beam above the bed and it gave me the creeps. The picture I'd had in my head last night, of Trey hanging from that beam, his sneakers dangling, was so vivid that I still couldn't banish it. I took some deep breaths and thought hard. I made a decision. I'd sleep here tonight, but tomorrow I'd leave. I'd go and find a motel somewhere down in Buchanansville. I couldn't stay in this house on my own. It would drive me mad. I needed somewhere else, somewhere where I could think more clearly about things. I'd pretend to everyone that I was in Buchanansville so that I could be nearer to Trey in hospital. I didn't want to admit that I was scared to be alone in the house; scared of what it would do to me.

I got one of my suitcases out of the wardrobe. I pulled handfuls of clothes and underwear from the chest of drawers and crammed them into the case. I threw a couple of pairs of shoes in on top and tried to close the case. And then, overcome by tiredness, I went to the bed, lay down and simply fell asleep.

I hadn't pulled the curtains before going to sleep so it was the sunrise that woke me. The first thing I saw was my suitcase, clothes spilling out of it, still not closed properly. And that was when I knew for certain that Sarah Swigert's death was neither suicide nor an accident. Someone had killed her.

44

Sarah hadn't finished packing her suitcase. That was how I knew she hadn't killed herself; that was how I knew it hadn't been an accident. She hadn't closed the suitcase properly. She was still trying to force her favourite clothes into the case. Think about it. She was eloping with her teenage lover, the father of her unborn child. She had no reason to doubt he'd turn up. He'd told her what time he'd be there, so she would have packed her case and got herself ready. After packing, she would have done her make-up. She would have sat on one of the couches in that cramped trailer and applied that shiny turquoise eyeshadow that she used to wear. What she wouldn't have done was half-pack her suitcase and then wander down to the river.

She was killed. Someone interrupted her while she was packing. Someone who was angry that she was eloping. And who would that someone be? Who was angry about her eloping with Trey? CJ Ferguson, of course.

It took me well over an hour to drive to Boone this time. Orange cones and teams of workmen were out in force, repairing the damage from the last few days' storms, and I was held up several times by workmen with *Stop* signs. It was a clear blue day with a welcome autumnal chill, and to my right I watched the bright sun climb into the sky. Bright tints of red and orange were showing among the massed green of the trees that covered the mountains.

Despite the delays I was still far too early to make a surprise call when I reached Boone. I pulled into the busy parking lot of a big restaurant and went in to have breakfast, picking a choice almost at random from the four-page menu. While I drank my sticky strong coffee and waited for my pancake platter I watched the local news on the giant TV screen in the corner of the restaurant. The Blue Ridge Parkway had been ravaged by the wind and rain, parts of it falling away and crumbling into the mountainside. Large sections of the road were closed as repair teams worked against the clock to get it reopened in time for the prime leaf-peeping season, just a couple of weeks away. A glossy female reporter in a bright red trouser suit stood by the side of the road, over-emphasising wildly, her eyebrows semaphoring the story she was telling. Another reporter, this time in Asheville: I recognised the area near the entrance to Biltmore House. Flooding: businesses wrecked, stores and restaurants closed. Again, a race against the clock. Tourism in this area was all about fall visitors. Just two weeks to get the mess cleared up. I thought back to the night before last, standing by that rushing river with Trey, chasing him through the night in Jerry's truck. He could have died. He'd escaped with concussion and broken ribs. Maybe someone had been watching over us. Maybe Trey was right to believe in God.

Trey's aunts were surprised and not particularly pleased to see me. I think they were about to go out. Nancy had a beret on, and was holding a coat in her hands when she opened the door to me. But I burst in like a force of nature and, being the polite Southern gentlewomen they were, they had to offer me iced tea.

'I need to know,' I said breathlessly, as though we were in the middle of a conversation that we'd already started. 'I need to know everything about that day. The day your father died. I need to know what happened to him, and I need to know what happened to Sarah Swigert.'

Nancy breathed in sharply and looked at Jean. Jean looked back at her and it looked as though some kind of unspoken agreement was being reached between them. 'Oh my dear,' said Jean. 'You know about Sarah Swigert.'

'Yes,' I said. 'She was Trey's girlfriend. She was pregnant. That's who Trey was planning to marry. That's why your father was so angry. Trailer trash, that's what he called her.'

Jean nodded. 'He always hoped he'd marry Missy. She was such a charming girl, and so musical. I'm sure he would have been quite happy if Trey had announced that day he was marrying Missy. But instead, he told him he had got that . . . waitress pregnant and was eloping with her. She was nearly twenty years old. She was four years older than poor Trey. He didn't know what he was doing.'

'Yes, he did,' said Nancy, unexpectedly. Jean glared at her. 'He did know. He was in love with her. He always knew his own mind, did Trey. Love. You remember that, Jean. Remember when you were in love with that boy who used to work over at the Hamilton place? But father wouldn't let you see him, and you had that fearsome row. Trey was just like you.'

Jean coloured, and looked at her hands in her lap. I'd swear there was a glint of something young in her bright blue eyes.

'Did your father know about Trey and Sarah before he told him?'

'Oh no,' said Nancy. 'It came as a complete surprise.'

'Did it?'

They both nodded vigorously. But something didn't ring true. I remembered something that Trey had told me, during that phone conversation after I'd been to see his aunts for the first time. 'If your father didn't know about Trey and Sarah, then why did he change his will?'

They looked shocked. 'What do you mean?' It was Jean who asked.

'CJ Ferguson changed his will, didn't he? He left you the rights to all his music and Trey just got the house.'

They both stared at me.

I continued. 'Surely Trey was the musical one. Surely your father would have left him the rights to his music. He saw him as his rightful heir, didn't he? He took him on stage with him. I've seen the photographs. So why did he change his will?'

It was Nancy who eventually spoke. 'Trey kept a diary.

He hid it in the fireplace in his bedroom. Our father found it. It was with some dirty magazines, and he was angry about those to start with. Until he started reading the diary. That was when he got even angrier. That was when he found out about Sarah.'

'He put the diary back.'

Nancy and Jean both gave me curious looks.

I was working it all out in my head. I knew what had happened. I continued: 'He put the diary back. So Trey wouldn't know he'd read it.'

Nancy nodded. 'He wanted Trey to tell him himself.'

'But your father definitely knew that Trey and Sarah were planning to elope on his birthday before Trey told him?'

'Yes.' It was Nancy who said it. Jean was staring at her fingers again.

'Last time we spoke, you told me about that day, the day your father died. You told me Trey was pacing around the house trying to pluck up the courage to talk to his grandfather. Was he? Was he just trying to pluck up the courage or was he waiting for his grandfather? Waiting for his grandfather to come back?'

Again, the look of unspoken communication. Eventually it was Jean who spoke. 'Yes. Our father had gone out.'

'Where?'

'We don't know.'

'He might have been doing some chores.' Nancy piped up in a hopeful tone of voice. 'There was a storm brewing. He might have gone across to see old Ma Hamilton, to check her storm doors were working. He might have been bringing extra wood in for the kitchen range.'

'You think you know what he was doing, don't you?' I looked pointedly at Jean.

This time her clear blue-eyed stare met mine. It held me with a long, steady gaze. Eventually she spoke, clearly and precisely, as if she'd often rehearsed the words. 'I'm very much afraid of what he might have been doing. I have always wondered whether he killed Sarah Swigert.'

I said nothing for a while. Jean stood up and went over to the window, and seemed intent on learning the view by heart. Nancy tried to smile, fidgeted for a while, fluttered her hands and then ran out into the hallway, clutching a tissue to her mouth.

'So why did you never tell anyone what you suspected?'

Jean continued to look out of the window. Then she said, in a voice that reminded me of Trey's at its chilliest: 'My father CJ Ferguson. The Preacherman. The god-father of country music. How could I possibly accuse him of having been a murderer?'

45

The front parlour of the old Ferguson homestead:
still dusty, still smelly. I looked around at the
furniture, the wallpaper, the picture above the
mantelpiece: Adam and Eve, hunched and ashamed of
what they'd done, expelled from Paradise, as storm clouds
gathered in the sky. I stood in the middle of the room and
tried again to take myself back to that day. Trey, nervous
and pacing, waiting for his grandfather to come back from
wherever he'd been. CJ Ferguson, in his seventies but still
fierce and strong and determined enough to push Sarah
Swigert into the river to her death. Then he'd staggered
up the muddy path from the river. It had been pouring
with rain; the old man would have been cold and
exhausted when he'd arrived back. No wonder the argument with Trey had been enough to kill him.

The smell of the room set my teeth on edge. I walked
around it aimlessly, touching walls, the curtains; sitting
down at the harmonium, getting up again. Leaning on the
mantelpiece, I kicked the boarded-up fireplace. I was
frustrated: I felt sick, claustrophobic, trapped. I grabbed
one of the porcelain ornaments from the top of the radio
and I threw it hard across the room, watching it smash
against the wall and then fall to the floor in pieces. I kicked

at the piece of board in the fireplace again, wanting to lash out in all directions. It wobbled and, impatiently, I knelt down to pull it out, meaning to chuck it across the room.

There was something there. Just as there had been in Trey's old bedroom. There was something in the fire basket, lying in the grate as Trey's secret stash had been.

It was a small red bundle. I looked more closely. Red Paisley with a fringe: a shawl of some sort. I touched it, hesitantly. The shawl was old and faded but looked as if it had once been good-quality. I touched it again, trying to work out if there was something wrapped in the shawl. I felt something hard under my fingers. I sat back on my haunches and put my hands in front of my mouth. I felt sick. The stale smell was stronger, and seemed to be coming from the bundle. I took some deep breaths and dared myself to pick it up.

It was light. Very light. My hands trembled as I gently removed it from the fire basket. It felt fragile, like something that would break, that could easily be crushed. It felt almost like a dead bird, a large bird that crashes into your window and kills itself and you have to wrap it in newspaper and throw it away. I put it gently on the rag rug by the fireplace. With shaking hands I began to unwrap the bundle. As I put one hand inside the shawl my fingers came into contact with something cold. I forced myself to continue. As I delicately peeled back a corner of the shawl I saw something creamy-white that looked like part of a ribcage.

It was a baby. There in front of me, lying on the red Paisley shawl, was a baby. The skeleton of a tiny baby, its skull, its spine and all its little fingers and toes still perfectly intact.

46

The sheriff's deputy had a star-shaped badge, a gun in his holster and a slow, reassuring Southern accent. He called me 'Mizz Ferguson'.

'Now, Mizz Ferguson,' he was saying as I sat on the couch in the kitchen, still in shock, trying to drink the glass of iced tea that rattled in my shaking hand. 'Tell me again how you came to look in the fireplace.'

'I don't know,' I said. 'I just noticed the piece of board was loose. I guess I wanted to know if we could use the fireplace. Maybe have an open fire. With the weather turning cold. You know.'

'Did you expect to find anything there? Did you know something was hidden there?'

I shook my head.

'Do you have any idea whose baby it might be?'

'I've only been living here since this summer,' I said. Not an answer to his question but not a lie either. 'Can you tell how old it is, just by looking at it?'

'Oh no,' he said. 'We'll have to get the forensic scientists on to that. The Campbell County Sheriff's office isn't really equipped for that kind of thing. We'll have to get the state boys in.'

I suddenly visualised the CSI team swooping on the

house, Gil Grissom and the rest of the gang, sticking yellow crime-scene tape across the doorway of the front parlour, dusting the whole room for prints. I wrapped my arms around myself, pulled my knees up to my chin and wished I'd never gone looking for answers.

It was Jerry who'd called the sheriff's office, not me. I'd simply knelt on the floor staring at the baby for a long time. I'd gone out to the kitchen, out to the field at the back of the house and paced around. I was hoping it would all just go away but when it didn't I rang good old Jerry and he took control.

'We'll need to speak to everyone who's lived in this house,' the deputy was saying. 'Everyone who's still alive, that is. That includes your husband, I'm afraid. I'm sure this has nothing to do with him, but—'

'You know, the house has been empty for nearly twenty years,' I cut in quickly. 'Maybe someone was squatting here?' I said it without conviction.

Jerry said quietly to the deputy, 'Mr Ferguson's in the hospital. Down in Buchanansville. You'll need to go down there to see him.'

'Will you let me go first?' I asked. 'I think I should be the one to tell him what we've found.'

Trey was sitting up in bed watching a daytime soap, his broken glasses mended with surgical tape and balanced precariously on his nose. He smiled at me and raised his hand hesitantly in greeting. 'Hi,' he said, a note of reproach in his voice. 'I was wondering if you'd be coming to see me.'

I leaned over and kissed him briefly, and then sat down heavily in the chair beside the bed. 'Trey, I need to tell you something.'

He hunched his shoulders with that apprehensive shrinking gesture I now knew so well. 'You're leaving me.' He picked up the remote control and turned the television off. 'You're leaving me, aren't you?'

I gave a loud laugh that made me sound as if I was on the verge of hysteria. I picked up Trey's hand and squeezed it to reassure him; to reassure myself as well. 'The thing is, Trey, I was in the front parlour and I found something in the fireplace.'

'In the fireplace in the front parlour?'

'Yes.'

'What were you looking there for?'

'Trey, it doesn't matter. Listen.' I rubbed his hand with my thumb, as he'd done so many times to me. 'Trey, I found a baby.'

'A baby?' He looked at me as if I was mad.

'A baby's –' I held my hand to my mouth as I gagged. '– body. The body of a tiny baby. Just a skeleton.'

Trey sat up suddenly, and then clutched his cracked ribs, his face convulsed in pain. His hand tightened around mine. 'Maeve, what are you saying?'

'There was a baby's body hidden in the fireplace of the front parlour.' I could hear my voice shaking as I said it.

I looked quickly at Trey. His face was almost green. I thought he was about to be sick.

'A baby? A dead baby? In our house? Why? I mean, who? Whose baby?'

'Trey, the baby was wrapped in a shawl. It was a red shawl. Paisley print. Quite old. It looked like it might have been second-hand, and the thing is . . .' I felt my voice shaking. I held his hand even tighter. I looked down at it, looked at the dark hair against the pale skin, the calluses on the ends of his fingers. 'The thing is, Trey, I thought the shawl might have belonged to Sarah. Your friend Sarah. The kind of thing she might have worn, from what you've told me. I think it might be your baby. The baby that Sarah was expecting.'

'Oh God,' said Trey. 'Oh God, sweet Jesus, no,' and his eyes suddenly filled with tears.

'Sarah had a shawl like that.' We were still holding hands as if our lives depended on it. Trey had dried his tears but he still looked green. 'She bought the shawl down in Asheville, at that thrift store I took you to. It must have been her baby.'

'Trey, what happened?'

He gave me a wild look. 'I don't know. I don't know. I just don't understand it.'

'Trey, you and Jerry went down to Buchanansville to identify Sarah's body, didn't you?'

He nodded.

'So you must have known that she wasn't still pregnant.'

'What do you mean?'

'I mean, you must have known that she wasn't still pregnant when she died.'

Trey turned and stared at me. 'What are you saying?'

'I suppose I'm asking you why you never wondered what had happened to your baby.'

'What is this? Some kind of accusation?'

I shook my head. 'No, Trey. I'm just trying to get you to work out what happened.'

'Maeve, I don't know what you're driving at. I was sixteen years old and my grandfather and my girlfriend had both died, on the same day. I had to identify her body, this awful, battered body. They showed me her face. It was Sarah. It was the hardest thing I've ever had to do. I didn't look at the rest of her body. I didn't know whether she was still pregnant. I didn't ask.'

'Trey, how do you think the baby got into the house?'

'I don't know.' He gave me a sharp glance. 'Why? Do you know what happened?'

Deep breath. I had to tell him what I suspected. What else could I do? 'I think your grandfather killed Sarah and the baby. How else could it have ended up in the fireplace? Nothing else makes sense.'

Trey let go of my hand. In fact, he almost slapped it away. 'No,' he said angrily. 'No. No, you're wrong. My grand-daddy would never do something like that.'

As I left the room I said gently, 'Trey, I know you're angry, but this isn't going to go away. The sheriff's on his way down here to talk to you. I don't know what they do then, how they identify the baby. I think they'll need to take some kind of DNA test from you or something. But anyway, it won't take long before he knows it's your baby and he'll want to know how it got there. So you're going to have to prepare yourself to face it.'

'Was the baby full-term?'

Trey's question took me by surprise. His voice seemed strangely cold. I snapped. 'Jesus, Trey, I just found the bloody thing. It doesn't make me an expert on baby skeletons. What difference does it make, anyway?' And with that I stormed out, not waiting for his answer.

47

It was a night full of bad dreams. I'd meant to get a motel room, of course, but somehow when I left Trey in the hospital I felt as if I needed to be back at the house, as if even more bad things would happen if I left. Julie came round in the evening, agog over the rumours that she'd heard. She had the idea that the baby must have belonged to one of Trey's aunts. She had this colourful picture in her head of the widowed CJ Ferguson having his wicked way with one of his unmarried daughters, and the family hushing up the whole incestuous business. I let her continue with her misunderstanding because I was too exhausted and confused to correct her. We drank wine and ate cheese and chips and olives – all I had in the house, still left over from the jam session that now seemed like weeks ago. She asked if I was all right to spend the night there on my own and I told her of course I was. And then the night was full of dreams about a lily-white maiden with eyes like diamonds, and CJ Ferguson with his hands around her neck, strangling her. Sometimes CJ Ferguson became Trey or even the sheriff, and the bundle in the shawl turned out to be a bird that fluttered away up the chimney, its wings flapping frantically as it tried to get out.

It was the wheezing noise that woke me.

I sat bolt upright in bed, sweating from yet another nightmare, and heard that sound. I looked at my bedside clock. It was late – past eleven in the morning. Outside the window the sky was grey and heavy with fog. I'd tossed and turned but must have eventually fallen into a deep, heavy sleep, because it was now more than ten hours since I'd gone to bed.

That sound. I knew it instantly. A wheezing noise, as someone pumped the pedals on the old harmonium. And then a tune began to play, a tune I knew only too well. The notes wound around each other like a twisting vine: an old, old tune that had travelled all the way from Scotland, or Ireland, or somewhere else back in the old country. An old, old tune about a lily-white maiden pleading for her life.

How can I tell you what it felt like, lying there in bed and hearing that tune? For a few moments I literally thought I was dreaming. I must still be asleep, I told myself. I even pinched myself, like they used to do in Enid Blyton books, just to check whether I was dreaming. I wasn't.

I shuddered. I gathered the bedclothes around me and tried to collect my thoughts. My heart was beating so hard that I thought it would burst out of my ribcage. I really do not believe in ghosts, I promise you that. But as I pulled on a T-shirt and jeans and gingerly made my way along the creaking floorboards towards the stairs, at least half my mind thought that I would find Sarah Swigert sitting at the harmonium, her hair dripping down her back, her face bruised and bloody from the battering of the river against the rocks, her eyes replaced by two diamonds, like in my nightmare. She'd come back to reclaim her baby, only to find that it wasn't there.

It's so easy to scare yourself stupid when you put your mind to it.

The harmonium stopped. As I reached the top stair it stopped, abruptly, in the middle of the tune. I thought I heard the front door swing open and closed. I thought I heard footsteps running away from the house. There was no one in the parlour – I checked. But the harmonium lid was open and the stool was crooked, as if someone had pushed it away in a hurry. I hadn't been dreaming. I slipped my feet into my sandals and pushed the front door open. It was unlocked. Through the fog I thought I could see someone – or something – slipping into the trees that led to the path down to the river.

Someone was leading me down there. Down to the trailer. I stumbled down that path again, catching glimpses from time to time of the person ahead of me. I couldn't shake the idea that it was Sarah herself. I got to the river. I could barely see the opposite bank, the fog was so thick. It was a dry, calm day, but despite that, the river was running faster than I'd ever seen it, the water full of mud and debris from the mountains. I looked around, but couldn't see anyone: no movement, no sign of colour apart from the leaves. I ran to the trailer and went inside – what was I going to find? The suitcase was still there, half-packed. I felt that it was telling me something.

I tried to put myself in Sarah's place. A nineteen-year-old pregnant woman in love with a weird, quirky sixteen-year-old boy? Why not? Or was she? Maybe she just judged him to be a safe bet. Talented and sweet – he'd be good to her, better than her father had been. Okay, what would stop her packing her suitcase? Think, Maeve. Remember what Jerry had said. She was only a month or two short of giving birth when she died. I suddenly saw the point of Trey's question: was the baby full-term? Maybe Sarah was further along than she'd said. Maybe it wasn't Trey's baby at all. Maybe the father was some old boyfriend she'd known before. Maybe she was nine months pregnant, not seven or eight. Suppose she went into labour. Suppose her waters broke. She goes into labour while she's still packing her case.

What would she do? Call for help? Who would hear her? Who would help? Could she make her way into town? No. No. Too far, too dangerous along that path. No sign of a phone, either. Think. Sarah Swigert: solid, practical, scared of nothing. Much like me. She wouldn't panic. It's childbirth, for God's sake. It's only natural. Women have been doing this for years. She'd squat down – here – in the corner of the trailer by the couch, one hand on the side of the built-in cupboard to support herself as each contraction racked her body in pain. She'd start taking those little panting breaths that they teach you to do – like this – and she'd feel the baby coming. She'd feel it slithering out of her as she screamed in agony. The baby would fall to the floor. She picks it up, cradles it against her. It's not making a sound. It isn't moving. She looks around her wildly, desperately, looking for help. And then, as if in answer to a prayer, she hears footsteps. It's Trey. But as she looks up at the tall figure that enters the trailer she realises it's not Trey at all. It's the one person in the world that she's scared of. CJ Ferguson. The Preacherman. Trey thought he didn't know about Sarah but of course he knew. He'd read Trey's diary. Why else would he have changed his will? CJ Ferguson, a man who made his own son give up his child so the boy wouldn't be raised out of wedlock. How could he let his own great-grandchild be brought up by a mother who conceived the child out of wedlock? He towers over her. He takes hold of what he assumes is his own flesh and blood. Clyde James Ferguson IV, maybe. And then what happens? Sarah pleads with him for her baby back. She crawls – staggers – out of the trailer, chasing after him. She begs for her baby back. Does he hit her? Does he knock her into the water? Does he fasten his big, strong hands around her lily-white neck and throttle her as she begs for her life? Or does he just leave her there, distraught, and then, overcome by the physical exertion and the wild swings of emotion of a woman who has just given birth, she throws herself into the ravenous brown river?

So CJ Ferguson, proud, unbending, self-righteous, still strong in his seventies, climbs back up the steep path to the house he built, clutching his great-grandson to his chest. And that's what kills him – the strain of the walk, or the realisation of what he's just done, or the discovery that the

baby is dead – and he gets back to the house and he hides
the baby in the first place that he can think of. A hiding
place he'd know about, because he'd found Trey's diary
upstairs in the fireplace. And then his beloved, misguided
grandson is telling him how much he loves the woman he
– the Preacherman – has just killed, and that's when he
has a stroke.

I was acting out the story, crouched on the floor in a
corner of that damp, mouldy trailer, and so when I heard
footsteps on the creaky wooden porch I was so convinced
it was CJ Ferguson that I started to scream.

'Hello, Maeve,' said a woman's tinkling, musical voice.
'Fancy meeting you here.'

48

'I t wouldn't breathe,' she said. 'The baby. It wouldn't breathe. It went blue in the face. So I wrapped it up in the shawl to keep it warm. I put it inside my coat so it was close to me. I wanted to look after it. I wanted to give Trey his baby. I thought he'd be so pleased. I thought he'd love me if I gave him his baby. But when I got back to the house I took the baby out and it still wasn't breathing. It was dead. I didn't know what to do. I was scared. So I hid the baby. That's where we used to hide things when we were children. In the fireplace. I didn't think anyone would ever find it.'

She was swaying backwards and forwards, twisting her perfectly manicured hands together, her glossy dark-red hair falling over her face; telling me the story in her musical, seductive, confiding voice. 'You're so clever, Maeve,' she said, reaching out and touching my arm. 'You worked it all out, didn't you?'

I shuddered. I couldn't move.

'You know,' she continued, in an almost exaggeratedly pleasant voice, 'When I found Sarah down here, in the trailer, she was in labour. And you know something strange? She was crouched in the corner almost exactly where you are now.'

I was tired. Exhausted. Drained. My brain wasn't ticking over properly. I was in a trance. My limbs felt like jelly.

'So I helped her with the baby and then I was going to take it to Trey, you see. But she wouldn't let me. She came out of the trailer and she could hardly walk, and she was pleading with me to give her the baby, but I couldn't make her understand that it wasn't hers, it was Trey's. And she grabbed me by the knees so what was I supposed to do? She wasn't making any sense so I pushed her into the river.'

I'm twice her size, I told myself. I can handle her. I can take her in a fight. I took a deep breath and then sprang up suddenly, pushing her away as I did so. I ran outside, out onto the river bank, but she was faster. She caught me. She grabbed the waistband of my trousers and I fell heavily into the mud.

She stood over me, Missy Ferguson, tiny but wiry, with her gym-toned arms and her strong harmonium-player's hands. 'Did you like the tune I played for you?'

Humour her, Maeve. 'Yes. Yes, I did.' I started to pick myself up.

'You see, I let myself in. I still have a key to the house. Trey told me you wanted it back. Would you like me to give it to you now?'

'Yes, please,' I said, thinking that I could reach out for the key and then somehow push Missy away again, this time into the river. But she was ahead of me. As I started to scramble, suddenly her hands were clamped around my throat, her thumb pressing on my windpipe so that I couldn't speak or scream. As I tried to stand, my stupid, stupid sandals got stuck in the mud so I twisted sideways to free them. But I felt myself lose my footing. I grabbed the nearest solid thing I could reach, and it was Missy's leg, and we both fell backwards into the raging stream.

Everything slows down when you go underwater. You sink – sink down into the embrace of the river – and for a moment it's like you're dead. It's almost a relief. But then I came back up to the surface, my mouth full of muddy water, trying to cough, trying desperately to breathe. Missy's hands were still clamped around my throat. I kicked my legs, trying to kick her off balance, but we were both floating – no, not floating – being *swept* downstream. Twisting, turning, like on a fairground waltzer. I had one hand at my neck, trying to claw Missy's fingers apart, and the other hand trying to steer myself away from the ragged rocks lining the river.

I couldn't breathe. I couldn't shout. In my head I knew how to fight off attackers. But everything they tell you is aimed at fighting off rapists and muggers – men – on dry land. Knee 'em in the balls, they say. But that's no use at all when you're fighting another woman in a fast-flowing river. The more I tried to loosen her hands from around my neck, the tighter her grip. I stopped trying for a moment. She relaxed her hold slightly. My hands were behind me, scrabbling for purchase on the sharp, rocky river bank. I clung on for a while with my fingertips. I gathered my strength, and then with one almighty surge

I head-butted Missy so hard that she lost her grip on my throat and sank under the water.

But as my head jerked backwards from the impact of the head-butt, it connected with a jagged piece of rock. Some impulse made me put my hand to my head and then look at the fingers of my hand. Thick blood. Missy must have seen the look on my face. She smiled. We were still being swept downstream together, and she took advantage of my distraction. She ducked underwater and took hold of my legs. She started pulling me under. I kicked and screamed and swallowed yet more mouthfuls of the water. I lashed out with my hands and feet. I was panicking, terrified, because while Missy had her back to the direction we were going, I could see where we were heading: over the falls and onto the rocks below.

Again, I kicked, for dear life. I managed somehow to manoeuvre myself into a narrow gap beside a rock. I shoved Missy up against the river bank. But she was faster and lighter than me. She slipped out of my hands and ducked under me again. I found a crevice in the river bank. My fingers were bleeding from trying to hang on to my tiny sharp-edged fingerhold, and I was bracing my legs against the rock in front of me, desperately trying to avoid being swept over the falls. Missy came back at me again, and I was hanging on to my crevice with my lacerated fingers and she was hanging on to my throat, and it struck me that neither of us would get out of this alive.

There was a disturbance on the river bank opposite. Through the thick fog I could see some sign of movement. A blur of colour resolved itself. Two figures were running down to the bank. I saw Jerry. He was carrying a rope, and he slung it around a tree. And then the tall figure of my husband, the rope around his waist. My brain registered the bandage round his head, the cuts on his face. He shouldn't be here, I thought. What's Trey doing here? Slowly, as if in a dream, I watched him tie the rope securely. He climbed into the raging stream. I watched the expression on his face as he winced with pain. I watched him as he half-swam, half-scrambled his way across, buffeted by the fierce flow of the river that was heading single-mindedly towards the waterfall. And until Trey reached us, I had no idea which of us he was going to save.

Trey came towards us and he reached out his right arm and he caught hold of Missy tightly around the waist. I saw her smile. It was a smile of triumph. And then I realised that Trey was holding out his left hand to me, and in that hand was the rope.

I'll never forget the look on Missy's face as Trey slapped her across the cheek once, twice, three times. Her eyes were wide and surprised – indignant, almost; as if to say 'Why are you doing this to me?' She lost her grip on me and fell backwards, splashing frantically.

I tied the rope around my waist and I stayed there, clinging on to the rope with one hand, the rocky river bank with the other hand, frantically treading water. I watched as Trey grabbed hold of Missy again. He wrapped his big, strong hands around her throat. He pushed her head underwater and he held it there. I watched his face as he did it. It was completely expressionless.

49

The Sheriff of Campbell County, Bruce Long-baugh, became our new best friend. He interviewed us both several times: firstly in the hospital in Buchanansville where we were taken to be stitched and bandaged, and later in the warm, friendly, cluttered kitchen of Trey's aunts' house in Boone where we went to recuperate. It was Sheriff Longbaugh who decided what the official line would be. The baby had been stillborn. Sarah, out of her mind with grief, had wrapped the tiny corpse in a shawl. Who was to say how it found its way into the fireplace in the old Ferguson house? Who was to say it was even found there, anyway? Sarah killed herself, of course. We all knew that anyway.

As he explained this to Trey and me, as the three of us drank coffee round the table in the kitchen, I realised just what the Ferguson name meant in Campbell County. Who would want to rock the boat? Who would want to implicate the two – three – most famous people in Bodie's Hollow in a baby-killing scandal? No one in Bodie's Hollow would have had the appetite to suggest that the town's most famous daughter, Missy Ferguson, had murdered her husband's lover and baby. Think what that would have done to the town's economy.

Missy's death was, of course, a tragic accident. A tragic accident in which neither Trey nor I were in any way implicated. A tragic accident that was entirely unconnected with anything else that might or might not have happened in Bodie's Hollow. It made the news. Of course it did. Missy Ferguson, one of the most famous stars in country music, dead at the peak of her fame: the story hit the front page of every paper in the South and Midwest. The *Campbell County Courier*, published weekly in Buchanansville, set the tone for much of the press coverage:

Bodie's Hollow: country superstar Missy Ferguson drowned this week in a tragic accident in her mountain home town. The 33-year-old singer, who was born in Bodie's Hollow, is thought to have lost her footing as she walked beside the river that runs through the town. Locals said the river was particularly fast-flowing due to the storms that this part of the world has suffered in the past few days. The Sheriff of Campbell County, Bruce Longbaugh, said: 'This was simply a country walk gone tragically wrong and we are not looking for anyone else in connection with this incident. We would urge all local folk to take extra care during this late inclement weather.' Mrs Ferguson's ex-husband, musician and producer Trey Ferguson, who still lives in Bodie's Hollow, witnessed the tragic drowning. Friends say he is being comforted by his second wife, Maeve O'Mara Ferguson.

We were staying with Trey's aunts. We wanted to avoid all press and publicity. Missy Ferguson's death was the biggest thing to happen to Bodie's Hollow since CJ Ferguson first went to Knoxville in 1928 to record those old-time songs onto wax cylinders. Jerry kept us informed. He told us that TV crews had flocked to town to take pictures of the river and the house where Missy had been brought up, the old schoolhouse, the café – and, of course, our house. Journalists were ringing our doorbell looking for comments and interviews, for background information and in some cases the true story behind what some were starting to suggest was a cover-up.

According to Jerry, Bodie's Hollow was bustling. As well as the TV crews and journalists, Missy Ferguson fans were coming to town to pay tribute. The Foggy Hollow Motel had cars in the parking lot for the first time in years. The café was buzzing as it'd never been before, and Patsy had taken Kayla on as a waitress to help cope with the rush. Jerry said that Julie had a feverish air about her as she brought out all her most expensive and difficult-to-sell stock, hoping for more drop-in customers. Valerie rearranged the exhibits in the museum to put all the focus on Missy Ferguson's career; she put the entry fee up to five dollars and was busier than she'd ever been.

I watched the way Trey's aunts looked after him, fussed over him. They tousled his hair, annoyed him and wrapped their arms around him with warm, motherly love: a love he'd turned his back on nearly twenty years ago. It was just what he needed, I thought. I felt a lump in my throat whenever I watched them all together.

Trey and I spent a lot of time in the cramped, over-furnished guest room talking about what had happened. He told me how he'd found me; how he'd worked out what had happened. Missy had visited Trey in hospital that morning. He'd been surprised but pleased to see her. She'd been expecting him back in the studio in Nashville that day and she came to tell him how sorry she was that he was ill. 'She was all sweetness and light,' said Trey, shuddering, sitting cross-legged on the frilly nylon bedspread and picking, as he so often did, at a loose piece of rubber on his sneakers. 'Sweetness and light, just as she always was. So I figured I'd confide in her. She knew about Sarah and me. She was around in the old days. So I told her about the baby, about you finding the baby.'

'What happened? How did she react?'

'She lost it. She went crazy. I've never seen her like it. She was really angry. Not surprised, angry. She was pacing around the room, her hands curled up into little fists. And then she said this one thing. She said, "What the hell was Maeve doing poking around in that fireplace?"'

'What did you say?'

'You don't get it, Maeve. The point is that I hadn't told her where you found the baby.'

I went cold all over.

'After she'd gone my mind was just trying to make sense of everything. How did she know about the fireplace? Jerry came in to see me and I told him, and as I was explaining what had happened, I realised. That day, when Sarah and I were going to elope, the day my grandfather died, Missy had been in the house.'

I gasped. Jerry had mentioned that to me in passing, but it hadn't seemed relevant at the time.

'I didn't think about it when you first told me about the baby, because Missy was always up at the house. She was a friend of mine. She got on real well with my grand-daddy. She liked to visit with my aunts. There was nothing unusual about Missy being in the house that day. Except I remembered something. I was so nervous that day. I was pacing around, waiting for my grand-daddy to appear so I could tell him what I was planning to do, about me and Sarah going off to get married. I knew I was going to get a thrashing but I didn't care. It was going to be my last one. So I was upstairs in my bedroom and I heard the harmonium playing. I thought my grand-daddy must have come back in, so I went downstairs into the front parlour to see him. Only it wasn't him. It was Missy, and she still had her coat on.'

'And because of that you guessed that she would try to kill me in the river?' I still couldn't see how he'd made his leap of deduction.

'Well, as I told Jerry all this, we just looked at each other and I said, "Maeve's in danger." You see, if Missy had killed Sarah then I figured she was going to kill you too. I checked myself out from the hospital and Jerry drove us back up as fast as possible. We went to the house first. All the doors were open. I knew you couldn't be far because the car was still there. And then we thought: the river. Of course. That was where you'd be, you and Missy. Thank God we found you in time.'

'Trey, did you ever realise how mad Missy was?'

He shook his head. 'No, never. She was always a little intense, if you know what I mean. I knew she liked me when she was a kid, but I didn't realise she liked me that much. You know, even when we first got married, I thought it was because she felt sorry for me. A friend doing me a favour, is what I thought.'

'If she was so possessive of you, if she was ready to kill me, how come she left you?'

Trey gave me a lopsided smile. 'She didn't leave me.'

'What do you mean? I thought she left you for her bass player?'

He shook his head again. 'I left *her*.'

'What?'

'I woke up one morning and I decided I'd had enough. I wanted to come home. You see, when I married Missy I was running away. It was okay, you know, our marriage. We had a lot in common. We'd always been friends. But I didn't love her. Not the way I love you. Do you remember the first night we met I said something about it always being a matter of time with Missy? That's what I meant. I always thought it would come to an end at some point.

'Missy had affairs throughout our marriage. She wanted to have her cake and eat it. She wanted me, but she wanted excitement as well. But I knew she was – how can I put it? – emotionally needy. Clinging. I felt bad about leaving her. So I didn't leave, until I saw she was attracted to someone else who'd actually look after her, someone who was prepared to marry her. I thought to myself: Trey, you've done your duty. Now it's time to go home. Time to stop running away.

'You know, I guess she might have been all right if you and I hadn't got married. That's what made her so desperate, so needy. She hated thinking about me with someone else. She hated seeing me in love with you.'

50

We stayed with Trey's aunts for a couple of weeks, until the papers got interested in another story and the news machine moved out of Bodie's Hollow. Jean and Nancy wanted us to stay longer, but there was something that needed to be done.

It wasn't Trey's baby. It was news that he seemed to be expecting. 'Sarah never actually told me it was mine,' he said. 'All she ever said was that she was pregnant. And you know the honest truth?' Trey looked straight at me as he said this, his pale blue eyes shining with tears. 'I didn't care. I loved her and I wanted to marry her, and I didn't mind whose kid it was. But I can't stop wondering whether Missy would have still killed her if she'd known that.'

We buried the tiny body on a chilly autumn day, a few weeks past what should have been the baby's eighteenth birthday. The undertaker had dug a small grave next to Sarah's in the churchyard of the Presbyterian church. Trey and I stood hand in hand. Jerry was there too, and Patsy and Valerie and Nancy and Jean. Our new friend Sheriff Bruce Longbaugh came as well, his cap in his hand. Bright autumn leaves fell onto the grave as we sang 'Amazing Grace', and Trey and Jerry and Trey's aunts put on some harmonies that were so spine-chillingly beautiful that they seemed to cut right through the air. And throughout the short service I could not stop myself crying.

After the burial Trey and I sat in the field at the top of the Ferguson land and admired the outrageous autumn leaves. The mountains were aflame with gorgeous, flamboyant reds and oranges and yellows. There were even some purples in the mix. The colours seemed brave and bright – too bright and brave for that sad, melancholy, subdued day.

'Missy never wanted to have children,' Trey said out of nowhere.

'Why not?'

He gave a humourless laugh. 'I don't know. Too selfish, maybe? Anyway, thank God she didn't. Thank God.' He pulled me towards him and rested his chin on my bowed head. He was wearing the black suit that had been his grandfather's, the one he'd been wearing the first time I saw him. He put his arms around me and kissed me, and I knew what he was about to ask me: he wanted us to have a baby.

He opened his mouth to speak so I put my fingers up to stop him. Instead, I took his hand. I entwined my fingers in his. I led him back to the house. I was about to do the most difficult thing I have ever done in my life.

Trey turned to me and smiled. 'The ghosts are gone now, Maeve. It's our house. Yours and mine. Can I carry you over the threshold again?'

I shook my head, very sadly. I was exhausted, but I knew what I had to do. 'No,' I said.

'Why not?' He was smiling, but when he saw my expression he stopped.

'Trey, I'm leaving you.'

His face fell. He frowned, sticking out his bottom lip, a line running sharply down between his eyebrows. He tried to laugh; to pretend that I was joking. 'What are you saying?'

I had to look away from him. I felt that old familiar ball of grief about to burst out of my chest. I wrapped my arms tightly around myself. I felt actual, physical pain in my stomach, my chest, my heart. 'I'm leaving. I can't live here. Not in this house, not in this town, not with you. I just can't do it any more, Trey.'

He crumpled. He was leaning against the back porch and his legs went from under him. I moved towards him to try to hold him up, but he beat me off with his hands.

'Trey, I'm sorry.' The words sounded so limp and inadequate.

'If you're sorry, then why are you leaving?'

I took a deep breath and tried hard not to cry any more. I'd tried to rehearse what I had to say; I'd run through it in my head so many times, but I hadn't taken into account what Trey would say to me, the way he would look at me. 'Trey, when we first met, you knew what I'd been through. I was so honest and open with you. I told you everything. I shared everything with you. You knew how sad I was about Martin, and you knew I wasn't over him yet. But you told me everything was going to be all right and I believed you.'

He was staring at me with his mouth slightly open.

'But you told me nothing about *your* grief. Nothing at all. You brought me back here to this house, this town, that's so full of your ghosts, and still you told me nothing. You shared nothing with me. You shut me out. Trey, I have had to be so strong for you. So, so strong. And I've done it.' The tears were streaming down my face now. 'I've stood beside you and with you, and I've taken everything in my stride, and still . . . still the secrets. You stood on that river bank and you nearly strangled me, Trey. I was so scared. I went searching for you in the pouring rain. I held your hand in the truck when you crashed it and I thought you were dead. And Missy. Missy nearly killed me. I nearly died for you, Trey, because of all your secrets, this past of yours. I've been strong and I've tried not to be scared and I've backed you every inch of the way – and now? Yeah, so you came to rescue me in that river. Well, great. At last. At last I know you love me. But you know what? I don't care. I'm exhausted. I'm dead. I'm through. I've got nothing left to give you. I don't know what I feel for you any more. I want to go home.' A huge sob shuddered through my whole body. 'I want Martin back, to tell the truth. And I know that's impossible, but at least I want some time to grieve. I don't want someone telling me it'll all be all right, because I don't believe it any more.'

I sobbed and sobbed, and Trey tried to comfort me, tried to shush me, tried to run his hands through my hair like he'd done so many times before. But this time I pushed him away.

I ran into the house and grabbed the suitcase that was still half-packed from that weird time: the night of the murder ballad, the night of the truck crash, the night of the hospital waiting room; the day I'd made up my mind to leave. I got into the car, started up the engine and drove away.

51

I t was eleven in the morning on a wet, grey late-October Tuesday when I unlocked the door of my little South London flat and went back home. It was still empty. I'd been away for less than three months. That was how long my marriage had lasted: not even long enough for the estate agents to find a tenant. There was a blank spot against the wall where Martin's CD collection used to stand, and I wondered what Nick would say when I asked for it back; how I would explain what had gone wrong with my marriage.

I went into the kitchen and put the kettle on. There, upside down on the draining board, were two coffee mugs: the mugs Trey and I had used on the morning after our wedding while waiting for the taxi to take us to Gatwick. I'd been expecting the flat to be full of memories of Martin. I hadn't realised there'd still be memories of Trey.

L ater, I rang Helen and she came round and hugged me for ages without saying anything. We drank a bottle of wine and I told her the full story: everything that had happened between me and Trey. The jealousy, the secrets, the hidden tragedies; the way he made me laugh and smile; the way he pissed me off. She responded just as I'd hoped. The right facial expressions, appropriate little sounds when they were called for, a tightening of her grip on my hand during the really tough bits. And then I asked her, 'Have I done the right thing?'

She stroked my hair. She kissed my cheek. She hugged me. She didn't say anything for a long time. And then she said this: 'Maeve, I don't know. You're the only one who can tell.'

Except I couldn't. I really didn't know.

Life went on. I told most friends that Trey and I were having a few problems. Of course they'd heard about Missy Ferguson's death and most of them put two and two together and made about seventeen. Fiona said, 'Of course,' and put her hand on my arm. I flinched and pulled my arm away. The gesture reminded me too much of Missy. Putting on her most sympathetic face Fiona said, 'I do understand. It must be so difficult for both of you. Trey losing his first wife like that. Of course it must put a dreadful strain on your marriage.'

Oh well, let her think that.

Nick was more perceptive, especially when I asked for Martin's guitar back. 'Was it too soon?' he said, and I cried in his arms. 'For both of us,' was what I replied.

I went back to work. I managed to pick up some freelance bits by ringing old contacts and telling them that I was back in London for a while. 'For a while': the words chosen to suggest that my marriage hadn't collapsed completely after less than three months. We were on a break. We were taking some time. We were trying to sort things out. It happens to the best of couples.

Of course, Trey e-mailed me. The first message was short. It was simply some kind of apology. 'I'm sorry, but can we talk some more?' Sorry. That word again. I deleted the e-mail as soon as I'd read it. A couple more came in that first week, as I got back into normal London life: the Tube, the rain, the crowds in the supermarkets, the bustle in the street. His third one said: 'You told me "Not in this house, not in this town, not with you." Do I dare see a chink of hope in that? Could you manage to live with one third of that equation?'

I didn't delete that one, and I thought about it a lot over the next few days.

After Martin died I used to see him quite often. I'd be walking through a crowded street somewhere or I'd be sitting in a bar, and I would see him: across the road, at the far end of the room – always too far away to talk to. It was never him, of course. He was dead, and there are no such things as ghosts. I'd look back and see that it was just someone who was vaguely the same height or build or who had the same hair colour; or even someone who looked nothing like Martin. Maybe some slight gesture had reminded me of him. But it kept happening. It was months before I stopped seeing him.

I'd almost forgotten what the experience was like, until I started seeing Trey. I was in the supermarket and ahead of me in the aisle, his back to me, was a gangly guy in jeans with a slouchy uncoordinated walk. I almost called out Trey's name, until I saw him put his hand into the back pocket of the girl who was walking alongside him. I saw Trey browsing at the book market under the bridge outside the National Film Theatre: a tall man with dark hair falling forward over a pair of heavy-framed glasses, a bottom lip thrust out in concentration. I actually spoke to him. I shouted, 'Hey!' and waved at him to get his attention, and then he looked across the trestle table at me, confused, and of course it wasn't Trey at all. He looked nothing like him.

I cried so much that evening. I wrapped myself in my duvet and cried until every part of my body hurt. I was confused and scared. I was trying so hard to be strong, to be brave; not to give up, not to succumb.

One day I was sitting in the coffee-and-sandwich place at the front of the Royal Festival Hall, watching people hurry by on the rainy South Bank. Nick, who had forgiven me for never completing the piece I'd promised him on CJ Ferguson, had asked me to interview a musician. It was a guy who performed a kind of jazz-folk hybrid and had released a Mercury-nominated album. I'd listened to the album and hadn't liked it much. I wasn't looking forward to the interview. The guy was bound to be a pretentious arse. It was a cold day, and I was picking at a piece of carrot cake and sipping a latte. I'd had a few days in a row of feeling – not happy, that would be an overstatement. No, what I'd had was a few days of feeling only vaguely unhappy, and that was a big improvement. I was telling myself that it was okay not to feel happy. I told myself it was nothing to do with Trey; it was to do with Martin. I'd grabbed at my chance of happiness far too early and of course I hadn't deserved it. I hadn't given myself enough time to grieve for Martin. I'd been greedy. I'd grabbed at the first piece of happiness that had come my way, like a greedy, needy child. Of course it had all gone wrong.

The musician appeared, and he was a surprisingly nice guy. He had dreads, a bit like Cornell's, and a nice gap-toothed smile. We spoke a little bit about the concert he was preparing and the new album he was working on, and it was all actually quite interesting. We chatted for about twenty minutes or so, and I felt the warmth of genuine human interaction. And then I asked him this question: 'So what are you listening to at the moment? What are your current influences?'

'Well,' he said, his voice suggesting that he was about to tell me something unexpected. 'I've been listening to a lot of old-time American mountain music. Those old folk songs. Those vocal harmonies. You know, sometimes the harmonies are so intensely beautiful that they're painful to listen to . . . hey, what's the matter?'

The tears had come from nowhere and were streaming

down my face. I fumbled in my pockets to try to find a tissue. I couldn't. The musician handed me the paper napkin, still with a question in his expression. In a choked voice I said to him, 'I'm so sorry. I miss my husband so much it hurts.'

I opened Trey's last e-mail and replied. 'Just a chink' was what I wrote, and I sent it quickly before I had second thoughts.

He turned up on my doorstep two days later, a hopeful smile on his face, carrying a cardboard sign that said, 'Maeve O'Mara'.

52

I married a man I barely knew. I married him within two months of meeting him, because I was afraid that the moment might pass. I married him on a whim. He swept me off my feet. It was a stupid thing to do. I wouldn't recommend it to anyone. But I think it's going to be okay, after all.

Trey said goodbye to Bodie's Hollow, to that astonishing view, mountain top after mountain top, the green fading slowly into the blue of the sky, until you think you can see infinity. He's replaced it with a partial view of the London Eye, if you crick your neck and look upwards out of the window of the flat, and there's not a car passing at the time. We thought about selling the old Ferguson homestead, but instead we paid a team of decorators to finish doing up the house, and we're going to let it out as a studio complex. Bands will be able to stay in the house and work in the studio, and soak up the heritage of CJ Ferguson. Jerry's going to manage it for us: he's very excited about the idea. Julie's talking about turning her gift shop into an upmarket bar and restaurant, to cater for the influx of major stars that she imagines will now be coming to the town. Apparently she's still talking about the impact of the *O Brother* phenomenon. So Trey and I haven't burned our bridges yet. We haven't completely left Bodie's Hollow. The house is still there if we ever want to live in it again.

But we probably won't. We've made an offer on a big Victorian house north of the river, in Crouch End. We both think it would be a good place to raise a family, although we haven't dared to say that to each other yet. I know Trey thinks that, because I watched his face light up when he saw the little bedroom that the previous owners used as a nursery. Ironically, we'll be able to afford the house because of Missy Ferguson. Her final – posthumous – CD is selling by the bucket load as Nashville continues to mourn its late lamented star. As the album's co-producer, Trey is raking in his share of the profits. 'Fearless Heart' didn't make it to the final cut. Curiously, Missy's version of the song got horribly and irretrievably distorted somewhere in the production process and was unusable. The engineer on the album is a good friend of Trey's. But now 'Fearless Heart' is on hold for Tim McGraw. I don't know exactly what that means, but Trey seemed very excited when he got told the news so I'm guessing that it's something good.

Trey's working on his new album at some studios in Camden. He's working with a really eclectic bunch of musicians. It's going to be a loose, punky kind of album, mixing bluegrass and old time and folk and anything else that takes his fancy. He says he left tradition behind when he drove away from Bodie's Hollow – no, when *I* drove away from Bodie's Hollow. I'm on the album too. I'm doing backing vocals and handclaps on one of the tracks.

It turns out that maybe I do have natural rhythm, after all. And also, I'm learning to play the guitar, although I don't think I'll ever be any good at it. But it's nice to take an interest in what my husband does.

We talk now, me and Trey. The day he arrived back in London we talked more than we'd ever talked before. We were making up for lost time. We shared stories about our childhoods, stories we hope we'll never have to tell anyone again. We talked about love and jealousy and what we really felt about each other, and then we fell asleep to the sound of sirens and traffic and rowdy drunks in the street, and big-city life in general. We still talk. We share: bad stuff as well as good stuff. It's a real effort for him, I can tell, and I don't think Trey will ever have therapy; he's altogether too stiff and Presbyterian for that. But I think that's probably for the best. Because some of the things he's seen and done are probably best kept secret. Occasionally I wake with Trey's arms wrapped around me, and I remember his hands on my throat on that wild, wet night. And then I remember his face as I watched him kill Missy, that complete lack of expression. That scared me more than anything, and I don't think I'll ever completely come to terms with what my husband is capable of doing.

Sometimes I think to myself that if we'd waited to get to know each other we'd never have got married. If we'd gone through the normal 'getting to know you' process, we'd have discovered that we had nothing in common.

We married on the basis of a whim, a mutual physical attraction and a few misunderstandings. We shouldn't have got married, really. That's not enough to base a marriage on, is it?

If we'd been sensible and cautious we would never have got married. And that would have been a real shame. Because I love Trey, and he loves me, and I think we're going to be all right together for a long time. I hope so, anyway.